Saxon Dawn

Book 2 in the

Wolf Brethren series

By

Griff Hosker

Published by Griff Hosker 2013

Copyright © Griff Hosker Third Edition

SWORD
BOOKS

Dedication

This is dedicated to you my readers. I am gratified that you continue to buy my books and, I hope, enjoy them. I will continue to write them, if only because I enjoy creating the stories and the characters and, I hope, bringing history to life. Thanks to my new readers in Canada and Germany; you are a new and welcome audience. Thanks to Eileen, my patient wife and editor.

Thanks to Rod Harmon for finding the other two errors my wife missed!

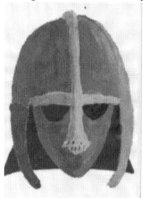

Chapter 1

Hen Ogledd 587 A.D.

Spring had come late to the last lands free from the domination of the Saxon and Angle invaders. The icy ground had remained hard, frozen and sterile while savage, vicious winds had ripped trees and homes into splinters. A late snow had killed many lambs and sheep and it would be a difficult summer with famine hard on the heels of hunger. Despite the problems he was suffering King Urien of Rheged had been adamant; he had promised King Gwalliog, his ally and king of Elmet, his aid against the Saxons who pressed his borders and he would send a force, even though it meant his own people would be hungrier as a result. That was King Urien's way. It is said by the holy men of the White Christ that he was the last great British king and I believe them. He had the vision to see that the Saxons could only be defeated by the remaining British kings banding together. We had done so before the winter and destroyed the invaders who threatened us. Now we would launch our own attack and attempt to retake the land further south which they were threatening. We were no longer just consolidating, we were attacking.

I looked around at my army. In truth it was little more than a large warband but they were all seasoned warriors and had fought with me for some years. I had thought that Prince Ywain, the son of King Urien, would lead the force but the king wanted his son to remain at Civitas Carvetiorum to learn how to govern the kingdom he would inherit one day. Ywain was not happy! But it mean much to me that the king whom I admired thought that I would be capable of the feat with such a small force. I had with me my brother Raibeart. He had married the daughter of King Gwalliog, Maiwen, and he was more than happy to be aiding his father in law. Maiwen, heavily pregnant, was with my wife and child at my stronghold, Castle Perilous. He led my troop of archers which had proved, time and again, superior to any archers the Saxons possessed. There were a hundred of them and they were all skilled fletchers and bowyers. We had pack animals with bundles of arrows strapped to their backs as we had learned, long ago, that you could never have too many arrows. My other brother, Aelle, would have commanded my slingers but he had lost an arm and now commanded the southern approaches to Rheged. The forty slingers we took were commanded by Raibeart.

The rest of my force consisted of thirty mounted and armed equites and two hundred mailed warriors on foot. The archers and slingers might damage the enemy but it would be my oathsworn warriors who would defeat them. Garth, my lieutenant, walked at their head whilst Raibeart and I rode with the equites. I had long fought against this as I preferred marching with my men, but it was they who forced me to mount for I was their lord and their leader.

The first week had been an easy journey as we had ridden south through a Rheged recovering from the hard winter. The hills which divided the island in two were sparsely populated and our scouts had an easy task. It had been cold as we breasted the hills which ran the length of the land, but now we were on the descent towards the east and the biting wind was a sign that we were now in greater danger, for the Saxons came from the home of the evil east wind; they would be close now and we did not want to fall foul of a roving band of raiders. Brother Osric, the priest, who ran Rheged for the king, had told me of the Romans who had built a camp each night when they marched in enemy lands. At first I had thought it unnecessary but now, as we headed closer to those lands captured many years ago by the Saxons I could see the wisdom. We did not make a camp as organised and as strong as those of the Romans, but we dug a ditch and embedded sharpened stakes around the perimeter. We all slept easier knowing that we could not be surprised. It did, however, slow us down and we were still at least a week away from the Kingdom of Elmet.

Raibeart and I huddled in our wolf cloaks as the wind whistled around us. I was chewing on a piece of dried venison and I ruefully pointed west. "Just think, I could be in my comfortable castle with a roaring fire and my wife with me instead of freezing out in here in this land which is fit for nothing." Raibeart was silent and I looked at him. He had taken my attempt at humour seriously and I remembered that we going to aid his family. "Of course, brother, when we do reach warmer climes we will become richer men when we plunder the Saxons we kill!"

I was relieved to see a smile break out on his face. "Aye brother, I am pleased that our enemies like to fight with their riches and treasures about them."

One reason for our success as an army was that King Urien used the treasure we collected to pay the men and to arm them well. It meant that most of our warriors had mail and helmets as well as shields. The Saxons liked to spend their treasure on bracelets and armlets to show their prowess in battle. Traders now brought their wares to Rheged for they knew that they would be given coins of silver as payment and not the barter of other kingdoms. Civitas Carvetiorum was a beautiful city and not a shell as many of the other Roman settlements had become. The riches we had accrued made us a popular market and was one of the few places left on the island to attract merchants from as far away as Constantinople and the Byzantine Empire.

"What of King Morcant Bulc?"

Raibeart's words cut like a knife. King Morcant Bulc was, supposedly, our ally but he had shown a reluctance to fight. I suspected that he had deliberately delayed when we had fought King Aella in the hope that he might achieve a victory at the expense of our warrior's bodies. He was part of the alliance but he had not offered any troops to aid King Gwalliog. I shrugged, "He is what he is and we do not trust him. If he fights for us then it is an unexpected surprise and if he stands and watches then we will not be disappointed."

Raibeart shook his head and spat out a piece of gristle. "No I meant about Bladud and him." Bladud was King Urien's champion and he hated me. I knew that one day I would have to kill him but King Urien valued him too much. For myself I thought that he was a snake and untrustworthy. Bladud had been with the King of Bernicia when he had delayed his attack and we both suspected some collusion and perhaps conspiracy, although we had no proof.

"I can do no more. King Urien still thinks that Bladud is a loyal warrior. At least he is now at Civitas Carvetiorum with the king and no longer with Morcant Bulc." I knew that Bladud was a good warrior and Rheged would be safer now that we had taken so many men to aid an ally. The equites of King Urien and Prince Ywain were sound warriors, much feared by the Saxons, but they were few in number. They were constantly on patrol seeking Saxons who were raiding our lands.

Elmet was but a short ride from our childhood home of Stanwyck but the warriors of Elmet had been busy fighting to the east of their land and left the north to the privations of the men from the sea. The first time we had met any of their warriors was when they visited King Urien. Both kings felt that it would not take much to secure Elmet's safety and then the alliance could close around the small Saxon kingdom of Deira and drive them back into the sea. The plan showed King Urien's vision for it would unite the last British kingdoms into one block and could halt the invasion.

One of the scouts, Adair, galloped up. "My lord I can see the stronghold."

I turned to Raibeart, "Then we will not have to dig a ditch this night and we shall taste your father in law's hospitality."

Raibeart gave a weak smile. He had only known King Gwalliog for fourteen short days and did not know him. He knew that he was not born of noble blood and was anxious to show that he was a warrior who deserved his daughter. For my part I had no doubts that the king would be impressed with my brother. I had heard other men, and not just his blood kin, speak of his valour and cunning on the field of battle.

Elmet's stronghold, Loidis, had a good position on a hill above a fast flowing river. They had cleared an area of forest all around its perimeter and it had a commanding view of the surrounding land; it could not be approached stealthily. It was not ancient, as were Civitas Carvetiorum, Stanwyck and Eboracum. It had been built neither by the Romans nor the ancient ones but the men of Elmet had been forced to build it when the Saxons came. It looked new. The palisade was sound and, doubtless, still a little green. The wooden buildings within still looked fresh and the ditch which surrounded it had sharp edges and fresh stakes in the bottom. The Saxons would not find it easy to take such a fortress.

King Gwalliog and his lieutenants were pleased to see us. A new warrior hall had been built at one end of the fortress and we could still smell the animal dung which had been mixed with the mud and straw for the daub. My warriors would not baulk at the smell; it meant they had no walls to construct and would sleep in the dry and warm beneath a roof. Raibeart and I left Garth to see to the men while King Gwalliog took us to his Great Hall. I know that the Elmet king was proud of his hall but, having lived at Civitas Carvetiorum and seen what a magnificent hall could be, it seemed primitive by comparison. I chided myself. I had grown up in a wattle and daub roundhouse and, if my father were alive, I would have received a clout around the ears for my uncharitable thoughts.

"Come, Lord Lann and Raibeart, my son. Sit and enjoy some ale. We have much to discuss." He and three of his leaders sat with us around a huge table laden with jugs of ale and cold meats.

King Gwalliog was not a young man and the years of fighting had taken their toll. His hair and beard were white and he had the gaunt look of a man who has seen four of his sons die. Raibeart could be the next king of Elmet if his last son fell and that was a sobering thought. The ale was good and we were both ready for it. Raibeart was still nervous and remained silent. "You have a fine fortress here King Gwalliog. The Saxons would lose many men trying to take it."

"What you say is true but it is the only one we have and the Saxons raid with impunity. It is why we, as your king does, use mounted men to hunt them down."

I had learned not to hide my words when speaking with kings; if they were good kings then they valued the truth and if not then it did not matter anyway. "Unless you have an army of horsemen you can never defeat the enemy, your majesty."

He nodded, sadly. "I know Lord Lann and I hope that your warriors and my son's famed archers can swing the war in our favour."

I saw Raibeart begin to smile and sit a little straighter in his chair. He was still my little brother. "How many men can you field?"

"When the crops are sown and the lambs born then a hundred mounted men and a thousand warriors."

I took a deep breath. "And what if we attacked them now? The soil is still cold and the lambs are unborn. I think the Saxons will be too busy to have begun the wapentake."

A frown creased the brows of his leaders and they began to murmur but he held his hand up. "What Lord Lann says is true. It will be a month before we can move such a number. Today, Lord Lann, we have the horsemen and three hundred warriors available."

I nodded, "Would I be right in saying those were your best warriors; the warriors of your household?"

"Aye they would."

"And they would all have a helm, arms and armour?"

He smiled proudly, "They would indeed, every one of them."

"Then we have an army my lord, for the Saxons will have the same problems as we do; frozen ground and inclement weather. They will not be mustered. We strike now for the men we lead, although small in number, will be worth ten of those we meet."

"But that would be less than a thousand men!"

"Eight hundred and seventy by my count," I smiled apologetically, "plus the six warriors beneath this roof."

He laughed, "Well that makes all the difference." He slapped Raibeart about the shoulders. "If you have balls the size of your brother's then I will have many fine grandchildren, my son." He became serious. "Are you sure that less than nine hundred will suffice?"

I had made the bold statement and now I needed to back it up. I saw the look on Raibeart's face and knew that I could not let my brother down. "Where is their nearest settlement?"

"There is the settlement of Wachanglen which is close to the Calder River. It is but half a day south of here. The chief there is a young warrior called Wach and it is said he is the son of King Aella."

Raibeart threw me a knowing look and I nodded. "I know Aella; we have fought him before. He is a wily king."

One of Gwalliog's lieutenant's said, "You defeated him last year did you not?"

"I was part of the army which defeated him yes, but it was not an easy win and he showed great cunning. His son may have inherited some of his father's skill." I remembered how close we had come to losing and how it had cost my little brother, Aelle, his arm. "Is the place defended?" I swept my arm around the hall. "As well defended as this, perhaps?"

The King beamed at the compliment and shook his head. "No. It is close to the river on one side and has a palisade as high as a man around the rest. There is a ford close to the settlement."

"Warriors?" Raibeart ventured.

There was an embarrassed silence around the table. They had not scouted it out and showed that they were fighting a defensive war; holding on to what they had. "No matter. Raibeart and I will take our men and scout it out. If you have your men to prepare to leave in three days we will give this Wach a bloody nose and then see who else we can upset."

King Gwalliog stood and embraced me. "I can see why King Urien values you, Lord Lann. For one so young you have a clever mind."

I hated compliments and praise and I felt myself colouring. "Have you someone who can show us this place?"

One of the lieutenants stepped forward. "I am Aiden and I lived close by until the men from the sea came. I will take you."

We found Garth who was organising the sleeping arrangements. "My brother and I will be taking the equites to scout the enemy. Have the men prepare for battle. We will be fighting soon."

Garth grinned. "Excellent. I hate them sitting on their arses too much; it makes them soft!"

Garth was a hard task master but a fierce warrior. When he guarded my right I never feared any danger. I told the equites that they would not need mail. Raibeart and I took our bows. This was a mission when we needed to be invisible but, if we were spotted, then we could delay any pursuit.

The land we had to cross was heavily wooded and that was a good thing. We could feed ourselves and remain hidden. However if they had scouts out then we could be ambushed. I sent four men forwards as scouts ahead of us. I turned to Aiden. "How do the people there live? Is it the same way you and your people did?"

His face became hard and cold as he remembered his childhood. "They fish the river and they tend animals such as cattle, goats and sheep. They have cleared much of the forest and they plant crops. My people were hunters and Vindonnus was good to us."

I had learned much from his words. He was, as were Raibeart and I, a follower of the old ways and he would be skilled with a bow and a javelin. These things were good to know. "So they are likely to be spread outside the walls?"

Raibeart looked over at me and grinned happily as he understood my words. "They will be as we were in Stanwyck with a few people remaining in the village while the rest work beyond its walls?"

"Yes and I am now wondering if these were the same warriors who destroyed our home for it is almost as close to Stanwyck as it is to Loidis." Aiden's face creased into a frown. "Do not worry, warrior of Elmet. We do not seek revenge. Those who did the deed are dead. We saw to that."

"The stories are true then, my lord, that you and your brothers, when little more than children killed a warband?"

"It wasn't a very big warband." I could see that he was impressed but, at the time, we had not thought of our own survival, just hitting back at the enemy.

Aiden pointed ahead. "The land drops to the river there."

I gave a long whistle and the scouts reappeared. "There is no-one ahead my lord. The edge of the forest is a mile distant beyond these trees." Aiden looked bemused. I smiled. We normally travelled on Roman roads with their mile markers and my men could estimate distances well.

"We will halt at the edge of the forest and approach on foot." I did not ask Aiden how far it would be from the edge of the forest to Wachanglen; his estimate would be of little use.

When we reached the edge of the forest I could see that the land had been cleared and there were a few sheep and goats there. Beyond them was another wooded area and beyond that I could see tendrils of smoke rising; it was Wachanglen. I left half of the men at the edge of the forest and I led the rest with our horses through the cleared area to the woods. Once there I left ten men with the horses and we took the other five with us. Raibeart and I had our bows strung and our arrows ready. My men had their javelins and spears prepared. Aiden just had a sword and shield. It was a small thing but I would need to speak with the king about arming his men more effectively. I had learned that you needed to be prepared for any eventuality.

I knew we were approaching the edge when it began to lighten and we heard the sound of activity. They obviously had a blacksmith for I could hear the clang of the hammer on metal. The sound of children playing also showed that they were not expecting trouble. We almost felt our way to the edge of the trees. My men were good at this and used the cover of the trees to mask our approach although I doubted that they were looking for an enemy. Aiden also showed his skill as a hunter and we soon found ourselves looking across the river to the village.

It was a large village and I could see a river gate with two bored looking guards who were fishing. Through the gates I could see many villagers moving about. There were a few guards on the walls but they did not appear to be concerned and, like the guards at the gate, were not alert. A column of men with a line of pack horses hove into view at the northern gate. They were warriors. We watched until the sun moved the shadows of the walls and I signalled for us to withdraw. Once back at the horses I asked them what they had seen. By pooling our information I discovered that they had a small herd of ponies and we had counted a hundred warriors, including the ones who had brought the pack animals.

"We can now return to the king."

Aiden started. "But we have not counted every warrior!"

"And we could not do that without alerting them to our presence. From the number of women and children we counted there could be over a thousand men in that settlement. But we could only see a hundred. We assume they have double that number of warriors available and make our plans accordingly." I left him to ponder that as we headed north again. Raibeart and I compared ideas.

"We need to attack in the late morning when the workers are away from the town." I nodded. An early morning raid, while it would have the element of surprise would leave us with a greater number of warriors to fight. I wanted to make a quick strike and cause more casualties amongst the Saxons than on our meagre supply of warriors. "What about the women and the children?"

I knew what he meant. Neither of us wished harm to come to those who were not warriors, our mother and sisters had been ruthlessly slaughtered, but neither could we allow them to remain. "They will become slaves. Some may do as Freja did and join us." Freja had been a slave whom we had rescued and she was now married to my young stepbrother Aelle. It was a harsh world in which we lived but this was a fight to the death between two cultures and we wanted ours to be the victor.

King Gwalliog had prepared a feast for us when we returned. All of his bodyguards were there as were his mounted warriors. Raibeart and I were seated next to him and I drank sparingly for I needed to explain my plan to him. I was arrogant still in those days. It never occurred to me that the king might have his own ideas. The fact that he had asked King Urien for help showed me that we had more skill than he. King Urien was diplomatic; I was not!

"We will use my horsemen to guard the road from the north and yours to guard the one from the east. Raibeart and his archers can attack the men on the walls close to the river while your men use the ford to attack the gate. My men will attack the northern gate. Even if there are two hundred warriors within the walls we will outnumber them four to one and our bows will outrange them. "

"But scaling the walls…"

"Do not worry. Raibeart will clear the walls and they can then be scaled. The gates are twice the height of a man but the walls are only as high as a warrior."

One of his lieutenants, Aidan, asked, "Will we need ladders?"

"No for your men have the means to scale the walls with them."

He looked puzzled and Raibeart smiled as he explained. "Two men hold a shield. A third man climbs upon it and then he is raised to the top of the walls." He saw the doubt in the warrior's eyes. "We have done this before and it works."

Garth and the leaders of the Elmet warband spent the next day rehearsing getting into wedge and shield wall formations. The fact that all of the warriors who would be making the assault were mailed meant that this would be a safer undertaking than had they been armed as the Saxons were.

We left well before dawn to allow ourselves the time to get into position and, as dawn broke, we were at the edge of the forest with the open ground before us. We waited until the sun warmed the ground to allow the shepherds and herdsmen to take their charges to the pastures. Raibeart and his archers quickly raced across the open ground to secure the woods on the far side. I left King Gwalliog with Aidan and his men. Aidan knew the plan and I trusted him. The king too had understood the need to coordinate our attacks. I led my column to the east. We would have to swim the river but Aidan had assured us that it was shallow enough for it to be a safe task. I used my thirty horsemen to scout the giver and make sure that there were no surprises. As we formed up on the far side I was concerned about the lack of people working in the pastures. So far we had seen none, despite the fact that it was approaching mid morning. Perhaps they were using the pastures to the east and the south. I still had a nagging worry at the back of my mind as we headed east.

I sent Tuanthal to the eastern gate while I led my band of men behind the pathetically thin line of slingers to the northern gate. There was enough cover for us to approach to within half a mile of the palisaded stronghold. I had to assume that the other parts of this puzzle were in position and I lead my men forwards. We marched in a four wide column for speed. I was confident that we could change to wedge formation in the blink of an eye. We moved swiftly across the open ground at a steady trot. The slingers were a good hundred paces before us and they would be the ones to initiate the contact. I heard the whirr and whizz of their missiles and the screams and cracks which told me that they had struck their targets. The gates swung closed as those inside Wachanglen realised their danger. I hoped that they would be over confident in their stockade and not realise the danger they were in.

"Wedge!" I ran a little faster to facilitate the change in formation and soon felt the comfortable presence of Garth on my right. I had drawn Saxon Slayer as soon as I had ordered the formation and it felt satisfying to hold the mystical blade once more. I saw at least two of my slingers fall to arrows and lead balls and I shouted, "Slingers! Retire!" They all disengaged and ran behind the wedge. They would still be able to use their weapons but would be afforded the protection of the shields. As we approached the gate I suddenly decided to change my plan as I saw that the gate was not reinforced; I could see through the gaps. "Men of Rheged, we are not going over the walls we are going through the gate!" I heard the roar and felt the excitement of combat course through my body. I moved my shield around to my front and lowered my head. Stones began to ping and crack off helmets and shields but they caused minor discomfort rather than serious wounds. My two hundred warriors in their mail struck the gate like a battering ram. I felt my arm jar and I went dizzy and then I heard a crack as the gate gave way and we poured through the wrecked gate.

A Saxon rushed at me with a two handed axe and he roared defiance as he swung it at my head. Even though my arm was still a little numb I held it forwards. His blade was sharp but it caught on the metal rim of my shield and Saxon Slayer slid up under his armpit to appear, as though by magic next to his right ear. He slumped to a bloody death. I looked ahead and saw that the Saxons were rushing to their broken gate. "Shield wall!" We formed three lines, each one seventy men wide with the boy slingers hurling death above our heads. I knew now that we would win for no army could stand against my seasoned two hundred warriors. I hoped that Raibeart and King Gwalliog were having the same easy time of it. The Saxons appeared to be waiting for something but I didn't know what.

One of my men growled. "They are scared, my lord. Let us end this."

I thought that he was right and I ordered the line forward. "Attack." We moved towards the enemy with a measured pace. We did not need momentum, we had skill.

Just before we struck their line I heard am urgent voice behind me. "My lord! It is an ambush! There are five hundred Saxon warriors coming towards you."

I turned and saw Tuathal and the remnants of my equites behind the slingers. "What of my brother?"

"They are still attacking the gate!"

"Ride and support them."

"My lord?"

I grinned, "We are going to join him! Wedge!" I turned to Garth. "There is no point going back to fight five hundred men. We might as well join Raibeart."

He too had the mad look of battle I recognised so well. I could hear the men moving into position and I lurched forwards screaming, "Rheged!" at the top of my voice. The cry was taken up and we hit the shocked Saxon line like a hot knife through winter butter. I smashed one man in the face with my shield as I stabbed a second. The line did not break, it disintegrated. I could see, through the gaps which appeared, that Gwalliog's men were on the ramparts. As we neared the gate I shouted, "Get the gate open. The last two ranks about face. The rest of you kill anything that moves!"

Those Saxons who still stood were quickly despatched as the gates were opened and I saw the smiling face of King Gwalliog. The smile left his face as I shouted, "It is a trap. They have more men behind us. Back over the river."

The old king just nodded and shouted, "Men of Elmet form a shield wall across the river!"

"Garth, get the slingers to safety. I will bring the rest over." He was going to argue but I just shouted, "Now! We have no time for a debate."

I turned and joined the fifty warriors who formed my rear ranks. I shoved myself into the front ranks. "Come on lads. Make way for me!" I heard them cheer. They were neither beaten nor cowed. "Now let us walk backwards. Lord Raibeart will be giving them a welcome once we get through those gates."

The Saxons had formed a shield wall and were less than fifty paces away. I knew that they had to be tired as they took some time to form a wedge. My men were fit and had only run for a couple of hundred paces. We still had a chance even though they outnumbered us ten to one. The narrow gates would slow them down. I tried to visualise the river and the walls. If we could make the river then we might still escape.

The leader of the wedge had a long spear and a helmet like mine. If he thought the extra reach of the spear would aid him he was wrong. As he thrust the blade forwards, aiming for the eye hole of my helmet I turned his spear and then chopped down on it with Saxon Slayer. As the heft broke in two I heard the clang as the warrior to my right fended off an axe. Before the spearman could recover I punched him in the face with my shield and, as he raised his to protect himself, stabbed him through the thigh. He crumpled to the ground. I could see that the ramparts were close and I shouted above the din and clamour of combat. "Left and right, through the gates. Shield wall!" My well trained men punched with their shields and disengaged leaving ten of us filling the gate and backing out slowly. A second hero swung at me with his axe and he aimed at Saxon Slayer. Although I punched it away it continued its arc and knocked the warrior to my right to the ground. A spear stabbed him in the throat and I was suddenly without any protection on my right hand side.

I brought Saxon Slayer up to slice savagely through the unprotected throat of the axe man and then whirled around to knock the two swords which came at me from my left with my shield. Although I had gained space I saw an exultant spearman stabbing down at me with his weapon eagerly anticipating a victory over the Wolf Warrior. I would have died there and then but a feathered shaft appeared in his throat and his joy died with him; I knew, without being told, that it was Raibeart who had loosed the life saving arrow. I heard Garth yell, "Across the river my lord, we are all."

Shouting, "Back!" I led the remaining four warriors through the icy river. Arrow after arrow hurled back those brave warriors who tried to kill the killer of champions and claim the Saxon Slayer. Soon they were forced to form a shield wall and watch impotently as we were dragged from the river, the whole army cheering as though we had won.

I felt Raibeart's arms around my shoulder. "That was too close for comfort brother."

"Thank you for your arrows. I would be dead were it not for you and your archers."

King Gwalliog's voice came from behind Raibeart. "And we would have suffered a slaughter had you and your men not made the charge and sacrifice you did."

I looked up at Tuathal; he seemed far away on the top of his horse. "You and the king's horses, cover our retreat. Keep them from pursuing us." I suddenly realised that I had given the orders to the King of Elmet's men and I looked at him. He smiled and nodded.

I tried to turn to leave the field with my men but my leg would not work. I had felt no pain but my leg did not move. As I crumpled to the ground I heard Raibeart yell, "Lord Lann is wounded. Fetch a healer!"

Chapter 2

I had not noticed that I had been struck; we had been too busy fighting our foes for that but the wound was deep. A blade had sliced down the back of my calf and the blood flowed freely. The priest bound it to allow us to journey home where it could be dealt with more effectively. As we trotted, in my case, painfully home I discussed with the King and Raibeart what had occurred.

"I think brother that we were spotted the other day when we scouted. I wondered why there were sheep in that open pasture but no shepherds. That also explains why we saw no one outside the settlement this morning."

I had to ask the painful question; made even more painful by the waves of pulsing agony with each footfall of my mount. "What is the butcher's bill?"

I saw the look exchanged between the king and his son in law. The king sighed, "The men of Elmet and your archers lost few men but fifty of your warriors perished and ten of your horsemen."

It was a heavy loss for those warriors could not be easily replaced. "And ten of the boys, my brother." That cut me to the quick for the boys, my young slingers, had died before their time. Their reckless bravery had cost them and Rheged dear for they would have been the future warriors. "But we killed many more of their warriors. We might have yielded the field but we left it sown with over a hundred and fifty dead Saxons. There were many others who were wounded. Their walls are wrecked. We have won my brother and they will not forget this day."

We rode in silence. I suspect the others thought it was my wound which silenced me but it was not. I had been bested and I did not like it. Despite my brother's words, to me it felt like a loss as we had left the field with neither victory nor booty. The next time we fought them I would make sure that we were not surprised and we would hurt them. Raibeart made my remaining horsemen take me to hurry me back swiftly to Loidis for my whitening face worried him. In the event it was a good thing he did so for my wound was bleeding more than we had thought and I fainted as we entered the Elmet stronghold. When I came to the first sight I had was of Raibeart's concerned face looming over me.

"You had me worried there; we thought we had lost you. The holy men have stitched it up but you will not be moving for a few days."

I struggled to raise myself but felt drained of all energy. "I will…"

King Gwalliog's voice boomed out. "You will be staying in that bed Lord Lann until I am satisfied that you are healed. The Saxons have been given a bloody nose and they will be on the alert for a while wondering if we will return."

Raibeart nodded. "We captured a couple of prisoners and they were terrified that the Wolf Warrior was coming to get them." My face must have displayed my thoughts for Raibeart smiled, "Aye brother. Saxon mothers frighten their naughty children warning them that the Wolf Warrior will come in the night and take them if they are naughty. That is why they fought so hard to get at you and also why the warriors inside fell back when your wedge broke through. Wach has sworn to have your head on his walls."

I slumped back on to the bed. All I wanted was to sleep but I still had my duty to perform. "Raibeart we need to find where their other settlements are. Have our scouts find them. We will keep them guessing where we will attack next."

"It is already planned. Garth and I will be leading the patrols on the morrow. Now rest and then you can tell us of the plan which is hatching in your fertile mind." My brother knew me well. I had already begun to devise a strategy which would defeat these men from the sea.

I drifted in and out of consciousness for the next two days. I suspected the priests had put some drug in my water but after three days I felt better and I was allowed to sit up. King Gwalliog and my brother joined me when they had returned from their patrols.

"You have a better colour Lord Lann. The priests tell me that you can walk soon."

"I will walk tomorrow." I was not as confident as I had sounded.

"We will see. Now what is this plan you have concocted. I am intrigued."

"It is obvious that they will outnumber us." I turned to Raibeart. "How many Saxon strongholds are there?"

"We found six although none are as stout as Wachanglen." Raibeart had deduced which way this was going and he pre-empted my next question. "I would think the six hamlets could field eighty men each, at least."

"If we add them to the force at Wachanglen then we can see that the enemy will be twice our strength."

"Not if we use our own people when we have sown our crops."

I shook my head. "I would rather fight now for we will weaken them. Did you see many workers toiling in their fields and meadows brother?"

"No. They were on the watch for us and, had they had horses, they would have chased us."

"You see, King Gwalliog, our very presence weakens them. Your people are preparing for the summer and autumn and you will have a good harvest. They will not and, in the long run, that will be how we defeat them. We will use nature and the earth to be our allies. Famine and hunger are fierce enemies."

King Gwalliog looked disappointed. "That does not seem glorious."

"It isn't but, when this is over, you will have more people than they do. We will strike at their smaller settlements using archers and horsemen. We are mobile. All of Raibeart's archers can ride and we can weaken them by constant attacks. We will make them watch for us, not knowing when or where we will strike. Eventually Wach will tire of this and he will come here to attack you. We will lay a trap for him. Our horsemen can watch for them and warn us of their arrival. Then they can stay without the walls while they hurl themselves at your defences. The archers will thin them out and they will not expect us to attack them. When they are weakened enough then the horse and the foot will attack at the same time."

Raibeart nodded. "They will have seen our dead warriors and as the only forces they see will be a few horsemen and archers they will assume that they have seen off the threat of our men."

I could see that King Gwalliog was not convinced. "Once they have been drawn here and weakened then you can call up all of your forces and drive them from your land. You can lead your mighty host." The beaming smile told me that I had used the right argument. He saw himself as another King Urien leading a mighty army and showing his people that it was he who had destroyed the Saxons. That was the difference between the two kings; one saw the end result while the other wanted their name enshrined in men's memory. I was pleased that I had chosen to follow the former. "While we harry them you can improve the defences of this stronghold to make them bleed upon its walls."

I defied the King and the priests by walking the following day. I knew that I would not be able to stand in a shield wall but I also knew that we had no intention of fighting the Saxon way. We would fight my way. The people of Elmet reared horses and we were able to procure thirty extra horses for our archers. They would not be fighting on horseback but we needed speed to achieve our ends. We would dismount them when the archers fought and then use them to evade any pursuit. Raibeart tried to dissuade me from participating in the raids. "Raibeart, I allow that you are the finest archer in Rheged but we both know that I am a close second. In addition I want my Wolf banner and my helmet to draw Wach to attack us. We need him to know who we are."

"Garth could carry the banner and wear your helmet."

I glared at him. "Do you know so little of me that you think I would let someone else risk his life for me. I command this force and I make those decisions."

He looked at me with fear on his face. "I only mean to protect you, Lann."

I relented, "I know and I am sorry that I spoke to you as I did but you must understand that I know my body better than a priest and I need to be on the raids so that I can gauge their success… or failure."

As we mounted our fifty warriors I could see that the boy slingers were unhappy at being left behind. I rode over to them. "I have a task for you warriors." I saw them puff with pride. "I want you to train as many Elmet boys as you can to be slingers. Show them how to make the missiles and hit as well as you do." I glanced up at the king who nodded his approval. "We have seven days to prepare. Do not let me down." I knew that they would not but I merely wanted them to be occupied. They were, after all, still boys and mischief would follow if I did not make them work.

We headed north east towards the first Saxon settlement. No-one had been near it for a few days and I hoped that, if Raibeart and his scouts had been seen, they had been dismissed as a nuisance rather than a danger. Raibeart and I had worked out our plans for all the attacks. We would ride into the heart of their village if the gates were open and kill as many warriors as we could. If the gates were closed then we would kill as many sentries as we could. The important factor was that we could afford no casualties but even four or five dead Saxons would serve our purpose.

The Saxons were a little less diligent than we were when it came to defending their settlements and they had only cleared forty or fifty paces of trees. That suited us for it allowed us to approach quite close before we were seen. We could see that the gates were open and there were just two men watching the track way. They would be the targets for Raibeart and me. Garth led my mounted men and as he charged them towards the gate we loosed our arrows and the two guards fell dead before they could even raise the alarm. We quickly followed our mounted men with our archers and we thundered through the gates. Garth and the equites were butchering the men who raced to fight the invaders. We dismounted and one in four of the archers held the horses. We aimed at those warriors who were further away or standing on the walls. It was a slaughter. We were mailed and prepared while they had been going about their normal business. It was not glorious but it was necessary. I heard the screams of the women, the children and the old as they raced out through the southern gate. I had made it clear that we could not burden ourselves with prisoners and they were allowed to leave. Soon all who could flee had fled and all that remained were the dead and the dying. "Burn it!"

My men quickly started fires in the Great Hall, the houses and the walls. Others took weapons and anything else of value from the dead Saxons. "Now back to Loidis." As I mounted my horse I was also aware of blood seeping down my leg and into my boot; the pain had become worse as the day had gone on and I felt a little light headed and weak. Although I had only stepped on to the ground briefly the movements of the horse had aggravated the wound while we were riding. I was determined that none would know and I led the column of jubilant warriors home keeping a smile I did not feel upon my face.

Wachanglen was but ten miles south and I knew that they would not only see the pall of smoke but would be receiving the first of the refugees. We had to return as swiftly as we could to the safety of Loidis' walls. "If they are all as easy as that my lord then this will be a swift campaign."

"I do not think, Garth, that it will be as easy the second time. They will be prepared. I expect them to keep their gates closed and to have more guards. Our next attack will be different."

"And when will that be my lord?"

"Tomorrow. Unless you are too tired from today's endeavours?"

Garth laughed, "I did not even break out into a sweat this morning."

"We must have killed fifty or six of them."

"There were seventy five my lord, I counted them." I nodded my satisfaction. That would shake Wach up and make him take notice. It had been a good start but I had meant what I had said to Garth; the next attack would not be as easy.

King Gwalliog was delighted with the results of the raid. The arms we brought back would be valuable additions when his farmers fought against the Saxons. The young priest, Brother Patrick, who had tended my wound when I had returned from the first raid watched me as I dismounted and hurried after me to my quarters.

"My lord you have burst your wound. Lie down!" I was unused to taking orders but I knew from Brother Osric and Brother Oswald that the White Christ priests were a law unto themselves. He almost pushed me to my bed and then he pulled the boot off and a pool of blood flooded to the floor. He tut tutted his annoyance. "You should not have ridden to war. All my good work is undone."

"Then stitch it again!"

"Am I a seamstress?" Despite his words he took the needle and held it in the flame. Suddenly an evil smile crossed his young face as he watched the blue and golden flame flicker. "If you are determined to go to war then there is but one solution." He went to the door and said to the two guards who stood there. "You two, carry Lord Lann to the blacksmith's!"

As I said priests are a law unto themselves and my men obeyed but they, and I, wondered why we were going to the blacksmith's. King Gwalliog and Raibeart saw me being carried and they followed, equally curious. Brother Patrick did not seem concerned by the exalted audience. The blacksmith's jaw dropped as the priest marched into his place of work. The fire was burning fiercely and we could feel the heat as soon as we walked in. "Put the lord face down and give me his sword." I had no opportunity to argue as Raibeart removed Saxon Slayer from its scabbard and my men place me face down on the dirt. It was undignified and I was about to argue when the piping voice of the priest sounded, "Hold down his shoulders."

Out of the corner of my eye I saw him plunge my sword into the fire which burned almost white and I knew what he was going to do. This would hurt. "Lord Raibeart, hold your brother's leg. Lord Lann is a brave man and he will not move the leg himself but I have seen limbs move of their own accord, even after a man is dead." I felt my brother's hands gripping my leg and it, somehow made, what was to follow, easier to bear. I felt the heat from the blade before it even touched my leg. When it did strike the flesh I felt such a pain as I have never borne before. It seemed to lance through my whole body but I dug my nails into my palms and did not utter a sound. The smell of burning hair and flesh almost made me gag and then suddenly I heard the priest's voice. "Well my lord that was bravely done but your leg will not bleed again. Your wife may find the scar uglier than the stitches I would have preferred to use but it was your choice."

I rolled over and sat up. I held my hand out to Brother Patrick and a brief look of fear erupted across his face; he thought I was going to strike him. "Thank you, priest; I am a poor patient but I will buy you a cross for your church as a token of my thanks." He beamed with pleasure; for some reason priests like to remember that their White Christ was crucified on a cross. I could never understand it myself.

Raibeart helped me up and King Gwalliog said. "We will need some ale tonight my lord to celebrate our victory and to ease your pain."

Later that night as we feasted and ate I knew that it was not a great victory. We had surprised them and we were lucky. Wach was a cunning leader as his trap at Wachanglen had shown. It would not do to under estimate him. "Your majesty when we next attack it will not be quite so easy."

"And when will that be Lord Lann."

"Tomorrow." I ignored the look my brother flashed at me. We had to use the time available to stir up this hornet's nest. "When we leave I would keep a vigilant watch from your walls and keep your gates closed. Have your mounted men patrolling the settlements."

"Why? What do you fear?"

"I fear that Wach may strike immediately. He is half a day away as we know and we do not know his mind." I could see the king sobering up. Perhaps he thought that we had won already. We had only just begun this war and there would be much bloodshed before it was over.

I was like a bear with a sore head the following day. Despite the ale my leg had kept me awake for most of the night. My brother and Garth recognised the signs and they made sure that no-one upset me. We had chosen a village to the south of Wachanglen. It was like the game with three cups and a pea. Wach and his men would be guessing where we would strike next. If I had been Wach I would have had men watching Loidis but our scouts found no evidence of scouts and we set off before dawn.

The gates on the walled village were closed, as I had expected for the Saxons were not stupid and we halted in the tree line. The archers tied their horses to the trees while the equites kept watch. "Well brother. What do we do this time?"

I pointed at the heads of the guards we could see. "Two things, first we light a fire and then we eliminate the sentries."

"Light a fire?"

"Remember Metcauld?" He grinned. We had used fire arrows against the Saxons there and we could do so again. A burning village would be as big a victory as one with a corpse covered field. He quickly found some kindling and some pine cones. "Garth, light the fire and we will take out the sentries." There were eight sentries we could see and I chose ten of Raibeart's best archers. Raibeart and I told them their targets and, as one, we loosed. All eight disappeared from sight. "Any head which appears then hit it."

The fire was going well and Raibeart had his men attaching pine cones to their arrows. Their flight would not be as accurate but they only had to hit a wall fifty paces away. We could afford some misses. I turned as a warrior screamed and fell from the wall. The beleaguered Saxons decided that discretion was the better part of valour and no heads risked the instant death which awaited an unwary head. As soon as the fire arrows began to strike the walls I knew that we had won for the wood was dry and flames leapt up from the ramparts. "Now aim into the village." We were firing blind but if we could light some of the huts or even the hall then we would force the Saxons to meet us.

Soon we could see flames rising from inside the village and the gates opened and the warband appeared. They formed a shield wall and began to head towards us. Raibeart's voice boomed out. "Shift targets!"

We all began to loose our arrows at the wall of shields which walked resolutely towards us. Few of their shields were as good as ours and I could see splinters appearing in the wood. They hurried forwards to meet us and to wreak revenge on their tormentors. That would not happen. "Archers mount and retreat!"

The archers sped into the trees to gather their ponies and escape before the warriors could attack them. Garth and the horsemen rode hard at the rear of the warband and began thrusting their spears and swords at unprotected backs. A second warband emerged from the village. It was time to leave. "Garth! Disengage and retreat!" As we fled through the woods I heard the cheers and jeers from the Saxons who thought they had won a victory. The dead bodies of their warriors and the blackened timbers of their walls was testimony to the fact that they had lost. We had not escaped unscathed and two of the horsemen had wounds as had three horses although none were mortal.

Raibeart was disappointed that we had no booty this time. "Raibeart, we have hurt them. Two of their villages have been destroyed. Wach cannot afford to allow us to continue this war. Tomorrow we begin a different attack."

He looked at me with that familiar quizzical expression on his face. "We do not hit the next village?"

"No. We leave the archers at Loidis and we will visit their farms and farmsteads. I want Wach to become angry and to attack us. If we enslave their women and children then they will have no option but to attack King Gwalliog."

"Aelle would not like that Lann."

"And you think I do? These are desperate times. We have to rid this land of the Saxons so that King Urien and the other kings can reclaim the rest of Britain. Would you have us surrender to the Saxons?"

He shook his head. "But there is no honour in capturing women and children."

"There is no honour in any of this." I swept my hand behind us at the smouldering, smoke filled sky. "But we are fighting for survival and we will do whatever it takes to preserve our way of life."

"You have changed brother."

"I know but then we have all changed a little, brother, even you."

King Gwalliog seemed almost disappointed when we returned. "Your fears were groundless Lord Lann; the Saxons did not appear."

I dismounted stiffly. My leg had ached all the way to the raid and back but at least it had not bled. "If we can launch a surprise attack, then so can the Saxons. They will come. I am leaving my archers here tomorrow and we go slaving."

"Slaving? And how will that defeat the Saxons?"

"There are only a handful of large villages but there are many hundreds of farms and farmsteads dotted all over the land. They are the warriors who will be fighting you. Besides which it will anger Wach and, when he comes, he will fight with his heart and not his head. I want him and his men desperate to rip out my heart. That way they will make mistakes."

"You will deliberately put yourself in danger?"

I shrugged. "I am a warrior and besides so long as I wield Saxon Slayer I fear no man."

"You were wounded in the leg during your last fight."

"And that taught me a lesson. I need to work with my oathsworn more. As soon as my leg is healed I will leave the horse behind and fight on foot. I am no equite. While we are away then deepen your ditches and prepare stones and rocks for when they do come."

There were just twenty five of us who rode away the next morning. I had commanded Raibeart to remain at the stronghold. I needed someone to command my men in my absence and I did not feel that there would be any danger that day. We rode east for a long time. By noon we had covered many miles and I rested the horses. "Now we can begin to hurt the enemy Garth. They will feel safe this far from our forces and we can attack with impunity. We will not take prisoners this far from home but, when we come closer to Loidis I want as many women and children taking prisoner as we can. Wach needs to bleed and this is all that we have."

We spotted the smoke from the two roundhouses and rode swiftly in. The two men who tried to defend it were quickly killed. I watched as the woman and her three children fled east. We burned the house and slaughtered the animals. We tied the corpses of the dead chickens and geese to our saddles and threw the bodies of the other beasts into the burning home. Starvation was a serious weapon and I would use any weapon I could. We headed west and destroyed another five farms. I could tell from my men's faces that they did not enjoy this butchery for the farmers who fought us were just defending their lands. We too had done as they had and our people had suffered. It was a harsh world.

"Now we take prisoners." When I gave the order I saw the sadness on men's faces. My warriors were noble. I could think of other warriors who would enjoy inflicting pain on women but Garth and I had chosen our men well. Four farms later and we had six women and four children wailing and bemoaning their fate. They were tied to our horses but we were now close enough to Loidis to be safe from reprisals. I assumed that Wach would have been drawn east and would be seeking us around our first burnings.

It was almost dark when we wearily trudged through the gates. My leg was an agony and I could see that the horses, too had suffered. We would not be riding the next day. We needed rest; besides I hoped that we had achieved our ends and provoked the Saxons into an attack. King Gwalliog was pleased to have slaves. They were a valuable asset and would be put to work in the kitchens. They were led to the blacksmith's to have their metal collars fitted. It gave me some consolation to know that they would not be treated as Monca, Aelle's mother was, and be made a sex slave for a warrior. They would be treated well for King Gwalliog and his people were kind. They would, however, still be slaves and the children would grow up serving their masters.

"You look tired, brother."

"I am, Raibeart. Tomorrow we rest and prepare for battle."

"Have you the second sight? Can you know that the Saxons will come?"

"If they do not come then we will go to meet them for it will mean that we have defeated them. We can strike as we did today and that will make the Saxons flee. He either fights us or leaves. Wach is the son of Aella; he cannot afford to have us rub his nose in the burnt out buildings of his people. He will come."

Chapter 3

It was two days later when we were about to leave on a patrol to find the Saxons that the scouts I had sent ahead of us spotted the enemy. The Saxons were filtering through the woods a mile from the walls and my men hurried quickly back to me. "We return to Loidis. Raibeart keep ten warriors with you and harry them. I will sound the horn when we are prepared."

We had discovered that King Gwalliog possessed one of the old Roman battle horns called buccina and we had begun to use it to signal in battles. Today we would frighten the Saxons with its cry. The guards at the gate were curious at our sudden return. "The Saxons are here. Prepare to defend the walls."

King Gwalliog was armed already and striding towards me, the joy of battle upon his face. "At last we meet them beard to beard!"

I could not help but smiling at the older warrior who still relished battle. "Let us show them who they face. Run up the standards!"

The men at the gates were ready with the two standards and they rose above the main gate. I knew which one would anger and annoy the Saxons; it would be my Wolf standard. The wolf cloak I wore above my armour marked me as the Wolf Warrior they both dreaded and hated while my shield had the image of a wolf painted upon it; I was not easy to miss. I dismounted and walked gingerly towards the walls. Today would be a test of Brother Patrick's skill and the ability of my leg to endure a battle on foot. I would not have the support of a horse and I would have to stand on the battlements to fight. One of the slingers ran towards me with my bow and quiver. "Here my lord, I thought you might need it."

"Thank you Targh and make sure you keep your head down. I would have you grow into a warrior to stand beside me in my shield wall." I saw him glow with pride and he ran to tell the other boys of the praise from his lord. When I reached the top of the ramparts I saw that Raibeart and his men were facing a couple of hundred Saxons. The walls were fully manned and I shouted, "Sound the horn!"

The horn gave a mournful moan. It did not have the same effect as the dragon standard of King Urien but, as our men galloped back, I saw that it made the enemy halt and look to their leaders. Wach was there. I had never seen him before but the warrior with the helmet like me and surrounded by similarly attired mailed warriors had to be the son of Aella. We had poked the bear with the stick and now he was here. The wily warrior showed his cunning by bringing his men from the woods slowly and aligning them with the better armed at the fore. My archers would score few easy hits. They kept coming from the greenwood like ants from an anthill. He had brought every male Saxon he could. The fate of Elmet would be decided this day.

I heard feet on the ladder and Gwalliog and Raibeart joined me. "That is a large army brother."

"I know. Put your archers on this wall and below. We can direct their aim from the walls."

King Gwalliog looked at me his face showing that he would brook no argument. "My men will defend this wall."

I bowed, "As you wish." It was his stronghold but I knew that my battle hardened men would do a better job. "Garth put our warriors on the other walls." Garth's face frowned then he shrugged his shoulders and nodded. At least the Saxons had few archers and they would have to close with the walls and our men who stood there; but we were outnumbered.

There were two thousand men facing us but only five hundred were warriors with shield and helm. I could not see any archers and, of course, they had no horsemen. I could see movement from behind the front ranks which were now two hundred paces from our walls but I could not work out what it was. I was suspicious and I remained alert to a trick or a trap. They were within bow range but I knew that we could inflict more damage at closer range. As I looked at the ditch I could see that we should have used a drawbridge as we had at Civitas Carvetiorum but it was too late for that.

The Saxon line came forwards steadily. Wach and his bodyguard were not in the front rank. I did not take this as a sign of fear but of strategy. He would not wish to waste his best men in the first brutal attack where they would face the arrows and swords of the defenders. It was one of his father's tactics and he had used it effectively before allowing his weaker warriors to be slaughtered. The warriors at the front held their shields tightly to their helmets affording them the most protection from any missiles hurled from the walls. They had learned. I could see that Raibeart and his archers were ready and I nodded. He would make the decision for the first loosing of the arrows. I aimed my bow at Wach. He was over two hundred paces away but it was worth the arrow just to let him know we had the range. I loosed. A sudden flurry of wind came up, *wyrd*, and the arrow moved to the left. It struck the surprised warrior to Wach's left in the throat and every warrior around the war chief raised their shields! I saw Raibeart shake his head but Gwalliog's men all cheered. It was only one warrior but we had first blood. I wondered how his farmers and untried warriors would feel knowing that we could kill them at two hundred paces.

Raibeart's command almost took me by surprise as one hundred arrows soared up and over the ramparts. The subsequent four volleys came in rapid succession. The plunging trajectories of the arrows and the relative short distance meant that over a hundred and fifty men fell and their bodies impeded the others. Suddenly the warriors at the front parted and I saw what had caused the disturbance at the start of their advance. They had a log on wheels. They were going to ram the gate.

"Brace the gate! They have a ram!"

King Gwalliog's men had spears and javelins and they began to hurl them at the straining warriors who were pulling the mighty oak. Some fell but other brave warriors took their places. I could tell that Wach had his warriors fired up and they hurled themselves at the wall. I turned to King Gwalliog. "Your majesty, if you mount your horsemen then they can leave by the south gate and attack in their flank when we are ready."

He looked at me dubiously. "Is this a trick, Lord Lann, to give your men the glory of victory?"

I shook my head. "The glory will come from the attack by your horsemen and mine as they slaughter the Saxons." He was not convinced. "They have no horsemen and the warriors at the rear have no armour. One hundred and twenty mounted men can cause large numbers of casualties if we time the attack well."

"Very well but I will lead them!"

"As you wish. I will sound the buccina when I judge the time ripe for an attack and we will time it to coincide with our own attack from within. Garth, send our equites to the king."

Just then we heard, and felt, the thump as the ram struck the gate. "Bring boiling water. Raibeart, target the men on the ram." The problem with this strategy was that it took the arrows away from their main battle line and that would allow them to close with the walls but if we lost the gate then we would lose the battle, and the war. I heard the clatter of hooves as the horsemen mustered and then Garth was at my side. "Bring half the men from the other walls; put half behind the gate to repel any who get through and put the others on the walls."

The men of Elmet had braced the gate as best they could but it would not hold. The redoubtable Brother Patrick led the women with the boiling kettles of water. "Good man. You men take the kettles and give the men on the ram a good dousing!" The archers were unable to strike the men on the ram as they were now protected by the shields of warriors sent forwards by Wach. "Raibeart start thinning out the warriors who are preparing to assault the wall." I heard the whirr of slingshots as the Saxons tried to hit my archers. "Slingers, take out the men with the slings."

Suddenly there was a hiss followed by screams as the four huge kettles were emptied over the ram. Boiling water found its way through mail and burnt and scalded the warriors. They dropped the ram and Raibeart's archers ended their misery.

It was a brief respite for more Saxons ran forwards to take up the ram and we now had no more water. "Raibeart, take command here and I will join Garth to attack those who breach the gate. Make them pay a heavy price for the entrance."

Raibeart's nod was worth a hundred warriors; he would not let me down and I joined Garth and my warriors at the gate. Garth grinned at me as he took his place on my right. "We will show them my lord. It is blade to blade that will give us victory and Saxon Slayer will prevail."

The hundred men with us gave a huge cheer, making those on the ramparts look around. I drew the sword which had come to me, as though willed from above and as I raised it the cheers became a crescendo. I hoped that their better and braver warriors had perished with the ram but I had seen Wach and his bodyguard and knew that there were at least a hundred warriors who would give a good account of themselves. I glanced up and saw Tadgh duck behind the ramparts; I caught his eye and he waved. "Remember you must survive to become a warrior of Rheged." He nodded and popped up to hurl a stone at an unseen enemy.

I watched as splinters flew from the gate and knew that it would not be long. We were in a wedge formation and we would have to hit them as soon as they broke through. Raibeart had sent down ten archers to kill those wielding the ram and I hoped that the ram would block the gate and make our task easier. I also wondered if my leg would support me; it still felt stiff and I would need to move swiftly. I was the point of the wedge. Much hinged on how I could lead my warriors.

With a groan and a crack the gate gave way and the ram lurched forwards. Raibeart's archers were good and ten of the men with the ram fell; the whole ram dropped like a stone and I leapt forwards. "Rheged!" I stepped over the two dead warriors. The first warrior I killed was prone on the ground and I severed his head. The man behind had no time to react as I smashed my shield into his face and stamped on him as I leapt over the dead bodies. I knew one of those behind would despatch him and I was eager to block the gate with my men. Suddenly we were ahead of the ram and outside what had been the gate; I yelled, "Shield wall!" My men's training took over and, quickly, we had two solid lines of fifty men. I could see the enraged Saxons who ran at us falling to Raibeart's arrows. It was vital for it splintered their wedge and they struck us piecemeal rather than a solid mass of men and metal. They had only fought the men of Elmet and, even though they were our allies, they were not the men who fought besides me that day. We had confidence in each other as we hacked and slashed at every Saxon we faced until their first wave was dead. It had been an unfair match up as each of their warriors faced two of mine.

Wach and his bodyguard formed up and I could see the anger and the hurt in their eyes. They were but fifty paces from us. These could not be damaged by Raibeart and his archers. The best that the bows could do was to weaken their shields. Tadgh and the other slingers had ended the threat of the enemy slingers and were adding their attack to that of Raibeart. It kept the shields of the Saxons up and that limited their sight. We had a chance. They would be expecting us to stand and take whatever they offered but we would take the attack to them. "Wedge!" I felt the men behind me move and I shouted, "Buccina, sound the charge!" I raised Wolf Slayer and roared, "For King Urien and Rheged." My men almost pushed me forwards as we raced across the body littered ground to meet their warriors.

Wach was not in their front rank. There was a warrior with an open helmet while wielding a double handed axe. I feared him not. I had already slipped a dagger into my left hand and my shield was studded with metal. There was no axe made which could dent it but I would use it as a weapon. I watched him raise his axe to swing it at my head. The man was brave but a fool. I ducked slightly and, as we met, punched hard with my shield. The men behind him meant he could not go backwards and the blow took all of his wind. I was too close to use Saxon Slayer and I head butted him to the ground. As I stepped over him I stamped on his face and felt his nose and his skull crushed beneath my boot. Their wedge was no longer whole!

I heard Garth roaring encouragement to our men and felt the whole line lurch forwards. Although they had more men to push forwards the constant barrage from arrows and stones was negating the effect of numbers as men tried to hide from the wicked barbs and stones which Raibeart and his men rained down upon them. As the men before us thinned a little I was able to swing Saxon Slayer over my head. Few warriors owned a helmet which could withstand it and I cracked open the helmet and the head of the warrior who bravely faced me. Many warriors wished to be the one to kill the hated enemy of the Saxons, the Wolf Warrior, but they had neither the skill nor the weapons to do so.

Wach and his bodyguard were forming up as the remnants of their vanguard were vanquished. They had endured much and, I suspect, had marched all night. My men had had a hearty meal and a good night's rest. We could fight all day without tiring. Wach and his elite warriors would be a true test of the skills of the Wolf Brethren. Two of the Saxons came for me with Wach close by. One had a spear which he jabbed at my eye while the other hacked over arm with his axe. The rim of the shield deflected the spear but the axe struck at the same time. I felt the spear head slice into my cheek. I raised the shield and thrust blindly with my sword. I felt it sink into flesh and saw the axe man's eyes fill with fear as the sharpened steel entered his groin. I sensed, rather than saw, the axe as it scythed towards me and then Garth's shield turned it away to embed itself in the dying axe warrior next to him. Before the warrior with the spear could strike me again I punched with my shield boss into his face. He took the punch well but he opened his body slightly and I slid Saxon Slayer through the mail on his left side; the blood which dripped from my sword told me I had wounded him and he stepped backwards. We all knew that to step back in a shield wall was to invite death and so it was. The warrior to my left pushed forwards and stabbed the wounded man in the throat.

Garth was busily engaged with Wach who was desperately trying to reach me. I heard the clash of arms from ahead and heard the wail as King Gwalliog and his horsemen struck the men at the rear of the Saxon line and began to butcher them. I noticed that the arrows were now falling further away and that meant that Raibeart could see the enemy lines faltering. "On, men of Rheged! One last push and we shall prevail!"

Wach's guttural Saxon almost spat in my face. "Not before you die at my hands, killer of women."

I did not bother to answer him and deny his lie. He was angry and that was a weakness. I slew the fierce faced swordsman who hacked at my shield and then turned to face Wach. There were two of us fighting him; no honour in that but we not seeking honour, we were seeking victory. He could not stand against two of us and his men, desperate to aid him were hacked to the ground by my shield wall which still retained its integrity. It was Garth who struck the mortal blow. As Wach's axe embedded itself in my shield Garth's sword took off his head. The Saxons who were oathsworn did not flee but pushed even harder to redeem themselves by saving their leader's body. They were slaughtered to a man. When we stood amidst the pile of bodies I glanced up and saw that Raibeart had led the garrison to pursue the fleeing Saxons. King Gwalliog and his horsemen were hurtling towards the woods and the last of the Saxons. I could not have fought any more for my leg was sending waves of pain through my whole body. All I wanted was to lie down and sleep.

I raised my helmet and Garth's face filled with concern. "You are wounded my lord."

"I think it is a scratch."

"I think not my lord, I can see bone. Brother Patrick!"

The priests and women had also followed Raibeart and were tending to the wounded. The young priest shook his head. "Are you determined to die Lord Lann? Your wife will not be happy when you return to Rheged."

I gave a painful grin. "At least spare me the fire this time." Suddenly my legs would no longer support me and I saw their faces get further from me as I slumped to the ground, to lie on the bloody, gore spattered ground.

Brother Patrick reached down and held a cloth to my face. "Garth, get your men to carry him. He has lost much blood. Another hour and he would be dead." He shook his head. "The sword may be magical my lord but you must remember that you are mortal. Take more care."

The last vision I had was of Raibeart's concerned face peering over the priest's shoulder and then all became black.

When I came too it was to see Brother Patrick and Raibeart still leaning over me but I was now in the priest's hut. Brother Patrick did not look concerned but Raibeart had the fearful look he had had when I had been stabbed in the leg. "You will live Lord Lann. You are tough."

"How long ..." I croaked.

"Just a couple of hours," said Raibeart with relief in his voice, "but it seemed longer. Brother Raibeart took his time with the stitches."

The priest shrugged and gave me an apologetic smile. "Having given you one scar I felt obliged to make the other as neat as possible." He stood up. "There. I would tell you to rest but I suspect you would ignore me. Besides unless you laugh a lot you will do your face no harm." So laughing he left.

"And the battle?"

"When Wach and his bodyguards all died the rest fled. King Gwalliog and the horsemen are still pursuing them. Our men are on the field, stripping the dead and despatching the wounded."

I asked the next question not wanting to know the answer. "And our losses?"

"Fifty two of our warriors and three archers died. The wounded will recover. We lost two boys. I know not of the horsemen for they are still with the king."

Our losses seemed light but even one was too many for me. I had fought alongside many of these men for some years and I would miss them. Old friends were harder to replace and old warriors even more so. "I think our work here is done brother and we can return home."

His face lit up. "I had hoped that was the case but I fear that my father in law may wish us to remain."

"There is little point. With Wach dead and the army routed then the king's horses can keep the Saxons at bay. I will suggest strategies to him but we will be needed at home. Besides I think we have shed enough blood for our allies eh?"

"You certainly have brother. Perhaps some mail beneath your helmet next time?"

"It is hard enough to move in my armour as it is."

"Then keep away from the thick of the fighting. I feel guilty for I am never in danger and I am always at the rear with the archers but Garth and you are the ones the enemy try to kill."

"And I am happy with that state of affairs. One of my brothers has lost an arm. I will do all I can to keep you safe."

I did not know what the priest had given me to drink but I felt little or no pain from my wound. Raibeart helped me to my feet and I went to see the other wounded warriors. I felt guilty as they all expressed concern at my wounds and yet some of them looked to be in a far worse state than I was. We went out into the courtyard and I could see that Raibeart had had the men clear all of the bodies but the dark patches showed where men had fought and died.

Garth and my remaining warriors wearily marched into the settlement, laden with armour and weapons. They added them to the pile near to the main hall.

"Good to see you upright my lord. There was so much blood I feared you would never stand again." Garth's face became serious. "I am sorry that I did not stop the spear. I have let you down."

I was going to shake my head and then remembered my wound. "You have no reason to reproach yourself, it was an accident and you managed to kill their leader. That saved many men's lives. My brother has suggested some mail beneath my helmet."

His face brightened. "A good idea. I will have the smiths make one when we return." He paused. "We are returning are we not my lord?"

"Aye. For our work here is done. We will leave within the next few days; as soon as more of our men are fit to travel."

Raibeart was right. When a jubilant King Gwalliog returned he was full of ideas for a war against the Saxons further away. "I am sorry your majesty but we will be needed at home. Besides with your crops sown and your animals born you can use your ordinary warriors to rid your land of the last few Saxons. We have much armour and weapons. You will have an army as well armed as that of Rheged. If you fortify and occupy Wachanglen then the enemy will be kept at bay. You will just need to be vigilant and use your horsemen to watch for the enemy."

"Do not get me wrong Lord Lann. I appreciate your ideas and I will implement them but my people like following the Wolf Banner as much as my own white horse."

"And my own people feel the same. We will fight alongside each other again your majesty and next time will be when we drive the Saxons back into the sea and finally defeat them."

We finally left after a three day feast to celebrate our victory. The King was as good as his word and his warriors now occupied Wachanglen. The Saxons, who could, had fled and the ones who remained became slaves. It was a cruel world. He also gave us some wagons for our wounded and our share of the enemy treasure. Garth now sported his own helmet like mine which he had taken, as was his right, from the dead body of Wach as well as his axe. The torc and his jewels we shared with the men. We would all return to Rheged richer but we had laid aside much of the monies for the families of those who had died. It was one of the things which marked us as different from those that we fought. Brother Patrick gave me a small jar of salve for my wound. Raibeart told me that it looked red and angry but, as it was itching, I assumed that it was healing.

The king and Raibeart had private words before he left. They had not known each other before our campaign but now the king recognised my brother as someone who could rule in his stead. My little brother would become a king one day and rule the land of Elmet. There were still five warriors who were not ready to travel but the king promised that they would be cared for and, when he came north to meet with his allies, they would accompany him.

We returned by a different route. We headed due west over the tops of the high hills and then headed through the land of the lakes. We both wished to see our little brother Aelle and we were told that it was a safer way for there were no enemies there. The Saxons had yet to discover the fertile west of Britannia.

Spring had taken some time to come but now that it had the world was green and alive with life. Warriors fight hard and know that death is just a blade away so we appreciate life more than the farmer or the merchant who just measures the quality of his life by possessions. We measured our success by enjoying life and the men laughed, sang and joked as we trekked back to our homes. We remembered the dead in our songs and tales. When we sat around our camp fires we made the songs to make the men live again.

My wounds healed well and Raibeart took out my stitches, ten days after the priest had put them in as instructed by the determined young healer. The men all watched as each stitch was cut and gently removed. There was a little pain but not much and I saw the sweat on Raibeart's face as he cut each one as though his life depended upon it. He sighed with relief when the last one came out. "Well you are no better looking brother but at least you are no uglier. The scar will become invisible when your beard grows again."

"I may not grow a beard. I have quite enjoyed having a face free of hair."

There was a gasp from Garth and the other warriors. A beard was the mark of a man although King Urien and his sons had neatly trimmed beards unlike the wild ones of Garth and the others. Raibeart shook his head. "I would wait until Aideen has made her mind up. In my experience it is women who make those decisions not their men."

Wide Water was beautiful in the evening sun as we crested the last ridge. We could see the smoke spiralling from my brother's stronghold. We would sleep beneath a roof this night and enjoy hot food. We were more than a mile away when the thirty horsemen approached us. "Hail Wolf Warriors. Lord Aelle has sent us to escort you the last part of the journey. My name is Scean and I am the leader of your brother's horsemen."

They formed a guard ahead of us and the leader rode next to Raibeart and me." How did you know we were not raiders?"

He grinned and gestured at the standard. "Even without that we would have know you and your brother by your wolf cloaks. Lord Aelle is forever boasting of his two brothers."

Raibeart pointed at the escort. "We could have found the fortress you know."

"Perhaps but Lord Aelle has made traps and ditches to foil an assault. Any enemy who tries to take our home will be defeated before he even gets to the walls. We did not wish you to come to harm."

There was pride in his voice. Aelle was still being as clever as ever. "It seems the loss of his arm has not inhibited our little brother."

"No he is as busy as he always was."

The whole family awaited us as we entered. Scean had been correct; it was a circuitous and complex route into the fort. With water on three sides Aelle had made the only approach a death trap. I could see the loopholes and gates which could be used to pour stones and arrows on an enemy who was foolish enough to attack. Aelle and his family would be safe and I would sleep easier from now on.

Aelle looked to have filled out and his two children had grown somewhat. Freja looked to be with child again but she was beaming. Aelle had his men as an honour guard and they roared, "Wolf Warriors!" as we halted.

Raibeart grinned at me as we dismounted. "It seems our little brother is making a fuss!"

As I embrace Aelle I noticed how much he had grown. "Thank you Aelle." I embraced Freja. "It looks like marriage suits you both, sister."

She held me at arm's length and looked at me critically. "And you have been wounded. "Whatever will Aideen think! At least Aelle's wound kept him from war but I fear you will continue to be a warrior."

I shrugged. "And what else would I do!" I bent down to pick up the children. "And these are getting bigger each time I see them. What do you feed them on?" They both giggled and squealed with delight.

"Welcome to you both. Your men can sleep in the warrior hall. You can sleep in our quarters."

Raibeart looked at Aelle in surprise. "You have a warrior hall? Isn't that a luxury?" Only Civitas Carvetiorum had one for it was an expense most of us could do without."

"As you can see I have made my fortress a stronghold. If the Saxons come then the people can all come inside and the warrior hall is their accommodation.

"We have missed your fertile little mind Aelle. And now lead us to some food. I am starving!"

Just then there was a barking and Wolf, our sheepdog bounded from the hall. He had been my dog originally and he leapt into my arms and began licking my face. That, too, nearly brought forth a flood of tears for he had been my companion for years. Now he was old and had outlived other dogs.

Aelle turned to me as Wolf fussed Raibeart. "He is a father now and has many pups. When they are weaned I will send you one." Aelle, who had had the toughest upbringing, was the most gentle and thoughtful of the three of us. I was lucky to have such a brother.

The meal was a merry one as we told of our victories and Aelle quizzed me about my wounds. "It is good that you are both back for King Urien needs his strongest generals."

There was something in my brother's tone which suggested danger. "What is wrong with the king?"

"Physically? Nothing but with Prince Ywain away in the north and you two in Elmet he has had much to think about. Morcant Bulc is being as devious as ever and Bladud, well Bladud is still Bladud."

Bladud was the champion of Rheged and he hated me and my brothers. He and Morcant Bulc had deliberately held back at the battle with the Saxons and it had cost Aelle his arm. The king could see no wrong in Bladud but none of the three of us trusted him. "I should have killed him after the battle but…"

"I know brother. You were too concerned about me and then the moment passed. Perhaps it is for the best. You are now the great general Lann and Bladud will have to walk carefully around you. When King Gwalliog comes to the kingdom and meets with the king I am sure that Bladud's sun will be eclipsed."

"I hope so." My thoughts belied my words. Bladud was cunning and I still feared his association with Morcant Bulc who was a snake in the grass.

Chapter 4

Before I could return to my home, Castle Perilous, I had to tell King Urien, personally, of the events; I had been Rheged and King Urien had high standards. Bearing in mind what Aelle had said about the state of affairs in the land I knew that it was vitally important. Both Aideen and Maiwen were staying with the King and the Queen but I yearned to be safe within my own walls again and master of my own life. I sent Garth and my warriors back to my castle to prepare it for my homecoming and it was a much smaller retinue which crossed through the magnificent gate and the reassuringly thick stone walls of Civitas Carvetiorum; I had seen how flimsy wooden walls could be.

The guards grinned and waved at us as we rode through the gates. I recognised both of them and I had fought alongside them at Metcauld. "Glad you are back safely my lord!" Their faces became more serious as they saw the scar on my face. It was a warning of what my family would think.

The courtyard was empty as we dismounted. The slingers took our horses to the stables and we headed for Brother Osric's quarters. He glanced up and then went back to his map making. "As you are back so swiftly then I can assume that you were victorious but from your leg and your face I can see that you are not returned unscathed!"

I was amazed, he had barely looked at me and yet he had assessed me in an instant. "The Saxons are defeated. It was one of Aella's sons, Wach, and Garth killed him. Elmet is safe."

"And was the expense of the weapons and men worth it?"

Raibeart laughed. "Ever the book keeper. What you really mean, you tight fisted old scoundrel is did we come back with treasure?"

He looked up, a wry smile playing about his lips, "And did you?"

"Of course. There are two wagons in the courtyard with arms, armour and treasure."

"You have, of course, taken your share?"

"Of course; you taught me well old man."

He suddenly seemed to notice how long the scar actually was. "Whoever stitched that face of yours did a fine job. Who did it for you? One of the Elmet women; I heard they are good."

"No it was another of your White Christ priests. Brother Patrick." I turned and rolled up the breeks to show him my calf. "He did it to make up for burning the wound on my leg."

"Only because you would not let it heal." Raibeart admonished me.

Brother Osric sniffed, "Then he was a fool for I would have cauterized it at once. It ensures no putrefaction and decay."

"Where is the king?"

"He is on patrol but the Queen and your wives are in the main hall. You can leave the wagons and treasure to me." He paused and actually smiled, "Well done and I am pleased that you are back safe and sound. The kingdom needs you, both of you."

As we left Raibeart said, "Things must be bad. That was almost gushing from Osric."

"Aye. Perhaps our wives might know more."

The guard on the Queen's quarters smiled, apologetically, as he knocked and peered around the door. We heard him say, "Lord Lann and Lord Raibeart are returned."

There was a chorus of squeals and then the guard was bowled over as Aideen, Maiwen and my son Hogan rushed to throw themselves about us. I saw the Queen smiling at the scene. She had lost one of her own sons in the last year and she could appreciate the feelings of our wives. I have to confess that I felt a little tearful. I had only been away for a few months but Hogan seemed to have grown a whole hand and his hair had changed colour! My fighting was stopping me from watching my family grow and I now understood why my father had not taken the warrior route. He was obviously a better father and husband than I was.

When Aideen saw my scar her mouth opened and she almost screamed. "What happened?"

Queen Niamh said, "Sit down my lords and tell us of your travails for I can see that serving Rheged and Elmet comes at a cost."

We spent the next hour giving an account of the small war. We cleaned up the horror but there was no escaping the description of the wounds I had suffered. I tried to make light of it but my brother told them the truth. I would have been annoyed with him but I knew that he cared deeply for me and had been worried that I might die.

"Well at least I have you now, at home." Aideen turned to the Queen, pleading with her words and her eyes. "Tell the king that Lord Lann needs to rest. It is not fair that he is the one who is always fighting."

"Aideen!"

"No, she is right, my lord, others should shoulder their share but, as the borders are peaceful, I think that we will be able to have a peaceful summer and autumn. It will do the king good to see you two again." She rose, a little stiffly, for she was old. "And now I will leave you to be reacquainted. I have a feast to organise although I suspect the Osric will already have begun the preparations."

Once alone I bounced Hogan on my knee. He put a tentative finger up to poke my scar. Aideen went to stop him. "Leave him. It does not hurt and he is only curious."

"I meant what I said to the Queen. I do not want to lose you so soon after finding you."

I put my arm around her. "You will not lose me." She drew back and gave me a sceptical look. "Neither of these wounds was life threatening. The leg is a little stiff but that will pass and, when I have regrown my beard the scar will vanish."

"But you could have died."

I said simply, "But I didn't so do not upset yourself with something which did not happen."

"I want to go home."

"As I do and when the King returns then we can leave and we will make Castle Perilous as fine a home as this."

The king did not look any older as he rode through the gates but there was sadness in his eyes which disappeared when he spied Raibeart and me standing next to Osric. "My warriors return!" The queen smiled at me and nodded; she could see a change in her husband already. He almost picked me up he was hugging so hard and he did the same to Raibeart.

Out of the corner of my eye I could see the black looks Bladud was throwing my way but I just smiled back at him. He stepped back. "Your early return tells me that you have succeeded quicker than we had hoped. Come, from that fearful scar on your cheek I can see you have much to tell me."

Later that evening when we had feasted and drunk well the king was a happy man. "I am pleased that we have aided your father in law Raibeart because it means we can plan our assault next year on Aella."

"He is still a threat then? I though the bloody nose we gave him last time might have made him less aggressive."

"No, he has a stronghold south of the Dunum and more warriors are coming from across the sea to aid him."

I threw a look at Bladud who appeared to be hanging on every word. "I would have thought that King Morcant Bulc would have finished off Aella. We left him with few men to deal with. Why did he not reclaim his lands? South of the Dunum is almost half of the kingdom of Bernicia."

"And the better half at that," piped in Raibeart.

The king shrugged. "I know and if I were king of that land I would have driven the Saxon and his hordes back to the sea." He shrugged, "But I am not. It seems we will have to fight him once again and, from what you tell me, he will be desperate to get to you, the killer of his son."

I saw Aideen and her face had paled. I wished that the king had kept his opinion to himself. I could do without my wife being reminded of the danger I had been in. I changed the subject quickly. "A year without war will help the kingdom to grow."

"Amen to that," intoned Brother Osric who was busily filling his face with wild boar. "War is expensive and we need to consolidate what we have before we fight again. I, for one, would have been happier had the King of Bernicia dealt with his own problems rather than waiting for his brother kings to solve his problems for him."

I swallowed a piece of boar and washed it down with some of the wine the Brother favoured. "And yet Brother Osric, as Raibeart and I discovered, having an army which is small but paid well can be more effective than taking men from the fields where they will be more productive. The Saxons may have outnumbered us at Loidis but our men were better armed and trained. King Gwalliog's farmers managed to sow their crops and tend to their flocks. The Saxons did not. Even had we not defeated them in battle, the king would have won for come the autumn his people would have starved."

Bladud snorted. "Your argument backs up King Morcant Bulc and yet you criticise him for not attacking his enemies."

I fixed Bladud with a steely eye. I had watched what I had been drinking but not so the leader of the king's bodyguard who was well in his cups and had made an unguarded remark. I noticed the narrowing of King Urien's eyes. He had heard and it had worried him. "I criticised the king who allows others to fight for his land and does nothing when he has the opportunity to reclaim it. We will be going to war in the spring and it will not be to secure our own land but that of our ally."

He could see that he had been indiscreet and he waved a hand of apology, stood and then staggered off to his quarters. Queen Niamh shook her head, "I do not know why you invite that man he has neither manners nor wit and he spoils every feast."

"He is a warrior not a jester and he is a brave man," the king sounded defensive and unconvincing.

The Queen smiled dangerously, she had the point and she would use it. "Lord Lann and Lord Raibeart, as well as your sons, are warriors, and yet they have manners and wit."

The king shrugged in defeat and Brother Osric coughed, "You may have something Lord Lann. I have noticed that the revenues from the southern part of the kingdom, the one ruled by your brother, have increased. He does not fight and yet he has warriors should they be needed." He looked up at me. "As, it seems do you and Lord Raibeart. Perhaps that is the model we should adopt." He gave a sly sideways look at the king.

"You know that I am for peace but, until the Saxon threat has gone then we will need every warrior we can muster to drive them back across the sea. You would agree with that Lord Lann?"

I was in a difficult position but I found that I agreed with both of them. "I think that we will need every warrior to drive the Saxons away but it will be just one battle, and at a time and place of our choosing. We keep our workers toiling and use our few warriors to watch for trouble."

Brother Osric nodded. "You have grown Lord Lann. That was as diplomatic an answer as I have heard. You manage to agree with both of us and yet disagree at the same time without offending either of us! Very skilful indeed."

Everyone laughed and the atmosphere lightened. "Verbal jousting seems easy after fighting off two or three Saxons who are trying to hack lumps off you."

As soon as the words were out of my mouth I regretted them for Aideen paled again and fled the room; Queen Niamh shook her head. "You might be a diplomat and a warrior but when it comes to being a husband you could take lessons from your brother Aelle. Get after her and make it up to her."

I gave a hesitant bow and left. As I passed the queen she slapped me hard on the buttocks. She smiled as she said, "But I have no doubt that, given time together you will become the fine husband you ought to be."

Aideen was lying on the bed sobbing when I entered. This was a world which was strange to me. I had never been gentle as Raibeart and Aelle could testify but I had been caring. My world was a harsh one where the tone of voice you used did not matter to the men who heard it, only the command that was given. I was learning that I had to think before I spoke. Perhaps it was best if I did not speak at all. I sat on the bed next to her and put my hand on her heaving shoulders. I could feel the sobs wracking her body. With my other hand I began to stroke her hair and gradually the sobs subsided. I leaned forwards and the sweet smell of rosemary and rosewater filled my nostrils and I nuzzled her hair and then, gently kissed, first her ear and then, moving the hair away, the nape of her neck. It was as though I had stung her with a whip for she suddenly turned and grabbed me, kissing me hard on the lips. Later as she lay sleeping in my arms I wondered if I had hit upon the right strategy; say little and be gentle.

The next day nothing was spoken of the upset I had caused and she was all smiles. I think the journey home was filling her mind and the thought that she knew she would have me alone and without war filling the horizon. As she and her slaves packed the wagons I went to say farewell to the king and Brother Osric. The Queen had a wry and knowing look upon her face. "You are learning Lord Lann!"

I suddenly turned. How did she know? The king smiled. "Welcome to the brotherhood of husbands who are kept in the dark!

"Buffoon!" was all she said and then she left the room.

"She is right though Lann. You need to enjoy the rest of the year for your words last night were wise. When the other kings come at Yule then we will plan our final assault. Until then you need to recover your strength."

"Aye your majesty but I also need to recruit more warriors. The war in Elmet might not have been a long one but it was costly in terms of the valuable men I lost."

Brother Osric chortled, "I would not worry Lord Lann for word has spread and young men will be coming from all over just to learn from the Wolf Warrior. Your fame has, indeed, spread beyond our borders. You cannot hide away any longer."

When I returned to the courtyard Maiwen and Aideen were saying their farewells and arranging to visit the other's home. That pleased me for it meant I would see Raibeart and it would be good to see him when we were not fighting for our lives. We could even go hunting and that thought put a grin on my face.

"Farewell brother I think I will try to make my home as strong as Castle Perilous. Our wars in Elmet have shown me the dangers of complacency."

"I too will be improving my own defences. I do not think that you can be too strong and our little brother has shown us the way."

Most of my warriors were with Garth and there were just ten men to accompany us. Some of those still rode in the wagon as they were recovering from their wounds but it was a joyous ride for me as I saw the land I ruled filled with growth and life. There were gambolling lambs and young calves friskily bouncing around the fields. The farmers and workers we passed seemed to be happier and healthier than I remembered. Perhaps I was comparing them to the fearful folk of Elmet. Hogan and Aideen also seemed caught up in the joy and we sang and told tales all the way back to Castle Perilous.

I felt strangely comforted when I saw the stout Roman gatehouse loom into view. Its position above the river and its clear views down the valley made it a vital fort to hold in the defence of Rheged. Each time I saw it I thanked the gods for giving me such a domain. As I had expected, Garth had sentries posted to watch for our arrival and, as we crossed the bridge, the Wolf Banner fluttered from the gatehouse. Brother Oswald which performed the same function for me as Brother Osric did for the king was there with the doughty Garth to greet us.

"Welcome home my lord and hopefully you will stay a little longer this time."

"Hopefully Brother Oswald."

"The money has been given to the families of those who died my lord and I gave the rest to the Brother here."

"And a tidy sum it was. Have you plans for any of it my lord?"

I looked at Aideen. "That depends upon my lady here."

Her face lightened and she smiled, "I can think of many improvements and we will make our house a home, at last."

We dismounted and crossed the drawbridge. It was a solid affair but I never like to overburden it. I could see that work had been done and the wood had been renewed above the gate and I could see fresh mortar. The priest saw my look and shrugged. "It seemed prudent my lord and we do live in parlous times. I also took the liberty of having a couple of extra rooms built next to your quarters." He looked a little embarrassed, "Privacy my lord."

Aideen compounded his embarrassment by hugging him. "You are a mind reader and I know not what I would do without you."

"When Garth and I first arrived we slept in a leaky gatehouse with no roof." I sniffed.

"Well thank goodness you now have a wife and a man who thinks of things other than fighting."

She hurried away with Brother Oswald and Hogan, keen to see the new quarters. "I want a warrior hall building, Garth. Just like my brother's. We have space over there."

"That is where we have the stables my lord."

I had been planning this all the way home. "We demolish the stables and rebuild in stone with a warrior hall on the top. The heat from the animals will keep us warm in winter and we can fortify it as a stronghold should the other walls fall."

Garth looked impressed. "You have been thinking my lord."

"It was at Loidis. I know that we are stronger anyway but when the ram breached the gate I knew we had nowhere left to run. We were lucky. There may come a time when we are outnumbered and need to reach a place of safety."

"Good. We can start tomorrow. It is summer and the horses can graze by the river."

"One more thing. Just use our warriors at first for I want a tunnel from the stables and an escape route for my family in case…"

Garth looked shocked. It was obvious the thought had never entered his head. "This castle could laugh away any attack the Saxons might make."

"True but one day they will learn to make machines of war such as the Romans used and then we would need such an escape. We can use the villagers to build the walls and the hall but the tunnel must be an oathsworn secret."

Oswald had done a good job and the rooms were well made. He was still trying to make the Roman hypocaust and baths to work. "The Romans were clever men. I should like to go to Constantinople one day and see their marvels of engineering first hand. I have read about them but to see them would be wonderful."

"If I can help in any way then I will do so but, for the present, thank you for your efforts. The people are well and prosperous?"

"Aye. The war seems a long time ago and they have short memories. There were many children born in the wake of the fighting and it is good to hear the sound of laughing bairns again."

He paused and look hesitantly beyond the walls. "Go on man, out with it. You should know me well enough to know I will not bite your head off."

"I took the liberty of building a small chapel by the river. The Christians amongst your people asked me to have somewhere close to water to baptise them."

"Baptise?"

"Yes, it is like a rebirth."

I enjoyed teasing the White Christ priests. "That seems a little pagan to me? Does your Christ approve?"

I saw him visibly relax at my reaction. "He was baptised himself." He hesitated. "You are not angry?"

"So long as my warriors fight for me and do not try to turn the other cheek as your White Christ suggests then I do not mind what they follow, so long as they follow me unquestioningly."

"They will do that because of who you are my lord." He became more business like now that the difficult matter had been dealt with. "We now have hives and can produce honey and some of the slaves you sent are busy making cheeses. I used the sheep we captured to begin a herd and one of the farmers loaned us a ram so we should have lambs soon."

I nodded my approval. "You have been busy."

"I was taught by Brother Osric, my lord. I think you will find that the land is now richer than it was and, if we can avoid war for a while then we will be even richer next year."

I put my arm around him. "I am pleased with your efforts and hopefully we will have a year of peace. We paid for it with our men's lives."

"Garth told me what you did for the families of the dead. It cannot make up for the loss but it can ease their burden. It was a very Christian thing to do."

I wagged an admonishing finger at him. "Then you do not know the old gods for they advocate that too. It seems there are many similarities in our religions Brother Oswald."

"And for that I am grateful, my lord."

The next few weeks were blissful. My wounds healed and the land flourished. Aideen was soon with child and I found Castle Perilous to be more precious than I had ever dreamed possible. Brother Osric had been correct in his predictions and young men flocked to join the Wolf Brethren. Some had come from Bernicia and remembered me from Metcauld. A few came from Elmet; while others were Rheged men.

Garth and I interviewed them when they arrived to find out how they left their lords. The last thing any of us wanted was an irate lord or king complaining that we had stolen their young warriors but all appeared to tell the truth and said that they had left with their lord's blessing. We divided them into three groups; horsemen, archers and warriors. The bigger men were put into either the warriors or the archers. We decided which the best option was when we had seen them work. With the training of the new men and the building of the warrior hall we were kept busy.

Brother Oswald proved his value when he advised us on the construction of the stables and escape tunnel. His wide reading had given him an insight into how it was done in the past and we were soon finishing off the stables and beginning the construction of the hall. The priest wanted an internal stairway but Garth and I dismissed that idea. Brother Oswald looked perplexed. "But it will mean you can move from the stables to the hall in winter and stay dry and warm!"

"Aye and if we are attacked then it allows our enemies into our building. With an external staircase one man can hold off an army." He had shaken his head, he understood the logic but it merely demonstrated the futility of war; he was a practical man and would have put comfort ahead of defence.

I had managed to avoid letting Aideen see my leg. Its appearance had not improved since the burning; the red, angry line snaked down my calf and the muscles had been ripped giving it a bumpy and uneven look. However we had one of those rare nights in Rheged when the night is hotter than the day and we both slept naked on the bed, allowing whatever breeze there was to wash over us. I must have been sleeping on my front when she awoke and as she stood in the first light of dawn she saw the savage scar which snaked from my knee to my ankle. Her gasp awoke me.

"When were you going to show me that?"

I rolled over on to my back. "I didn't want to upset you and you could do nothing about it anyway."

"That is not the point. We can have no secrets from each other." She ran a long finger down its length. "Does it hurt?"

"No but it aches in the wet weather."

She laughed, "Then we live in the wrong place, husband, for Rheged is wet almost every day."

"I know," I said ruefully.

The best parts of the day were those spent with my warriors. The recruits were each placed under the care of one of my more experienced warriors. This was where I missed Raibeart for he was the greatest teacher of the bow. I could also teach the bow but, as Garth pointed out, I needed to have a wider view. He tried to do all those tasks which he felt was beneath the Wolf Warrior. Tadgh had grown bigger over the summer; in fact he had grown almost a hand span and broadened out considerably, to join the ranks of the warrior. I knew that he had a good eye and, although he was disappointed I put him under the tutelage of my senior archer, Miach. Miach had shown himself to be calm under pressure and Raibeart had spoken highly of him.

Tuathal had become a good horseman and he trained my new horsemen. They were the smaller warriors as we did not have enough horses of a larger stature. I had seen the effectiveness of horse against Saxons who deigned to use the hoofed beasts. I only had ten such warriors but they were all well armed and mailed. Tuathal also trained up my slingers to ride ponies and act as scouts. I had worked with slingers the previous year and seen their potential. We showed them how to find sign and read the land for clues.

Garth, of course, trained the warriors. He was a hard task master. He made them work from sun up to sun down and he made them use their armour to strengthen their bodies. Once he felt they were fit enough and had the right skills he drilled them remorselessly in the formations we would use. Although I was not looking forward to our next battle I was eager to see how my men would perform in war but at the same time I wanted a time of peace and prosperity for my people and my family.

Brother Oswald was unhappy at the expense incurred with the new warriors but he was an obedient man and he kept immaculate records. "So my lord, you now have twenty archers, ten horsemen, twenty slingers and one hundred warriors." He sighed, "They have expensive appetites and horses are not cheap to feed."

I shook my head, "Will it be a fine harvest this year? Are my people not renowned as pot makers and we sell them throughout the land? Do we not make the best swords and sell them too?"

"True my lord but think how much better off we would be with fewer soldiers."

"And with fewer soldiers we would be in danger of attack."

He had no argument to that and he went off to his bees; I suspect he moaned and complained to them when he lost an argument with me. Garth was the next to report to me. I enjoyed these times in the solar. I had not known the name until Brother Oswald had told me. I had just thought that the south west facing room was bright and pleasant in the evening, looking out, as it did over the river, the valley and the sunset. "How are the men coming along? When I visited they looked to be almost fully trained."

"Aye well they are better than they were but they are not battle ready for me yet."

"You have high standards. And the new men are they fitting in?"

He looked troubled. "Most of them are but…"

"Come on Garth. You know me well enough to keep nothing from me."

"It isn't their skills that worry me. They are all good warriors but I am not sure about one of them."

"This is not like you Garth; out with it. What is the problem?"

"It is one of the Bernician warriors, Llofan Lilo. He is a good warrior and he is the best swordsmen amongst the men but he, well, he is a bully and there is something about him. Perhaps it is me; maybe it is the fact that I do not trust anyone from Bernicia."

"But you said there are other warriors from Bernicia. What of them?"

I could see from his face what the answer would be and he looked crestfallen. "There are two others and they work well with the rest of the warriors. It is just this one."

I shrugged. I did not want my captain to be upset by one man. "Then get rid of him. Send him back to Bernicia."

"He is a good warrior. He would be valuable in a shield wall."

"Bladud would be valuable in a shield wall but would you want him in our ranks?"

"No but I will persevere. It may be he needs a different approach."

"As always Garth it is your decision but we must be able to rely on our men next year when we have to fight."

Chapter 5

The arrival of midsummer saw a visit by my brother and his wife. A rider galloped through the gates, the day before their arrival. Aideen and Oswald became frenetic with their preparations. The warrior hall had been completed and my brother's warriors could easily be accommodated. Thanks to Brother Oswald's work in the spring we now had two spare rooms in the main building and Aideen fussed about making them homely. I left them to it. My policy of speaking as little as possible was paying off and Aideen did not appear to get as upset as she once had and I did not have to think up things to fill the silences.

I was superfluous and I sought my lieutenant. "Garth, we will go hunting. Let us see if we can get some meat for my brother's visit." When I saw his grin I knew that he was as eager to be away from the sweeping and cleaning. I pitied the garrison for my wife and the priest would make their lives a misery. I took my bow as well as a couple of hunting spears and we took a pack horse in the optimistic hope that we might actually return with something!

We headed west for there were few farmers there and game was more plentiful. The woods, two miles to the west, were full of fruit bushes and oaks and beech. Wild boar and deer were drawn to it. We rode along the Roman road for part of the way as it afforded us a better speed. We turned south towards the wood and tied the pack horse we had brought in the hope of a kill close to a stream and we moved further into the woods with our horses. Once we had dismounted and tethered our mounts we armed ourselves. Neither of us wore armour although I wore my wolf cloak as did Garth. He had managed to kill his own wolf during the winter and took pride in the fact that only my brothers and I had such cloaks. We had light, doe skin boots on our feet and we carried our weapons upon our backs. We would string our bows when we found signs of the animals. I found that that the little wind there was blew in our faces and that helped as we were following the stream downhill and any game would not catch our smell. That suited me; we would be more likely to find signs close to water. It is a strange thing about men; they do not feel the need, as women appear to, of filling up silences with chatter. Both of us needed no words. When you have fought alongside a man you learn to trust both him and his instincts. I led and Garth watched my back. It was how we fought and there was no reason to change it while hunting.

We spotted the deer tracks five hundred paces from our mounts. They looked to be fresh in the muddy banks of the small brook and they headed down the valley. I strung my bow and placed three hunting arrows in my mouth while I notched the fourth. Garth hefted his best javelin and we followed the tracks. I suddenly heard a snuffling and knew that there was some animal ahead but it would be unlikely to be a deer. Deer were silent creatures. It could be a badger or a boar. They were both edible but one was easy to catch while the other could kill a man with its vicious tusks and teeth.

I drew my bow half way back. If something suddenly hurled itself at me I would have a heartbeat to react. I was fast with a bow, but not that fast. Suddenly a black shape erupted from our left and threw itself at Garth. I could see that it was an old boar and it was enormous. I drew back and loosed. I was but ten paces away and the arrow went into its neck. I had not struck an artery and, although my wound would kill the beast it would take hours to do so. Garth had thrown one javelin and hit the animal in the chest but it still hurtled towards Garth who was trying to draw his second javelin. I threw down my bow and drew my dagger; I leapt at the beast and grabbed a tusk with my left arm, avoiding his sharp teeth. The boar had the smell of death about it. The tusk was covered in slime and blood and I found it difficult to hang on but I knew I must. I am a big man and even a powerful boar finds it hard to run with a man on his back. It turned its head and its fearsome teeth towards my left arm and I threw my right hand around its neck and pulled my dagger sharply across its throat. Boar skin is thick and it is tough but my dagger was razor sharp and I felt the hot arterial blood spurt over my hand as the animal slowed and lurched to his death. When I was sure it was dead, I stood and found that I was shaking. That was as close to death as I had come since I had become a warrior.

I heard a groan and looked down. "If you could my lord, I would appreciate you taking our dinner off my chest so that I may thank you for saving my life." It was a struggle, but between us we managed to roll the dead animal off Garth who stood and clasped my arm. "Thank you my lord. You have saved my life."

"Do not worry yourself about it but just do not say anything to lady Aideen. It will only worry her."

We retrieved our weapons and looked at the magnificent animal we had killed. "You can see the scars on his skin. This one has been hunted before."

Garth shuddered, "And I fear has killed those who would kill him. He was cunning.
"

"He let us walk beyond him and then attacked." I shook my head. It is almost as though he were a warrior." I looked through the trees. It was still some time off noon. "Shall we try to get a couple of deer as well?"

"As it looks as though we have felled the beast of the woods then why not."

An hour later saw us with a doe and a fawn. Both would be far tenderer to eat than the old boar. "Let us leave them here and then use the horses. I do not know about you but I have had more than enough exercise for one day."

We headed up the slope towards our horses, cutting off five hundred paces from our journey. Suddenly I stopped. "Look at that!" The tree next to me had three parallel lines carved into it. Both Garth and I knew what that meant; we had used the same technique ourselves. It was to mark a meeting place or a way out of somewhere. These were fresh and we both drew our weapons. Now that we had seen one we soon saw the others and they led us to a small clearing. There were the remains of a fire and hoof prints. "Someone has been meeting here."

"Saxons?"

"I do not think so. The signs we followed led from the west. That suggests someone coming from Rheged." We searched the other side and saw the same marks on the trees coming from the north. "These could be Saxons but the hoof prints seemed to be of larger horses than the Saxons use and they would come from the east, not the north. If I did not know better I would have said that these were Rheged horses."

"But none of our men could have done this; we would have known. Who else is there who could be meeting here?"

"That I do not know and, until I do, let us keep this between ourselves. But what we will do is take out regular patrols on horse to visit the dell again. I want to know if there is fresh sign."

"Won't that make the men suspicious?"

"We just take two men each day and make it a different two. We can vary the route to get there but always use the Roman Road. Soon they will expect it. We can tell them we are training them to be scouts."

"I suppose we could say it is part of the initiation and include the archers and warriors as well as the horsemen."

"Excellent idea. Good thinking Garth." Garth had much in common with my brother Aelle. They both thought deeply and said little but what they said was worth listening to.

Aideen and Brother Oswald had finished their efforts to make Castle Perilous match their incredibly high standards. I would just have made sure there was food and ale to hand. They were both much calmer when we returned to complete the preparations with the food for the feast. I smiled although inside I was still worried about the implications of what we had found. Garth was quite correct in his thinking and we both knew, even though we had said nothing to each other, that we had a spy in the camp. I suspected it was one of the new men for I could not believe that the warriors who had fought alongside me would betray me. That meant there were sixteen potential spies and I had no idea for whom they were spying but I suspected the Saxons. Aella was a cunning king and it would be just like him to fool us by sending his man from the north rather than the west. My castle guarded the entrance to Rheged. It was, in fact, outside the old kingdom of Rheged but it was in the sparsely populated part of the land. We would need even more men. I shook my head; Brother Oswald would turn purple when I asked for more arms and men.

Later that night, as Aideen lay in my arms she asked, "You have been quiet tonight is there anything the matter?"

I forced a smile upon my face. "No. It is just that Raibeart and Maiwen will be our first visitors and I want the castle to be as perfect as it can be."

I didn't like lying to Aideen but it appeared to work for she sighed contentedly. "You need not worry my husband we have made our home as good as any in the kingdom, save the king's, of course."

I smiled back at her, "Of course." But, as I tried to sleep images of Saxons pouring through the pass to Rheged filled my dreams.

We had a surprise when my brother arrived for Maiwen had given birth to their son. There was now a grandchild for King Gwalliog and I knew that the old man would be pleased. While Aideen fussed over the babe and the mother I took Raibeart on a tour of the castle. "You have done well brother. I remember when you had just a gatehouse in which to sleep and now you have stone walls, a warrior hall and a water filled ditch."

"That was Brother Oswald's idea. He pointed out that if we diverted the river then it would cover our stakes and our enemies would suffer grievous wounds when they fell into the water."

"For a follower of the White Christ Brother Oswald appears to have a bloody nature."

"No, he abhors violence and death, but he sees it as a way to keep our enemies from slaughtering, what does he call them, his flock."

"Seriously brother I would not like to assault this castle."

As we stood in the gateway looking down to the river I suddenly knew why there had been meetings in the clearing. There was a plan to invade Rheged but they would not attack the castle. "I have been a fool!"

"What do you mean?"

"We have less than a hundred and fifty men we can call on as a garrison. They would not need to assault us. They could just pass through the valley and leave a small force guarding the bridge. We would be trapped within these walls and the road to Civitas Carvetiorum would be open." I could tell from the silence that Raibeart thought the same as I. His face fell. "What we need is to extend the walls down to the river and fortify the bridge and road."

"Could you do that? Surely it would take a long time to build a wall? Would you know how to start?"

I turned and looked over to Brother Oswald who was busily directing Raibeart's bodyguards to the warrior hall. "No but I think my clever priest could."

I was quiet during the feast and allowed Raibeart to have all of the attention; as a new father and the leader of the king's archers he was popular. He was telling amusing stories of us growing up and everyone was laughing and enjoying the moment and the food. I saw Aideen giving me strange looks but I did not worry. I could explain it to her later and no one was offended by my silence. I was also thinking about my plans for the building and how I would defend against such an invasion. It was now obvious to me that we would be outnumbered and could not inflict much damage; unless we had archers. I would seek more archers and horsemen. We needed better intelligence. The markings in the woods had unnerved me. I had thought that the Saxons would not come until the following year. How little did I know! Just because that was what I wanted did not mean that was what they would do. My victories had made me become complacent and overconfident. I determined to be more vigilant in the future. When our guest had left I would meet with Garth and Oswald and make plans.

Raibeart and Maiwen left to visit my brother Aelle two days later. Aideen had become what one might call broody and was overly affectionate. It came with motherhood and pregnancy. I did not mind; I had put her through much with my wounds and she began to make plans for Hogan and the child she knew would be a girl. For my own part I couldn't wait for Hogan to be big enough for me to teach him how to become a warrior although I knew that Aideen would fight against it. Her nest building, however, afforded me the opportunity to meet with Oswald and Garth.

I explained to them both my thoughts on the possibility of an invasion. Neither of them tried to argue against me. I think that they too realised that we had made assumptions about the Saxons based upon our limited victories. "So could we fortify to the river and make some sort of gatehouse there?"

In answer Brother Oswald said. "Have you been north to the Roman fort they call Chesters?"

"Aye. It is where Aelle lost his arm and we defeated Aella."

"Then you have seen such a fortified bridge. We will first build a wooden wall and ditch joining the castle walls to the river and then we will have to get some stone to build a second wall behind it. When we have the stone then we build a smaller version of this gate to deny access to the bridge. Finally, we complete the fortification on the bridge by building a second gate on the other side."

Garth shook his head. "That sounds like a lot of work and it seems to me that it would be expensive."

"Not if we use our men to build it."

"What about their training?"

"Think about it Garth. We would be building up their strength and building them into a team who had to rely on each other."

"And, my lord, that is how the Roman legions constructed roads and forts in the first place. It was the soldiers who built not the civilians. But he is right we would need to get the stone and it would need to be cheap."

"Raibeart! His fort is close to the Roman wall and when I visited there last I saw the quarries the Romans used. There is still stone within and it is but a day's ride. How much stone would you need?"

"It is a hundred or so paces to the river. We would need to make it at least two and a half paces wide and as tall as two men. If I could go to the quarry I would have a better idea."

"Draw up your plans and begin work on the wooden walls. When Raibeart returns you can travel north with him and Garth and make your investigations." I paused to allow my words to sink in. "I want the building finished by harvest time. I do not want to be surprised by the Saxons as we surprised them." Oswald opened his mouth to argue but saw my face and nodded. Garth just grinned.

Surprisingly Aideen was all in favour of the new wall. "With two bairns we need all the protection we can get."

The wooden wall and ditch was erected within two days. I had deferred the patrols until we had at least part of the defences built and, as we worked from sunrise to sunset, there was little opportunity for any of our men to slope off to the clandestine meeting place.

When Raibeart and his party returned he was amazed at the progress we had made. His brow furrowed, "But why brother, have you heard something which I have not?"

The women were busily talking of Freja and her home and I took him to one side. I explained about the marks in the woods and my plans. He cast a look over his shoulder. "I cannot believe that any of the men who fought alongside us at Loidis would betray us."

"Nor do Garth and I. It will be one of the new men."

"Then send them home."

"And what good would that do? We need more men and any other recruit would be suspect. This way we know whom to watch."

He grudgingly agreed with me. "But listen, you do not need to send all the way to the wall for stone. There is ample just ten miles to the south west of this castle, on the way to Aelle's fort. We passed it on the way here. You could cut your journey time by half." I slapped him around the shoulders. "But I will build up my defences, for, if what you say is true then any enemy denied this passage into the heartland of Rheged would then travel north and my home would be in the way."

"Is it defensible?"

He laughed. "It is said that the old people who lived before the Romans built a mighty castle there and the Romans made it stronger. It is defensible and, like you, I will build up my forces although, unlike you, I will have to draw on the treasure I captured from Wach!"

After he had gone I mounted five men and Brother Oswald and rode towards this cache of stone. I gave Garth his instructions. "Begin building the gatehouse over the bridge today and deepen the ditch. With luck and, if the gods are on our side," I saw Oswald's stern look, "all the gods, even the White Christ, then we can begin the wall in three days."

As we headed south west Oswald, seated uncomfortably on the gentlest horse we had, admonished me. "There is only one god Lord Lann."

"And how do you know this?"

It was as though no one had ever asked him the question before. "Well his son…"

"No, I did not ask about this White Christ but about this one god. We have gods who fathered sons on earth. I do not deny your White Christ was the son of a god, I am just not convinced that he is the son of the only god."

He seemed perplexed by this. "Well the Bible…"

"Who wrote this Bible?"

"Men such as me who lived in the past."

"And did they all live at the same time?"

"No, they spoke of God over thousands of years."

"So how do you know it is the same god? Perhaps there were a number of gods who spoke at different times to the different men. Your god may well be the same one as one of my gods but I am not convinced that there is only one. I look around and see the differences in men: the noble King Urien and the cowardly King Morcant Bulc; the cunning King Aella and the incompetent King Ida. And it is the same with ordinary men, we too have many differences. I am a warrior and you are a man of peace. I believe it is the same with gods."

I smiled as I saw him consider these arguments and I concentrated on finding the stone. I had not yet travelled this route for we had normally been heading east to face the Saxons and not south through this lush and verdant land. It was a land of high hills and, as soon discovered deep lakes. None were as big as Wide Water but the hills were like mountains in places and I was hopeful that we would find a source of stone. There was a narrow valley and then the trail began to climb up a steep sided hill. Once we crested the rise I could see the stones which littered the side of the hill. This was perfect; we would not even need to quarry.

I halted and turned to Oswald. "Will this stone do?"

In answer he dismounted and brought out the small hammer and chisel he had had the smith make for him. He found a rock the size of a small child and searched it with his fingers. When he seemed satisfied he placed the chisel at an angle and then struck the rock. He repeated the action along a line I could not see and then he returned to the middle and this time, when he placed the chisel in the now visible groove, he hit it with all his strength. The rock cracked in two and I could see that there were clean lines. "Yes my lord, "he beamed, "this will indeed do."

"Is that magic priest?"

"No, my lord, it is what the Greeks called science. I read how the Romans used to break rocks and it worked." He held up the hammer and the chisel. "We will need bigger ones than this of course but I ordered the smith to being making them." He gave me a wry smile. "You will have to wait a while for your new weapons of war."

We found four wagons that we could use to haul the cut stone the next day and I left half the men with Garth to continue working on the wooden wall and gate whilst I took the rest with me. I took the recruits with me for I needed to gauge their mettle and to see if I could discern if any was the spy. I half wanted it to be one of them, for that would vindicate my belief that my other warriors were loyal but, at the same time, I wanted these men to become part of my retinue.

Brother Oswald took charge. He was a good teacher with patience far beyond mine. He knew the men slightly better than I did for he had to deal with them on a daily basis. He chose his eight stonemasons carefully. He chose pairs of men. One of them was always a huge muscled warrior but the other sometimes looked as though a strong wind would blow him over. As they started to cut I wandered over to him and asked him about the choices.

"The man with the chisel needs to be clever and make wise choices. If you hit at the wrong point then you may split the rock but make it unusable for a level wall." He shrugged. We can use all the stone but we need regular sized pieces for the gate and foundations."

As we watched the first stones split I asked him about the wall he would build. "The men will dig a deep wide ditch. It will be as wide as a man and as deep as his legs. We will put the larger flat stones on either side of the ditch and build it to the height we require. The odd shaped stones will be rammed into the middle."

"Will you be using the Roman mortar you told me about?"

"If I had the materials I would but we will use river clay. It will bind it and make it hard but we will need to renew it each year." He stroked his bald pate reflectively. "It might be a good job for the time after the harvest before the frosts. Even children could do it."

I had noticed that one pair was working faster and more efficiently than the rest. "What can you tell me of those two? They seem to work well together."

"The smaller one is Myrddyn. He comes from Wales and travelled a long way just to serve you. He is both clever and resourceful. He can both read and write. I am not sure he is cut out to be a warrior; it might be a waste to misuse his talents."

"How might you use this warrior then, if not as a warrior?"

"I would like to train him as a healer. He shows potential and it would be an asset to your retinue. A healer could save wounded men." He pointed at my leg. "Had you not had a healer, Brother Patrick, you would now be lame."

I could see the wisdom in his words. I will consider it but there will be no harm in his training as a horseman anyway would there?"

"No, my lord."

"And the other?"

"He is from Bernicia. He is the brother of someone called Riderch. He says you know of him?"

"Aye, he is a good warrior and the best man that Morcant Bulc has in his army. What is his name?"

"Ridwyn. He is a powerful warrior. See how he swings that hammer. That is why they are working faster than the others. Myrddyn has seen that he needs fewer blows and he spaces his chisel differently to the others."

I watched the men working well as a team. The ones loading the wagons did so diligently and clearing the quarried stones to enable the stone cutters to work quickly. "Which one is Llofan?"

He threw me a curious look and then pointed at a warrior who was almost as big as Ridwyn. "The tall one there, the warrior who looks as though he has a bad smell under his nose." I had noticed him before because whilst the others were working happily and bantering with each other he worked alone and seemed not to care whom he caught with the stones he carried. "I am curious my lord, why did you ask about him?"

I drew him to one side. "Garth said something about him which disturbed me. That he did not seem to work well with the other men. I can see for myself that this is true but what is your opinion?"

"He works hard it is true but he is a solitary man. When I was paying the men their stipend I heard them talk and he seems to be one that they all fear in some way. The other two from Bernicia, Ridwyn and Ardal, do not bother with him much which is strange as all the others who came together still sleep in the same part of the warrior hall. Llofan sleeps well away from the others."

"Perhaps it would be wiser to send him back to Bernicia."

"It might be wiser my lord, if you train him as a warrior and an archer and then when the kings come for the Christmas celebrations you can suggest to King Morcant Bulc that this man is so well trained that he would be a valuable leader for the Bernician army. That way you will ingratiate yourself with the king and rid yourself of a problem."

It was a solution but there was something about this that I did not understand. "But why did he join if he is such a loner?"

The priest shrugged. "Perhaps some kind of feud at home, who knows? One of the others from Bernicia might be able to tell us. I will ask questions." He saw my worried look. "Discreetly of course."

Llofan apart, I was happy my recruits. They worked hard, Llofan included, and there was none of the griping and moaning I might have expected. I would never truly know them until I had fought alongside them but I was happy. I would speak with Garth about Myrddyn. What the priest had said had made sense.

Garth had finished the wooden wall when we returned. I told him of the plans for the stone wall and he smiled. "You were right my lord. This makes the men even stronger and digging such a ditch will be good for them. I explained to Garth about Oswald's thoughts on Myrddyn. "He is a good man my lord. I had him earmarked as a future leader. Tuathal speaks well of him but I agree with Brother Oswald. A healer would be worth more than five warriors. We can always get more horsemen but unless we take Brother Oswald with us..."

"No. The Brother is too valuable here and if we take a healer with us then it should be one who can fight as a warrior too. I am glad that I spoke with you it has helped me to make up my mind. Send the young man to me after the meal and I will talk with him in the solar."

A day in the open working hard gives a man an appetite and I ate well. Brother Oswald had used some of his honey to make some mead and it washed the food down well. I played with Hogan for a while until one of the slaves came to me. "My lord there is a warrior waiting for you in the solar. He says you sent for him."

"Thank you. Take my son to his mother." I could see, as I approached him, from the look on Myrddyn's face that he thought he was in trouble. I smiled. "Sit down Myrddyn, you are not in trouble but I need to speak with you about… well we shall come to that. First, tell me your story. How does a man from Wales find himself in Rheged?"

He visibly relaxed. "My family lived on the Holy Island close to Mona. My parents were killed and sisters enslaved by Hibernian slavers." He saw the question in my eyes. "It was *wyrd* which saved me. I had been looking for one of our lost sheep; I heard it bleating from below the ground and, when peering for it, I fell down a cleft in the rocks. I must have banged my head. When I came to the sheep was licking my face and I was at the bottom of a ravine. I shouted but no-one heard me. When I became accustomed to the dark I saw that the ravine became a cave with a pool. I led the sheep there and we drank. I thought that we were doomed to die in the deep, dark hole. I lost all hope." He looked shamefaced. "I am sorry to say my lord that I cried."

"There is no shame in that."

"I must have fallen asleep but I had a strange dream or perhaps I was awake, I know not. A woman came to me from the water. She was beautiful and said that I would not die and there was a way out. She said to reach for the sun. And then she said, and this part made me wonder if I had misheard the first thing she had said, for she said that when I escaped I should serve her son in Rheged," I suddenly felt an icy shiver run down my spine, "her son with the magical sword and the cloak of the Wolf. She told me to seek you, my lord."

I would not have believed the boy but I could see no reason for a lie and the water and my mother were part of my dreams too. There did not appear to be deception in his eyes. Was it possible that two people could share the same dream and fate? I saw him looking at me. "And you obviously did escape. How?"

"I was confused which son she meant but I could see light above me and I knew that if I had fallen down then I should be able to get up. I had a coil of rope about me. We often carried one for sheep were always slipping down the cliffs. I tied the sheep about me and I began to climb. At first it seemed too high but I persevered. I kept putting one foot in front of the other and just climbed. The words of the water spirit kept running through my mind. I had heard of Rheged and its powerful king but I knew nothing of a sword and a wolf." He nodded at me. "I can see it now but while I was climbing I was confused. I think that helped me to take my mind from my task and I suddenly found myself at the top of the cleft. When I emerged I could see the burning buildings that had been our village. I found a family which had escaped and they told me of the raid. We buried the dead and I decided that another power, greater than man, had determined my fate. "

There was silence in the solar, as the last rays of the sun dipped into the west. I still had many questions for the young man before me. "When was this?"

"Over a year ago."

"Over a year? It took that long to find me?"

He laughed. "No, my lord. My mother's father still lived. He was a holy man in a different part of the island. I went to him to tell him of my mother's death and of my dream. It was he who told me of you and he said that it was *wyrd*. He said I needed preparing and he taught me some spells and some healing. He told me that he had waited for such a vision and then he could pass on his knowledge to me." Myrddyn paused. "It seemed he was waiting to die but could not until I was trained. I learned many spells and much of his magic. He died in the spring and I journeyed north to find you."

I did not doubt one word of his story and I could see the hand of *wyrd* and the gods all over this. "I believe you for I will now tell you why I have summoned you. Brother Oswald tells me that you would be wasted as a warrior and would be better employed as a healer. I agree with him but you joined as a warrior so what are your thoughts?"

He looked suddenly relieved. "I joined to serve you my lord and warriors were what you wanted. I would like to serve as a healer but my training was not complete when my grandfather died."

"And *wyrd* has delivered you to the land where Brother Oswald will teach you what you need to know. But you should know that he will try to convert you to the White Christ."

"That will be an interesting experience," he paused, "for both of us!"

I laughed. "Welcome, then, Myrddyn my healer. Brother Oswald does not know what is about to befall him. For the time being you will continue to train as a warrior; the skills will not come amiss and I will speak with both Garth and Brother Oswald to arrange your future training." And so Myrddyn entered our lives and nothing was ever the same again.

Chapter 6

I spoke with both Garth and Brother Oswald the next morning and explained my decision. They both nodded their agreement. I sat back in my chair. It had been ordered to be made for me by Aideen and it was padded; it was the most indulgent thing I had ever owned. It was as comfortable as sleeping on a bed. I looked at Brother Oswald. "You know, of course that he is a pagan and he believes in magic and witchcraft."

Garth looked in amazement at both of us. Brother Oswald did not seem ill at ease with the idea. "There are many things the pagans believe which do not contradict my beliefs as a Christian and, to be honest, Lord Lann, I relish the meeting with a new mind. If I can increase my knowledge then that is a good thing and the boy seems Christian in attitude if not religion."

I laughed, "As pragmatic as ever. Garth, he will continue to train under Tuanthal but tell him that he has my permission to spend as much time with the Brother as he needs; without, of course, drawing attention to himself."

"And what of the spy?"

Garth was suddenly aware that he had spoken in front of the priest and his face went white. I held up my hand. "You can always speak freely before the Brother. He has my complete trust." I saw the holy man swell with pride and I wondered what penance he would have to do for such a sin. "Garth and I suspect that there is a spy or traitor within these walls." I explained how we had gleaned our information.

"Your logic is good my lord. Like you I cannot believe that men who have fought and bled with you would betray you but there are others within these walls who are not warriors; slaves, smiths, cooks, maids. Any of them could have connections with the Saxons."

I slapped my leg. "This is why this man is so invaluable to me. We need to keep watch for anyone who leave the fort after dark."

Garth looked puzzled. "Why after dark my lord?"

"We have patrols out during the day but not the night. " I looked at the priest. "Can you arrange a shift system which rotates my officers? I want one of us on duty at night."

"That would be Garth, Tuathal and Miach."

"No, Brother Oswald, you are forgetting that I am an officer. I will share this burden." I could see from their faces that they were not happy about this but I would share this burden with my men. I had to feel what they felt and experience what they did otherwise, like great kings, I would lose touch. I remembered my beginnings which were humble. I had been lucky to achieve what I had but I would not throw it away for the lack of a little sleep. "And we need to find other officers to work below us. We can pay them more. I think we need another three for the warriors and another one for the slingers and the archers. That will be a start. And I want older warriors to be recruited to be the garrison. When we war next year I want to leave a garrison here to protect my wife, my family and Brother Oswald and his bees!" Their laughter told me I had the gauge of my men.

Aideen became not only broody about the castle and the family but about the warriors. One evening as she lay in my arms and we listened to the heartbeat of our unborn child she said. "It would look better if all your men looked as you do."

I looked at her. "What do you mean?"

"I mean if they all looked the same... colour. You are the Wolf Warrior and you wear a wolf cloak."

"Yes but we..."

She waved an impatient hand at me. Women are far quicker than men sometimes. "I know, you cannot give a hundred men a wolf cloak but you could give them a black cloak which would look the same and, if it were made of leather or hide then it would protect them as your cloak does."

I looked at her in amazement. Was she becoming a strategist? "That is a clever idea." I looked at her sceptically. "Where did it come from?"

She put on her innocent look, "I reasoned that if your men were more fearsome and better protected then you would live longer!"

"And I am all in favour of that. Could we get the leather and could we dye it?"

She waved another imperious hand. "The leather needs acid to bleach it. Your men are all full of piss so that will not be a problem and there is a stand of maple trees close to the river and the bark makes a fine black dye. By the spring they will all look the same. They will all truly be Wolf Warriors."

I was so glad that I had returned to Castle Perilous. Since my return from Elmet my life had been much better and I began to see a future beyond the Saxons. That was a mistake. *Wyrd* is a cruel bitch and likes to play tricks with men and their minds. I will say that that year was the most contented of my life.

By the time the days grew slightly shorter the new defensive wall which ran to the river was completed. It still needed steps building inside to enable warriors to reach the platform and the gatehouse needed a better gate but the barrier was in place. If the Saxons came we could hold them and prevent them engulfing the land. The despatch riders had brought us word that Aella had sent for more of his people from the sea threatened land of the Angles, Frisians and Saxons. There were reports from Bernicia of fleets of ships sailing down the coast. Had they had a fleet they might have engaged them but the Saxons sailed down the coast with impunity. There was a mighty army coming to our land again and our preparations were none too soon. Aideen was heavy with child and Oswald predicted that the babe would be born after the harvest.

Aideen was not a Christian and she had snorted her derision. "What do a man and a priest know of a woman and her babies? You keep to building your walls and counting my husband's money and leave babies to those who know best, The Mother and we women who worship her!"

Brother Oswald was used to the derisory tone employed by my wife and the other followers of the cult of Mother Earth. He was not at all put out by her attitude. "I have read books by Greek writers and from the position of the baby and your health I am making a prediction."

"Aha! You are not the logical Christian after all. You use prediction and prophesy." She went off laughing to play with Hogan, leaving Brother Oswald shaking his head.

"Do not worry Brother Oswald. As you are unlikely to take a wife you will never have to understand the strange ways and thoughts they have. Every husband will tell you he never wins an argument with his wife."

"True my lord, and I am ever grateful that I am not encumbered by females. No offence intended."

"And none taken. Now to much more important matters. How goes Myrddyn's training?"

"He has great knowledge, much more than I, about herbs and plants. He has shown me how to brew a potion which eases the pain of wounds. It will be invaluable on the battlefield when we have to deal with deep wounds. He has also told me of a way to stop an infected wound from killing; you put maggots on the dead flesh and they eat it."

I shook my head. Brother Oswald was always seeking knowledge. "Excellent so your training is going well. What about Myrddyn's?"

"What I am trying to say, my lord, is that he could be your healer on the battlefield now for he is more skilled than I am. And it pains me to say that for he is not a Christian."

"Good. Pride aside then, you are happy with his progress?"

"Yes my lord."

"Then he will be our healer. Adjust his pay to that of Miach and the others." He looked sharply at me. "He may not want it but I will have fairness in all things."

I led the small patrol out along the road. We had halted them for the time it took to cut the stone and build the wall but now that we just finishing off, it was time to begin them again. So far we had seen no recent signs of any clandestine meetings and I was considering halting the patrols, or, at least varying the route. Garth and I had told the men we were combining the patrol with hunting expeditions and we had managed to bag ourselves some game but I felt that the ruse was wearing thin.

The three men I had with me were all experienced warriors; we tried to use those men we could totally trust rather than the recruits. The wall building and stone cutting had been a boon as it had kept the men busy doing other tasks. As we headed off the road Targh suddenly pointed to the ground. "My lord, men were here recently. And they were on horses."

I dismounted with Aiden while the other two kept a wary watch in case this was an ambush. It soon became obvious that two men had ridden this way. I handed my reins to Targh and back tracked the prints to the road. They had come from the north and merely crossed the road. That, in itself, was suspicious in nature. Any Rheged warrior would use the road. Only an enemy would wish to remain unseen. We mounted again and, with weapons drawn, headed in the direction of the tracks. I knew which way they headed but I could not let my men know that and we arrived at the dell. Targh jumped down. "They lit a fire here and it still has some warmth." He looked at me. "There were unknown riders here last night my lord."

"Tie your horses to the tree and search for tracks, see which way they went." I took a breath, "And see if anyone else was here."

I took the westerly direction. If anyone from my castle had come here then I would find their tracks in that area. Annoyingly there was a path of sorts and it was covered in pebbles and small rocks. It made tracking almost impossible but I persevered and headed further west. The pebbles stopped and I began to sweep from north to south and I was rewarded by one footprint. Whoever had left the castle was very careful and had stepped on wood or stone to avoid leaving tracks. I put my foot next to the one faint print. It was about my size which meant it was a big man. That was useful as some of the smaller men, Myrddyn and the other horsemen, could be ruled out. We were left with just nine men who were suspect although as Brother Oswald had said it could be a slave but, again, it had to be a big slave; the women and children were ruled out. We were making progress.

I made my way back to the clearing and met the others there. "They rode off to the east my lord. Do you think they were Saxons?"

"Could be; let us find out. Mount up and we will follow their tracks."

The tracks headed east and then joined the road. We followed them for half a mile and then sharp eyed Targh spotted them again. "My lord. They have turned off the road and are heading north west!"

They had deliberately left a false trail. If they were not behaving suspiciously before they were now. "Let us follow." We finally lost them after a mile when they entered a wide boggy area. We could have searched for a month and not found out where they emerged. I led the patrol back to the castle. I could end the patrols now for we now had confirmation that there was a spy in the castle. The only way we could find out who it was would be to catch them. I began to formulate a plan to trap the spy as we rode back to our home.

"Garth, fetch Brother Oswald and meet me in the solar." Apart from being a beautiful room the solar also had the advantage of privacy. No-one could eavesdrop and the guard was stationed at the foot of the stairs, more than five paces away. I nodded to him as I went up the stairs. "When my guests have arrived I want no disturbances."

"Yes my lord."

Neither man was surprised by my request. They waited for me to impart my news patiently. "Our spy exists. It is someone my size which rules out the boys, female slaves, most of the horsemen and the shorter archers. If it is a recruit then we have a limited number to check."

Brother Oswald recognised the signs. He knew I had a plan. "And how do we catch him then, my lord?"

"There is little point in staking out the meeting place for that would merely let him know that we were on to him. We need to watch for men who leave the castle after dark."

Garth shook his head. "Surely that is impossible. We have guards and sentries. He would be noticed."

"Then those tracks I found… where did they come from?" I could see that Garth now understood the implications of my comments. "So whichever of us is on duty at night will also check the beds in the warrior hall. It is a simple enough task to count the men and, if one is missing, then we can identify him"

"And what do you want of me my lord?"

"I want you to check the warrior hall too. Just before you retire and as soon as you rise." He gave me a quizzical look. "You say prayers at those times do you not?"

"I do but why would I visit the warrior hall?"

"At the moment where do you say your prayers?"

"In my cell."

"And it is cramped is it not?"

"Very."

"Then, as we have Christians now amongst the warriors you can make a small… you call them altars?"

"Yes my lord."

"A simple altar with a cross can be made in the far corner of the hall. The non Christian warriors have their own places of worship in the warrior hall; it will not seem strange. You can tell the Christian warriors that you suggested it to me and persuaded me to allow it." I paused to let them take in all that I had said. "As they met last night I think that it is unlikely they will need to meet again for a few days. We can begin the new system now and then our spy will not become suspicious."

"And if we find someone missing?"

"Then, Garth, you find me, and we will deal with this promptly."

The next few days were filled with the activity of finishing the gate and the wall. I was proud of the achievement of my men. The wall was higher than a man and well protected. There was a step on which archers could stand and rain arrows on an enemy whilst remaining protected by a thick wall of stone. We might not stop the Saxon hordes but we would slow them down and we would definitely thin them out. I was also delighted because the training was complete and my men had become an efficient working army once more. True, some had never faced a foe but more than three quarters had and I would stack anyone of them against any ten of the Saxons.

The harvest came and we celebrated heartily for it was the finest harvest any could remember. The crops were abundant and even dour Brother Oswald was happy with the bounty. The festival was a joyous occasion and the Christians also felt obliged to celebrate the pagan festival although they praised the bounty of the White Christ rather than Mother Earth. What made it even more special was that Aideen gave birth to Delbchaem. We named her so because it meant pretty one and she was. Hogan is a dear son to me but she was so beautiful it made you feel as though your heart would burst and I always found myself smiling when I saw her. She was truly gorgeous and the name fitted well.

The year was going wonderfully for me. My wounds had healed and I felt no stiffness from my leg and my beard hid my scar and then Garth awoke me one early morning. "My lord!" I knew that it was serious when he awoke me.

"Yes Garth?" Aideen murmured in her sleep. She was still tired from the child birth and she rolled over without waking.

"It is urgent my lord." He whispered.

The fact that he had awoken me told me so and I put a cloak about me and stepped outside of the room. I could see that he was nervous and I made a joke. "Are the Saxons without?"

He relaxed and gave me a nervous smile. "No my lord but we have discovered a warrior trying to leave the castle."

I stiffened. I had been both hoping for and dreading this news at the same time. "Who is it?"

"It is one of the Bernician recruits. We have him in the gatehouse."

When we reached the gatehouse I saw Brother Oswald and two of the sentries. The fourth man was Ridwyn, Riderch's brother. I could not believe the treachery. He looked white and shocked. I dismissed the two guards. Garth threw me a look which suggested I needed protection. I gave him a rueful smile. "As we are both armed and he is unarmed, Garth, I do not fear him." Garth nodded. "Now what is this about Ridwyn? Why were you trying to leave the castle?"

He remained silent. Garth grumbled and pulled his dagger from his belt, "Let me have him my lord and he will speak."

I held up my hand. "Come Ridwyn, I owe it to your brother to hear you out but if you speak not then I will have to assume guilt." The look on his face bespoke innocence but I needed more. "Come, you know me to be a fair man and the priest here should tell you that I will do things honestly. Why were you leaving the castle and where were you going?"

He took us all by surprise by bursting into tears. "I was going to the village. There is a woman…"

I looked at the other two and we all relaxed. This was not acting. This was a young man who was ruled by his loins. Between sobs he told his story. He had been seeing a young girl from the nearby village. She had finally agreed to a tryst and he was going to meet her. It was too ridiculous to be a lie and his reactions were not those of an enemy.

I put my hand on his shoulder. "Next time speak to one of us. We are not inhuman and we understand. Send him back to the hall." After he had gone I turned to the other two. Well we have now alerted our spy to the fact that we are on to him. Unless he has the brains of a mule he will go to ground but I am happy that Ridwyn was ruled by his dick and not by treachery."

As I returned to the comfort of my warm bed I now knew that there were fifteen men for me to suspect but that I would come no closer to finding their identity. It was annoying and it was frustrating but sometimes events did not turn out the way one hoped that they would.

The next month seemed to fly by. We were still busy training the men and the new recruits who seemed to arrive daily. I was torn between my new daughter and the running of my castle and, before I knew it, the despatch rider arrived inviting us to Civitas Carvetiorum for the Yule festival and the meeting with the allied kings. At one time this would have been simplicity itself but suddenly we had wagons and children to think about. I left Garth and Brother Oswald to guard my home and I took but twenty horsemen and Myrddyn as my companions. I thought he might benefit from meeting Brother Osric. For his part he was excited but, as we rode towards the capital, I discovered that the main reason was that he would be closer to me for a whole week. The dream he had had made him keen to understand me and find out why the other world had both saved him and joined him to me. I was happy to be talking with someone so young, quick and clever.

The ground was hard with frost but, mercifully, free from snow and rain. I could see, as we rode along the old Roman Road that we would soon need to repair it before the frost and ice damaged it even more. I would not have thought of it myself but Brother Oswald had told me how the Roman soldiers worked to keep their vital roads functioning. I knew that they were crucial as they enabled us to move large numbers of men to meet any threat.

Civitas Carvetiorum loomed into view and Myrddyn was silenced by its size. It affected everyone the same way. It had been occupied constantly for over four hundred years and it showed. There had been no stone robbers to strip the walls as Raibeart and I had found with our own refuges. Roman leaders and then the kings of Rheged had improved it so that it always looked different and new but the constant was that it was a powerful statement of who ruled the land.

"Is King Urien a powerful king then, my lord, to live in such a magnificent abode?" Myrddyn's words showed his awe.

"I suppose I am biased as I swore allegiance to him a long time ago but I think he is the greatest king in this whole land and the only hope we have to stop the Saxon threat. But to answer your question, he is as powerful as we, his warriors, make him."

"They say that you are the leader and King Urien reaps the reward of your efforts."

I looked at him sharply. "Who says so?"

I knew that my words were harsh and he recoiled in fear. "I am sorry my lord. It was just what some of the warriors at Castle Perilous said."

"When we return I will speak with my warriors. King Urien is the leader and I merely serve. It is his ideas and his battle plans which have kept the land safe. I merely do as the others do and carry out orders. Do not speak those words again."

"I will have to learn to be as Brother Oswald and think before I speak."

I smiled. Myrddyn reminded me of me when I was younger and more outspoken. "I forget sometimes that you were recently a boy and you are still learning but that is a good creed; listen more than you speak." I slowed my horse and leaned over to speak quietly to him. "You will be close to me when we are in the castle. You will need to keep your wits about you. Some of the people you meet will try to deceive you. Keep your eyes and ears open and you mouth closed. I will ask later what you saw."

"I will be careful."

I kicked my horse on and we approached the drawbridge. "Brother Osric is one of the men you can trust implicitly. I believe the two of you will get on well."

I was the first of the leaders to arrive and King Urien welcomed me warmly. I introduced Myrddyn but I did not tell him of the dream. It seemed to be a private matter. King Urien was impressed that Myrddyn had travelled such a long way. "Did you not have trouble with Saxons along the way?"

"No, your majesty. The lands are emptier than here. The Hibernians raid the coast for slaves. They took my family and that may be why the Saxons have, so far, shunned it."

"That may well be why your brother is so untroubled by raids. Perhaps we can settle the lands there, Lord Lann."

"It is good land your majesty. We used some of the stones to improve the stronghold and I believe it could be farmed and protected easily."

"I will consider it and speak with my sons. Welcome Myrddyn of Mona."

I took my acolyte to meet with Brother Osric. As usual he was in his office with inky fingers. He never seemed to age and looked to be the same now as when I had first met him. "This is Myrddyn. Brother Oswald has been training him as a healer. When we war again we will be better prepared."

He looked up at the young man with appraising eyes. "You are young to be a healer." It was a bald statement which asked for an explanation.

Myrddyn looked him in the eye. "Yes I am young; I will have a long time to perfect my skills so that when I am as old as you I will be the greatest healer in the land."

Brother Osric laughed; a cackling laugh and he slapped his desk. "I like that. Not intimidated by an old man. Your lord here was young too but age does not necessarily bring with it wisdom. I was young once and there were many who dismissed me because of that. I will not make that mistake with you young man."

"I would like him to pick your brain Brother Osric and see if he can pick up some of your skills."

"A magpie too. Well the magpie is a clever bird and survives well in these parts. Leave him with me Lord Lann and we will talk. A healer from the Holy Island intrigues me."

"Will you take him to the barracks where he is to stay? " The priest nodded. "I will see you later Myrddyn."

I walked towards the quarters I used when staying at the fortress. I was in a good mood and meeting with Brother Osric had given me hope that Myrddyn would pick up even more skills. My mood was soured when I saw Bladud and two other warriors approaching me. I did not recognise the other two but they were wearing the same as Bladud and I assumed that they were bodyguards. Bladud said something to them and they all laughed. I assumed it was some joke at my expense. I did not give Bladud the pleasure of seeing a reaction and I just stared at him. I noticed that he had the swagger back he used to have before I bested him in combat. That was always a dangerous sign. I resolved to watch him just as carefully in the future. I knew he still had something to hide and I was determined to discover it.

Raibeart arrived along with his wife and child. He was a little closer than Aelle and myself to the fortress but the wagons he had been forced to use slowed him down more than u. I felt much better now that he was here for I felt I had protection. I knew that I should not have needed protection at Civitas Carvetiorum but Bladud had that effect on me. Prince Ywain arrived at the same time. It was some time since I had seen him and I was surprised at the change a year had wrought. He looked far heavier and his face looked flabby. I wondered if he had been working as hard as my brother and I. Combat and training kept a man slim.

They both greeted me warmly and effusively. We all made the right comments about the wives. "Where is Aideen brother?"

"She has only recently given birth and we thought it wiser to leave her in the castle. She is happy enough but she is sad that she could not see your ladies."

When the ladies had left us we could talk. "I hear you two had a fine and well earned victory at Elmet?"

"It was costly but we did win. I think Raibeart's father in law was more than happy with us. And you Prince Ywain, how is life treating you."

"We only have the Hibernians to worry about and I have fortified the towns on the coast. It is very peaceful now." I now knew why he had grown so fat. He had given up the patrols. I suppose I couldn't blame him for his northern borders were protected by his wife's father but it made me wonder if he would be prepared for battle the following year.

"Like my brother I have had to improve my fortifications for if the Saxons come then we will be the first to know."

Ywain laughed, "Raibeart we have cowed the Saxons. When we fight them again it will be the battle which seals our victory."

I looked at my brother. It was as though we were thinking the same thoughts. "Have you not heard that Aella has more warriors coming from the east? He will outnumber us again."

Ywain seemed unconcerned. "We defeated him before when he outnumbered us and now we are better armed and have more men." I was not convinced but he was the heir to the kingdom and perhaps he was right. "Come I have an amphora of wine from Italy. Let us try it."

As we headed for the great hall I wondered if this was another reason for the change in the prince. It was early to be drinking. It was a good wine but Ywain drank three beakers to the one Raibeart and I enjoyed. When Aelle arrived Prince Ywain was florid and slightly drunk. Aelle looked at me and I gave a slight shake of the head. We could talk later. As the allied kings were only arriving the following day that evening was almost a family feast with the king's sons and my brothers and me sharing the huge table with the king and queen.

The queen had aged more than the king and I think she still grieved over her dead son. The three she had left were even more precious to her and I saw her pride in the boys. It was even sweeter for me because Bladud was not there and the food and ale were appreciated all the more. Maiwen and Freja retired early after the meal and we left the king and his family to enjoy some privacy. I wanted to speak privately with my brothers in any case. I wanted to let them know of my spy and discover if they had a similar problem. We headed for the gatehouse. It was quiet and the guards who were there would give us the privacy we sought. They all knew us and would ensure we were not overheard.

When I had told them they both looked shocked. "I have seen no signs near my castle but then I did not stumble upon marked trees."

"Me neither. Perhaps I will take my men out on a patrol as you did."

"It cannot hurt, Raibeart, but I wondered what the spy would be reporting. My defence improvements are there for all to see. My escape tunnel is known only to a handful of my men so why would the spy need a couple of meetings?"

Aelle stroked his beard with his stump. "It is perhaps more worrying than the passing of information. If he is in your castle then he could be there to bring harm to you, or your family."

An icy chill grabbed my heart. I had left my family at the castle and the suspects were all there. Raibeart saw the look of horror on my face. "I think brother that they would try to hurt you, rather than your family."

"Sorry Lann. I should have thought before I spoke." Aelle looked appalled at his lack of discretion and thought.

"No Aelle you were right to voice your thoughts but I think Raibeart is correct in his judgement. It is more likely to be me who will be the target but I had not thought of it before. This is a hard thing to bear. The next time I fight will I be watching those behind me for a knife in the back?"

Chapter 7

The three allied kings arrived the next day. For two of them it was also a family reunion with their respective daughters and both kings looked as happy as each other as they played the grandfather. King Morcant Bulc looked decidedly unhappy as he was ignored by everyone. He liked to be the centre of attention. He had dressed in a highly polished mail shirt with a helmet inlaid with gold and silver. No-one noticed apart from me. I just thought that it would be impractical on a battlefield; although the Bernician king was too careful to be found where there was danger. King Urien looked on as though he, too, was part of the family. There was just me, along with Brother Osric who could see the resentment on Morcant Bulc's face. The priest leaned over and said, quietly, "Our friend from Bernicia does not look pleased."

"When does he ever look pleased, unless, of course, someone has fought a battle for him?"

"You need to watch him Lord Lann. King Urien is too trusting for his own good. The kings of Elmet and Strathclyde are honourable men, as we know, but the Bernician…" I nodded. I had learned not to trust him but the priest was a wise man and I heeded his comments.

When King Urien finally greeted him he was all smiles but the smile was not in his eyes. I saw Riderch and strode over to him. He gave a slight bow. "How is my brother, Lord Lann?"

I shook my head. "We have fought together, it is Lann. Your brother is a fine warrior, however. "I saw the shocked look on his face. "No, Riderch, it is nothing to worry about but he has taken up with a girl in the village and he fell foul of Garth and me. It is all forgotten now."

He looked relieved. "I had hoped that serving on the frontier would give him some sense."

Brother Osric smiled. "Young men often think that their brains are located between their legs… they are of course wrong!"

The evening feast was a more formal occasion than the previous night and, once it had ended then the women left. There were just the four kings, the king's sons along with my brothers and me. Brother Osric joined us after the women and children had departed. He sat next to the king with parchment and quill at the ready. I could see Morcant Bulc looking around the table and I could almost sense that he felt like an outsider. We were all joined by ties other than a military alliance and it gnawed at him. Had I not been watching him then it might not have been obvious but he was the focus of my attention.

"This year has been a good one for us. Elmet is now a safer place for its people and the Saxons have been dealt a blow to their ambitions."

King Gwalliog slapped the table. "Thanks to these fine warriors of yours King Urien!"

Brother Osric shook his head, disturbed by the interruption but the king did not seem discomfited."True and we are grateful to them for their efforts." King Urien's voice showed his concern. "However we now face a new and more dangerous threat from the east. King Aella is gathering a huge army and I have no doubt that he will attack us again next year. I fear, from what King Morcant Bulc tells me, that we will be outnumbered."

Morcant Bulc stood. He had the centre stage and he would milk the attention for all it was worth. "They are gathered all along the Dunum. I have had to fortify the old Roman fort at the bridge on the river to give us some protection but they can cross the river in their ships. It is not a case of if but when they choose to attack."

He paused and I said quietly, "Have you engaged them yet, your majesty?" He flashed me an angry look and I affected an innocent look and spread my arms wide. "I merely asked to find out if you had gauged the mettle of their warriors. If these are new troops, fresh from their homeland we do not know how they fight. The Saxons we know fight in a predictable way, as the King of Elmet discovered and we can counter that."

The King of Bernicia appeared mollified. "A good point Lord Lann but I have been loath to cross the river and risk losing a battle." I saw Brother Osric catch my eye and give the slightest shake of his head. I gave a slight bow to Morcant Bulc as though I agreed with him. "What we will do however is to try to gather some prisoners to find out the enemy plans."

"I am not sure that will provide useful information as we already know how cunning King Aella is. The last time he fought us he even used his brother king as bait. Unless we capture him then we will not know what his plans are." King Urien's brow was furrowed as he spoke. I knew from my conversations with him that he could not understand the lassitude of the Bernicians. "I am going to suggest that we meet at the Dunum at Easter and we will march to meet and defeat Aella."

There was much nodding. I coughed and they all looked at me. Once again it was left to me to be the dissenting voice. "We raided and defeated Aella's son Wach before Easter while his men were still sowing crops. What if he does the same? He can strike in any direction and he will outnumber whichever king he meets, if he chooses the time and the place for the battle."

"Are you suggesting that we attack early and risk starvation later in the year?" I smiled; King Gwalliog had learned his lesson.

"No, King Gwalliog, I am suggesting that we each provide some warriors to watch the Saxons so that we can delay an attack if he makes it early; much as we did last year when Raibeart and I aided you. It does not need to be a large force but it should be both mobile and well armed. We need to know when and where they will move. Although the land to the south is surrounded by our three kingdoms the Saxons can bring many more warriors across the sea and they can choose when and where to attack."

That began a debate amongst the assembled leaders. Eventually the noise became so loud that Brother Osric was forced to bang on the table. "Let us talk in an organised manner." He turned to Rhydderch Hael, "Your majesty, give us your views."

"I like the idea but I could only spare fifty of my men."

"King Gwalliog?"

"I know it would work and I owe much to Rheged. I could give fifty horsemen and fifty warriors." I nodded my thanks.

"The King of Bernicia."

"I am not against the idea but I would be the first to be attacked and I am not sure I could provide any men." There was just the hint of a smile playing around his lips.

My eyes narrowed. Once again he was allowing others to fight his battles for him. "What of the troops at the Roman fort?"

The smile which had been on his face was replaced by a scowl, "What?"

Brother Osric caught my eye and winked. "Well your majesty, you said you had garrisoned the Roman fort. As that would be the place this force would be mustering could they not be used? After all the force would, as you just said yourself, be fighting to save your land."

I saw the nods and smiles from all the others as King Morcant Bulc realised that he had been pushed into a corner and he had no escape route. "Well, I suppose some of them could be used..."

Brother Osric's face brightened. "How many men did you send to the garrison?"

"A hundred and fifty warriors and fifty horsemen."

"Perfect. The horsemen would be better employed outside the walls of the fort and a hundred men could easily defend the river crossing."

Morcant Bulc's face fell, "You know the place?"

"I know it well. I visited all of the Roman forts to gain ideas for improving the defence of this castle. The one over the Dunum is perfect for it controls the bridge. Why, even I could probably hold it with fifty men. So we can add fifty horsemen and fifty warriors to this force. King Urien?" The old priest had outwitted the king. He could not argue against his suggestion.

"As this kingdom is somewhat safer than the others, Strathclyde apart, I can provide a hundred mounted men and a hundred warriors as well as forty archers."

"Lord Aelle?"

"We are well protected in the south; fifty archers and fifty warriors." He spread his hands apologetically. "We have few horses."

"Prince Ywain?"

"It is quiet in my domain; fifty horsemen and fifty warriors."

"Prince Pasgen?"

The youngest son of King Urien and the least experienced leader looked embarrassed. "We have few regular soldiers in my domain. I could spare but forty warriors."

"Forty would be more than enough Prince Pasgen. Prince Rhun?"

"I have some fine slingers and archers. I could provide forty archers and slingers and twenty warriors."

"Lord Gildas?"

"I have forty horsemen but I am afraid that I only have ten warriors to spare."

Brother Osric raised an eyebrow as he looked at the three kings. "Fifty from a small domain such as yours is as many as many others, with much larger armies, are contributing." Having insulted the three kings he turned to my brother, "Lord Raibeart?"

"Like Prince Pasgen we do not have a large force but I have the best archers in the kingdom. I have fifty archers and twenty horsemen."

"Which just leaves Lord Lann."

"My fort is now well protected. I could bring all my horse, all thirty five of them, forty archers and fifty warriors."

King Urien look concerned. "Would you not be stripping your castle of its garrison?"

"No I will be leaving some archers, slingers and fifty warriors." I looked pointedly at King Morcant Bulc. "Fifty warriors are more than adequate to defend my fort for the despatch riders could reach you your majesty if it was threatened."

"Good. So, Brother Osric how does that force add up?"

"I will list them alphabetically. Bernicia would be providing one hundred men. Elmet would provide a further hundred, Rheged, six hundred and forty five men and Strathclyde fifty warriors."

The other three kings looked suitably shamefaced while King Urien nodded proudly to each of us. "As the majority of the force will be Rheged I will appoint the commander." He looked at each of us in turn. Prince Ywain, my son, and Lord Lann will jointly command. They have commanded together before and I believe they will work well together." He saw the looks on the faces of his sons and Raibeart. "The ones who are not chosen will be needed to organise the muster of the remaining forces but I think that almost nine hundred such warriors could give a good account of themselves. Aella would not easily roll over them eh?"

There was an outbreak of cheering and slapping the table from all apart from the isolated Morcant Bulc who sat stony faced. I could feel the animosity from his eyes and I could not work out why. We would be defending his lands, once again, what did he want? I decided to ask Brother Osric later on. I knew that he would have some idea for he was the cleverest man I knew although I suspected that Myrddyn would run him a close second.

As the others all had families I took a turn around the castle walls. It was an icily cold night but the cold air helped to refresh my tired eyes and clear my head. I had much to think about. How would we protect our thousand warriors so close to the enemy? How would we ensure that we had good intelligence? How would we hold up the enemy and yet not risk losing what were the best warriors we possess? None of the problems was insurmountable and I knew that I would have the advice of Brother Osric as well as the mind of Myrddyn but there was another problem, Prince Ywain. He had not looked to be overjoyed at the command. There were two possible reasons: either he did not want to share command or he did not want the command at all. The former was not a problem as I knew I could work with him but the latter was. Warriors want a leader who is keen and eager. They want someone who wants to fight as much as they do. I would have to speak with him the following day.

"My lord?" The voice came from so close to me that I actually jumped and my hand went to my dagger. "I am sorry my lord, it is me, Myrddyn."

I turned to see my healer but two paces away from me. Had he been an assassin then I would have been dead. "I am sorry too Myrddyn for I am slowing up if I did not hear you."

The moonlight made the ramparts as bright as day and I could see his gleaming teeth as he grinned. "I was always able to move quietly. I enjoyed the game as a child."

I relaxed and I smiled too. It was my fault I had been startled and not Myrddyn's. A warrior should always be aware of danger. "No matter," We began to head back to the stairs. "Have you learned much from the Brother?"

"A great deal my lord. He seems happy enough about my healing, my reading and my writing but he thinks I need to develop skills in language."

"Language? You mean Latin and Greek?"

"Eventually but he first suggested that I learn Saxon. He pointed out that it might be useful to have a healer who could speak with any wounded Saxons and discover information; if only by listening to their words." It made sense and I nodded my approval. "He said that you could teach me."

"Indeed I could but I will just start you off. M y brother Aelle was brought up in a Saxon camp as a Saxon and he can make you sound like a Saxon."

"Thank you my lord... I"

His hesitation told me that he was holding something back. "What else bothers you?"

"I have been listening to the other warriors, as you suggested, and I am learning things which disturb me."

"Such as?"

"The warrior you mentioned, Bladud, has been charged by the king with increasing his horse warriors and bodyguards."

"I know that we all need more horsemen. The Saxons do not possess them. That is a good thing."

"True. But the men Bladud is choosing appear to be more loyal to Bladud than the king. There have been arguments and fights between some of the other men and Bladud's."

I now remembered seeing some of the bodyguards with blackened eyes and bruises. I had put it down to training accidents but this was more serious. The king did not need warriors at his back who were fighting each other. "You have done well and you did right to tell me. Never hold back. I must know all that you do. I shall tell you now, because I trust you, that I have been given joint command of a thousand men and we are to watch the Saxons from early spring."

His face lit up and I suddenly saw that he was a young man and he was keen for the thrill of war and battle. I had been the same. Soon the idea would pale a little but it was good to see his enthusiasm. "And now I think back to our beds. We will leave at noon tomorrow. I will leave it to you to tell the men."

"Do we not stay for the Yule festival?"

"No I would see my wife and children. We have learned all that we need to learn and we need to begin our preparations for war."

I rose early for I had a clear head having stopped feasting well before the others. The rest had caroused until late. I knew that Brother Osric would be awake and I joined him in his cell-like office. He never seemed affected by drink, no matter how much he consumed. He briefly looked up from his inevitable writing and spoke, "Interesting last night was it not? It seems that the other kings want Rheged to bleed for their lands."

"At least this way we control the force which, I believe, is powerful enough to give Aella pause for thought."

"It is but," he looked at the door and nodded. I shut it. "But I am not sure that Prince Ywain is keen to lead."

"I was not sure of the reason for his diffidence. I thought that it might be the joint command which was the issue."

"No. He has grown too comfortable now that he is married. He rarely leads his patrols anymore and delegates that to his men. I am not saying that he is not still loyal but he has lost the hunger he had and which you still maintain; despite your marriage."

"I still seek revenge for the loss of my family. The Prince has yet to lose." I paused. "I think I will return to Castle Perilous today." I looked for a disagreement but he just nodded. "Will the king be disappointed?"

"No, my friend. He will know that you miss your family. I am afraid that the next few days will see a repetition of last night's debauchery. It will not be a pleasant sight."

I was relieved. I was fond of King Urien and did not wish to offend him but the priest's words had told me that I ought to speak with him personally; just as soon as I had had conference with Prince Ywain. "There is something else. Myrddyn…"

He leaned back and his face beamed a grin at me. "You were right about him. What a bright lad! If I were not a Christian I might believe that fate had sent him our way for other purposes. I could teach him nothing about healing and he has knowledge greater than mine. Some of it is a little arcane but still… I suggested he learn Saxon as well as Greek and Latin."

"Yes to question their prisoners."

"He told you that?" I nodded. "He has not yet fought or he would know that we take few prisoners. I was thinking of using him as a spy. He could pass amongst them and bring valuable information."

I had not thought of that. "And that, Brother Osric, brings me to some information he did pass on to me last night. Bladud is recruiting warriors who are more loyal to him than the king. There have been fights."

"I was aware of that but the king still has faith in Bladud. I think I agree with your brother, one day you will have to kill this man but I am at a loss to see how, without destroying the kingdom." He smiled. "So, Myrddyn already possesses skills as a spy. As you might say, *wyrd*."

King Urien was walking in the small, walled garden. It was a peaceful place and, even on a frosty morning was quite beautiful with the hoar frost hanging like silver jewels on the trees and shrubs. He smiled as he saw me. "Ah Lord Lann. I hoped that you did not mind being put forward as joint leader of the expedition." He pointed at my scar. "I know that the Queen and your wife think you have bled enough for the kingdom."

"Until the Saxons are driven back into the sea I will do everything that I can to fight for Rheged."

"Good." He could sense that I had not come just to chat. "There is something else?"

"I would beg your majesty's permission to return to my family. I mean no disrespect to you or the other kings but…"

He came over and put his arm around me. "Were I in your position I too would wish to go to my family. Go with my blessing but before you go… I chose Prince Ywain to go with you for I fear that he has lost the appetite he once had for defending this land. I know how he feels. I would prefer to stay at home with the Queen and watch our grandchildren play but one day he is to be king and he needs fire in his belly again and not the good food and wine with which he has been over indulging. I know that with you at his side he will make the right decisions and become the king he will need to be when I am gone."

I felt a sense of relief. I had thought I was betraying the two men who had given me my chance to be a warrior. "I was intending to speak with the Prince before I left for we have much planning to do."

"I would suggest Lann that you hold future meetings at your castle for he is easily distracted by his young wife." His twinkling eyes spoke volumes.

"I will do so. I will not be here to speak with the other kings; we would need their warriors within ten weeks from now. We can gather the warriors from Rheged and Strathclyde at my castle and march to the Roman Bridge where the men from Elmet and Bernicia can meet us."

"A good idea." He shook his head and a sad expression suddenly made him look much older. "I cannot understand King Morcant's reluctance to drive the invaders from the southern part of his land."

"Neither can I for he seems to want the glory without the risk."

"I hope that we can soon defeat the enemy and then you and I can get back to our families. Take care, Lord Lann for I believe that our hope lies with you and this wonderful cunning you have on the battlefield."

As I left the greatest king on the island I felt myself glowing with pride that he thought so highly of me. I would not have let him down in any case but I now had even more reason to do my duty. As I waited in the main hall for Prince Ywain I rehearsed how I would approach the man who was still a dear friend and closer to me than any apart from my brothers and Garth. I decided to just pretend that I had no worries about him and let him make his own decisions.

My brothers arrived just before the Prince and I gave a slight shake of the head. They both nodded and headed for the table which was laden with the cold meats left from the previous night's feasting. I put on my best smile as I strode over to him full of enthusiasm. "So, my lord, we lead again together! And what a force of warriors eh? The best that Rheged and her allies have to offer."

He returned a wan smile and drew me to one side. "But will we not be in danger Lord Lann? From the reports of the Bernicians the enemy could have more than five thousand men assembled ready to war. We would be outnumbered five to one."

"We have fought against great odds before and besides we are not there to fight them but to watch them. If we mount our archers then we will have almost half our force which can outrun the enemy and that just leaves me with four hundred warriors." I was giving him the excuse to be with the mounted men who could flee if necessary. I was not worried by the thought that I might have to escape the army with four hundred warriors. I knew the country well along the Dunum and the Saxons did not but I hoped it would not come to that. It was with some relief that I saw the hints of a smile appear on his face.

"With four hundred mounted men we could run rings around lumbering warriors. That is a good plan Lann and I will acquire us the horses."

"I also intended using the despatch riders who are slingers to be scouts. They did well in the last campaign and they are more experienced now." He nodded. I had kept from him Brother Osric's idea of using Myrddyn as a spy. The fewer who knew about that the better for I was still aware of the spy in my camp. What I did know was that the only men I would leave guarding my home would be the warriors I knew I could trust and all of the recruits would be going to war. If I was the target then I was not taking the chance that my wife and children might end up as accidental casualties. He was now nodding eagerly. "I will spend the next few weeks planning. If you could come to my castle in four weeks then we should be able to finalise them."

His face fell, "Your castle but…"

I remembered the king's words. "I will have the maps that we will need at my castle and we will be closer to where we intend to fight."

He could see no argument and he nodded reluctantly."It will have to be a short meeting. I do not like to leave my wife and castle alone."

"Just one or two days and we will be ready."

"Very well then. Four weeks." He clasped my arm. "I am pleased we had this talk for it has cleared my thoughts. Thank you; you are the rock of Rheged."

As soon as he had left my brothers came over; eager to speak with me. "I wish I was coming with you."

"I know Raibeart but I know that you will watch over my castle when I am away."

"As I will Lann."

"I know Aelle. I would also like you to teach my new healer, Myrddyn how to speak Saxon. I will give him the basics but you can make him sound Saxon."

He nodded. "He is to spy then?"

"You are a clever one but keep that to yourself. Only Brother Osric and you two know of this. He will be our secret and may give us the edge."

Raibeart looked over to where the prince was filling his platter with food. "And what of the Prince? Last night he did not look happy about the prospect."

"I have made him happier but the king is keen for him to go."

Aelle gave me a shrewd look. "And that tells me that you command. Good I am happy about that."

"Little brother you are so sharp, that you will cut yourself one day."

Chapter 8

Aideen was delighted to see me; the welcome I received made the journey through the blizzard worthwhile. The snow had come from nowhere and we had struggled through the driving windows and biting ice. Had we not been travelling home we might have turned around but we knew that if we kept on we would, eventually, reach home and so we finally did. It was after dark and we were chilled to the bone but we were home and it seemed so much more comforting for that. Aideen was not only a good wife she was a kind woman and she chivvied the kitchen slaves to make sure that the men who had accompanied me were as well fed as I. Brother Oswald had just brewed a new batch of mead which was gratefully consumed. For me, the journey had been alleviated by the Saxon lesson I gave Myrddyn. He was like a sponge and, by the time we had reached Castle Perilous, he had enough phrases to hand to speak with an unsuspecting Saxon. It boded well.

It was good to spend Yule amongst my own people and warriors. My family were delighted with my early and unexpected return and I was able to relax and enjoy comfortable and familiar surroundings. Brother Oswald had tinkered with the rudimentary hypocaust and the old prefect's quarters from the days of Roman occupation were the warmest part of the castle. It was a good time.

I was aware that we might have a spy amongst us and, although the men all knew we would be fighting later in the year, I kept my plans to a handful of those I knew I could trust. After we had celebrated and life began to get back to normal I met with Garth, Myrddyn and Brother Oswald. Garth had looked askance at the young man who sat in on our meetings. He had only recently been a recruit and here he was with those who planned and gave orders. I smiled at Garth's discomfort and I began the meeting by obliquely giving a reason. "Now, Myrddyn will be leaving within the week to spend a month with Aelle learning to speak Saxon. Then he will be charged with infiltrating the Saxon army to discover their plans. It is vital that we know what they are about. It is a difficult and dangerous job but I am sure that Myrddyn is up to it." He blushed and I saw the firm nod from Garth, "Brother Oswald, we will have two hundred archers. I know that Brother Osric will provide most of the arrows but I want a healthy supply here should we need them. Prince Ywain is supplying the horses but, Garth, I want every one of our archers taught to ride well. Their skill might just be the difference between victory and defeat. We need to be mobile. We need the armour of the warriors to be perfect. Have it checked and oiled regularly. We can have no weaknesses for we need to be better armoured than our enemies who will be more numerous. The shields, too, should all be reinforced with iron."

"The Lady Aideen and her ladies have finished the leather cloaks. Our warriors will all look the same and that should afford them more protection."

"Good and I want every warrior to have a dagger attached to their shields. I know that I found it useful. We need caltrops. The Roman supply has been used but they are not difficult to make."

"Not difficult but expensive."

"There is money available Oswald. Do not quibble over those things which can save men's lives. Now, Garth it will be up to you to organise and lead the four hundred warriors. I will be there, of course, but I will also have charge of the archers as well. Our men will be the point of the wedge and you will have to train the others on the march. Can you do it?"

"As most of the men are Rheged men, then yes, but I am not sure about the one hundred and fifty allies."

"They can form the rear two ranks. The men from Strathclyde and Elmet will be sound warriors, of that I am certain. One final point; no word of the date we depart should leak out. Keep the men trained and prepared. We will give them but one day's warning and then we will go."

After Garth and Oswald had left us I took Myrddyn to one side. "I will not order you to spy on the Saxons and I will not think badly of you if you refuse for you should know that it will be dangerous."

For one so young he looked both mature and calm. "It is my destiny to serve you my lord and the vision I had tells me that we shall have a long association together. Besides," he grinned and was suddenly a boy again, I will play the part of a Welsh healer; a throwback to the Druids. From what your men have said that has a certain aura about it." I felt relieved. I did not like sending men to their deaths but he seemed confident and I knew that Aelle would give him the skills he needed.

My next task was to summon my slingers and despatch riders. Garth stood with me for I had already briefed him about my intentions. As they were all boys there came a point when they would either become warriors or horsemen. Those who had skills with the bow were taken to one side by Miach and trained in that art. I gathered them all in the Great Hall; I could see the interest and trepidation on some of their faces. It was rare for them to be called to speak with their lord.

"I want you to stand in a line with the smallest on one side and the tallest on the other." They quickly obeyed me and I could see the disparity in height. There were three at the end who were almost men. "You three go with Garth; it is time you became warriors." I could see the uncontained joy on their faces and the disappointment on the rest. After they had gone I pointed to the six tallest. "You six will be warriors next year but now you will need to be trained to be scouts as well as slingers." I looked at the others who were still looking unhappy. "All of you will, eventually, need this skill and I want you all to learn how to scout. When we go to war it will be you who tell us the numbers of the enemy and help us to prepare our attack. If you do your job well then you will save men's lives. You six go and find Adair. He will begin your training. As for the rest of you I want you to collect the perfect stones for your slings. When we go to war you will need many, my young warriors." They raced to the river, oblivious to the cold. They would collect them until they were summoned to food for all felt the bond which tied my warriors to Castle Perilous.

When Myrddyn left for Aelle and his stronghold I felt a strange loss. I had grown close to the young healer and I missed him and our conversations in the solar. Garth and I concentrated on forging the warriors into a tightly knit group. It was difficult because of the Bernician, Llofan who was like a piece of grit in the eye; it was always there irritating. The others worked well together but he was the one out of step and yet, I agreed with Garth, he was the best warrior amongst the recruits. The problem was solved when Prince Ywain arrived for our meeting. King Urien had come with him and the warrior hall was full for the first time. It was a bustling and busy place filled with warriors. Bladud had to be polite to me as it was my home but I saw him and three of his warriors scowling at me every time I passed by.

I took my two distinguished guests to my solar to enjoy some privacy.

"You have some fine warriors Lord Lann."

I shrugged. I am generally happy but…"

King Urien looked troubled. "This is not like you, Lord Lann. We cannot afford any weakness in the man who will lead our warriors against the Saxons." I reluctantly explained about Llofan Lilo. "He is a good warrior?"

"He is the best I have but he is also from Bernicia and I do not wish to offend our ally by returning him to his homeland."

King Urien beamed. "Then I can solve the problem. Bladud has been faithfully gathering warriors for my bodyguards. We have ten Bernicians amongst our ranks and I am sure one more will not come amiss."

I brightened. It would solve my problem. "I would not wish to weaken your bodyguard."

"Do not worry about that. The bodyguard will be the core of my army. They will all be heavily armed equites and they do not need to fight as your warriors do in a shield wall. I will speak with Bladud."

Garth was also relieved at the possibility of a solution. "I still feel as though I have failed my lord. I should have been able to train him."

"Do not worry Garth. I saw that there was something different about him. There is a hidden story there."

When I entered the warrior hall I could see King Urien deep in conversation with Bladud and Prince Ywain. Two of Bladud's men stood nearby. I was waved over. "Which is the warrior you spoke of?"

"Llofan!"

The Bernician warrior strode over. He had an arrogant walk and, that too, had annoyed me. "Yes my lord." He managed to say '*my lord'* and make it sound as though it was an insult.

Bladud looked at King Urien, smiled and nodded his approval. I wondered about that because Bladud never smiled. "Would you like to join my bodyguards? I have other Bernician warriors and Lord Lann has given me permission to ask you."

I saw Llofan also smile for the first time. "I would be delighted my lord."

"Good then you will now join my guards. Bladud will explain your duties." From the expressions and embraces I realised that Llofan knew the two warriors standing beside Bladud already. It confirmed my dislike of both men.

Later Garth came to me, his face filled with anger. He held in his hand a black leather cloak. "I was thrown this by Llofan who said that now that he was serving with real warriors he did not need your wife's needlework!"

I could feel myself becoming as angry as Garth but over the years I had learned caution. I suspected that Bladud had something to do with this and I would not cause offence to King Urien in my own home. Aideen was not insulted because she had not heard the words. "We will let it go for now Garth but, fear not, the dishonour will be remedied one day."

Once I had met with Prince Ywain and his father all thoughts of Bladud left me for we had much to plan. I could see a change in Ywain already. He was a little thinner and looked as though he had been exercising. Some of his old enthusiasm and confidence had also come back to him. "I am training my archers to be horsemen and I hope that the others are doing the same. I know that Raibeart is. When the warriors are gathered we will work with them whilst marching to make them one." I explained our idea of keeping the allies as a reserve at the rear of the wedge.

King Urien frowned, "I would not have our allies insulted."

I shrugged. "There are but one hundred and fifty of them and we do not know how they are armed; at least the warriors of Rheged fight in the same style with the same weapons. But I promise you that I will do what I need to diplomatically. I have also begun to train some of my boys as scouts. We need eyes out there and scouts who can move swiftly. We need to be one step ahead of the cunning Aella at all times. I have armed my men so that they can fight any foe we meet. I too will work with the allied horse but the majority will know our tactics for I have one hundred and fifty with me now."

The king smiled. "This is excellent and I am pleased that we made the right choice; you two are a formidable force. You will gather in eight weeks and get to the Roman Bridge and I will bring the rest of the army when we are mustered but that will not be until after Easter."

"We will use my horsemen to keep you informed, father. We will set up relay stations with horses to enable you to get messages quickly."

"You could use homing pigeons."

"Homing pigeons?"

"Brother Oswald mentioned them to me. You have pigeons at Civitas Carvetiorum and that becomes their home. Then you put some in cages and they go with us. We attach messages to their legs and they fly home to their roost. They could do the journey which would take a horseman a day and a half at least in half a day."

"I will see Brother Osric when I return. It would be an advantage to have two methods of communication."

When they had left us I felt happier that the prince looked more like the old Prince Ywain who had valiantly fought at my side and we had solved a number of problems. The first heavy snow in a few weeks fell the day after they left. I took Garth to one side. "Now would be a good opportunity to see if we have had any visitors to the wood again. We can see their tracks in the snow."

When we reached the glade there was no sign of any human visitors and the fire which had been there before was long dead. I did not trust to chance and for the next twenty days either Garth or I visited the site but we saw no sign of clandestine meetings. If anything that made me even more worried. At least if they were meeting we knew they were still planning. The fact that they had, apparently, stopped meeting did not bode well and I found myself scrutinising the recruits, who now seemed like all the other warriors, very closely. I wondered what they thought.

By the time Myrddyn returned the snow had gone, the arrows and arms were ready and my contingent of warriors was as ready as they ever would be. We had made enough spare arms, albeit of a lesser quality, for the ordinary warriors who would be joining us with the king when the army of Rheged was mustered in spring.

My main problem was Aideen who had become increasingly fretful and fussy as the weather had improved. It was almost as though she was willing the snow to return for it would stop me leaving. I had not confided in her the plans we had made. It was not that I didn't trust her; I just did not want her worrying unnecessarily. Eventually, a week before we were to depart I had to tell her. We were in bed, and it was a cold night. I would miss the cuddles and the comfort of her warm body over the next weeks. She lay in the crook of my arm. "I will be leaving with my men soon." I felt her stiffen in my arms but she said not a word. "We will be but two day's ride from home and, hopefully, we will not have to do any fighting."

There was a pause and I felt moisture dripping down my arm. He voice was thick and deep when she spoke. "But you will be facing the Saxons?"

"Until they are destroyed by the gods or pestilence before I reach them then yes I will."

"I want to lose no more men to those sea devils." She remembered the men she had already lost; she hated the Saxons but not enough to lose me too.

"And I promise you that I will not die."

She sat upright in bed and I could see her eyes flashing with anger. "You cannot promise that! It is a hurtful thing to say for it is a lie."

"No it is not. I will be leading and I will put neither myself nor my men in harm's way. This time I am to watch. Fighting will be a last resort. I will have to order the men and be as a general. I will not be in the shield wall." I was not sure that would always be the case, but my intentions were good." I now have a daughter as well as a son and I want to see them both grow up."

She seemed mollified and cuddled in again. "Will we ever have a peaceful world again?"

"I hope so. I would dearly love to leave Saxon Slayer in its scabbard but, for the present, it must be unsheathed."

As the days grew longer and the earth warmed up Garth and I began to spar every day with the wooden swords and heavy shields we used. Then we began to spar together against four or five other warriors. It developed quick reflexes but, more importantly it helped the two of us to fight as one. We then spent a whole week with the thirty five warriors I would be taking with me practising the wedge and shield wall formations. With so many new warriors in its ranks it was vital that they worked as one. Garth had performed wonders over the winter and it was hard to discern any difference between the recruits and those who had fought Aella the last time.

When Myrddyn returned he was escorted by Aelle's contingent. Although they had fought in fewer battles than my men I knew that they would be well trained and their early arrival meant that we could train with those. Raibeart brought his own men down and I could see that he was longing to be part of it but he was loyal and the king wanted him in command of the army's archers. Of course I took the opportunity of some expert tuition for my men while I used the time with the one hundred and five warriors who would be the nucleus of our attack.

Myrddyn spent but a short time with us for he rode away east to find the Saxons and become our spy. I had said all the words I needed to and the confident young man gave me a cheerful wave as he rode east towards the Roman Road. When he left then I knew that our undertaking had begun in earnest. We had finished training and we would now begin the business of war.

Finally, and on time, Prince Ywain brought the rest of the Rheged vanguard four days later along with the Strathclyde contingent. We had no opportunity for training these men as we had to prepare for our journey the following day. The archers were assigned horses while the rest of us sharpened weapons and checked that we had all the arms we would need. We would not be taking wagons for we were to move swiftly and could not be encumbered by lumbering vehicles. The archers would carry their own quivers of arrows on their horses. As the warriors feasted and bantered in the warrior hall I took the five scouts I had chosen to lead our expedition. "You will leave tonight. I want you to find the Saxons but not to let them see you. Do not return to the Roman Bridge until you are sure that you have found the main force. I would begin at the Dunum; they will want to be close to their ships. Adair this is your command."The young man nodded seriously. "Next year, if you continue to grow you will begin your training as an equite but for now there is no more vital task in the whole army than this one. If they see us before we see them then we will lose." I could see from their faces that they would not deliberately let me down. May Vindonnus guide you and help you, for today you hunt Saxons."

I felt sad as they slipped through the gate and into the night. They were not much older than I had been when I had first fought the Saxons but I knew that I had been lucky. I wished for some of that luck for them.

I was leaving more of my warriors guarding Castle Perilous than I was taking with me. Some of those I left behind would join the king later but I wanted my family protected while we were absent. Brother Oswald gave me a reassuring smile as he stood next to Aideen, casting a paternal eye over her and my children. I was happy that my home was in safe hands and we rode east to find our allies.

The weather was an ally as we rode the road for it rained hard. It made it difficult to see a long way ahead but, as we had more of our scouts out before us, I thought it unlikely that we would be spotted first. Of course it made for uncomfortable travelling and the men grumbled about their armour becoming rusty. My men were the exception as they wore the leather cloaks about them; tightly fastened and covering both their head and bodies. Apart from keeping them protected during combat it also shielded both them and their armour from the rain and I saw some of the other warriors looking enviously in their direction.

The first night we camped just east of the high moors. There were wooded areas on either side of the road and it gave us some shelter. Those warriors who had not been training as hard as my men suffered from the inevitable blisters but it was not as bad as it could have been. We had fresh meat and foods with us and our supplies would last until we reached the Roman Bridge. After that it would be dried meat and whatever we could forage. I smiled as Ywain looked ruefully at the rain coming down like arrows and the meagre rations his servant brought to him. He would fit into his armour a little easier within a few days, that was glaringly obvious.

The rain relented by dawn but it was still both grey and overcast. There was a damp smell as we trudged towards the Roman Bridge. Although the Bernicians held the vital river crossing until we were safely there we all worried that we might run into the enemy and we wanted to do that on our terms not theirs. Our advance scouts had not returned. That could be good news; the Saxons might be many miles away, or it could be disastrous and they had been killed or worse, captured.

I breathed a sigh of relief when the road dropped down towards the old Roman fort on the Dunum. I smiled to myself as I remembered gathering my cache of treasure when I was a boy: armour, swords, caligae and nails. How long ago that seemed now. I rode with Prince Ywain into the fort while Garth organised a camp close to the walls. We would have more shelter this night than the previous ones. Some of the warriors recognised me from my time at Din Guardi and they called out a welcome. I waved back at them. I wondered who Morcant Bulc had put in command. Some of his leaders were even less keen to fight than their king and the Bernician in charge of this outpost was keystone to our success. When Riderch strolled to meet us his arms outstretched in welcome I felt hope course through my veins. He was the best of the Bernicians and would be the most solid of commanders but I had thought he was still the leader of the bodyguard.

He took us into what had been the Praetorium in the old fort. It had been made water tight and warm with a cosy fire burning; my old friend had learned the lessons of campaign well. There was hot food and wine on the table and Ywain looked happy for the first time in days. "My men saw your scouts and I thought hot food would be appreciated." It was. A soldier learns to eat as much as he can when he can for he never knows when he will be on half rations. We both finished two bowlfuls and drank the jug of wine before we spoke.

"Riderch, I thought that you were the leader of the king's bodyguard."

"I was," he said cheerfully, "but I upset the king by not being one of the yes men who fill his court these days. I pointed out that we should have our army closer to the Dunum and not have to rely so much on our allies. This is a punishment. I am the commander of the advance guard."

"You do not look unhappy about it."

"And I am not. I do not want to wait behind the walls of Din Guardi while you do the fighting and get the glory. I want to be a part of it."

"We may not be fighting and I think there will be little glory. We are here to stop the Saxons from moving through our land with a free hand. We need to tie them down," I pointed towards our camp. "It is why we have so many mounted men. We will always be able to move faster than they do."

"I know but where Wolf Warrior goes there is bound to be fighting and booty. All the men here are volunteers. They all want to fight with the man who freed northern Bernicia from the Saxons. I am leaving just fifty men to guard the fort. You will have me and another one hundred and fifty warriors when you leave."

"Isn't that dangerous? Disobeying the king? He said to leave a hundred here."

"He never told me how many men to leave here and he did put me in command." He had such a look of happiness on his face that it was hard to believe he was talking about going to war with an enemy who outnumbered us many times over.

Prince Ywain and I had decided that there was little point in trying to find the enemy. That was the job of the scouts. However we could be prepared. We had the warriors dig double ditches to the south of the river. I was not convinced that they would approach from that direction but it paid to be prepared. Aella was too crafty a leader and he knew that the bottle neck of the bridge would play into our hands as a smaller army could hold his up. He had, I suspect, respect for the qualities of my warriors who had repulsed him before and killed his son.

While my warriors were digging, Prince Ywain took a small patrol in a circuit covering the land five miles ahead of us. It was a precaution only. I also sent out more of our scouts to travel further afield. We had been there for a week and were well prepared when the advance scouts under Adair finally returned. They all looked dirty and tired but all of them had returned and I was pleased about that. Adair showed great skills as a leader by telling his scouts to rest and he joined Prince Ywain, Garth, Riderch and myself in the fort.

"They are many miles to the east my lord. They have made their camp below the bluffs where the old hill fort lies. Their fleet is anchored in the Dunum and they are encamped between there and the bluffs and out towards the mouth of the river."

Prince Ywain was nervous and he blurted out, "How many men are there?"

Adair gave him a very serious look, his young face filled with frowns. "From the hills to the river their tents fill the valley bottom. We could not count them all but there have to be more than five thousand. We counted the boats and there were more than five hundred of them."

"Where were the boats? Were they in the middle of the river or closer to the camp?"

"Close to their camp, Lord Lann."

Prince Ywain gave me a curious look, "Are you planning something?"

"Not if their boats are close to the camp but if they had been in the middle we could have fired them. Aella is too crafty for such a ruse to work. Adair, was there any sign of horses or movement?"

"No horses my lord but we saw them practising their formations, much as you do."

"You have done well. Get some rest."

"What do you make of it Lann?"

I noticed that all three of them were watching my face. I could now see why the king had asked for me. Prince Ywain was brave and a doughty warrior but planning was not his strength. "I think he means to cross the Dunum by boats. If he were heading west then he would have sent out probing patrols. Riderch, when is the tide at its highest?"

"There is a spring tide in about seven days."

"Then that is when he will cross. We all assumed that he would wait for the crops to be sown and the animals born. He is not waiting for he has brought fresh warriors from his homeland. He can strike at any time."

"But our forces will not be here for another four weeks."

Riderch looked anxious. "King Morcant Bulc has no forces in this area. They all guard the homeland. If Aella crosses the river then he can ravage the whole land. The people would be defenceless."

I looked at the map we had brought with us. If we left the bridge we were risking Aella heading east with nothing in his way. He would destroy all before him but if I was right, then he would capture the whole of Bernicia before we could assemble. "We need to slow him up and make him turn in this direction."

"My lord, could we not march along the north bank of the Dunum and meet him as he lands. We would have the advantage."

"We would indeed Garth but if he uses his ships then he can choose where he lands. He could even split his fleet and surround us; it is one of the perils of having such a small force. We must send messages to King Urien and King Morcant Bulc and tell them of the danger. If your king can move his forces south, Riderch, then it may help to slow down any advance they might make."

"What of Elmet?"

The warriors promised from Elmet had not arrived. "They can fortify this place when they do arrive and supplement your men. What I propose is that we take the archers and the horsemen and make a night time attack on his camp. I will speak with Adair when he wakes but I suspect their numbers means that they will not have a strong guard."

I could see that the Prince was not convinced. "Will he not then attack us here in the west or even begin his attack prematurely?"

"Either action works for us. If he attacks us here then we can do as we were ordered and slow him up. If he attacks early then we can harry and hinder him for he would have to do that piecemeal." I shrugged. "It is less than perfect but I can see no other way."

"Who would we use to attack the camp?"

"The equites and the archers; I would lead the archers in an attack while you and your horsemen were ready to support."

Riderch smiled, "Fire arrows?"

"Fire arrows and we can try to fire some of their boats. I suspect the warriors they brought from over the sea might not be happy at having their means of escape taken from them. When we have stirred the nest of wasps then we retreat. They have no horses and any pursuit would be slow."

"And if they did not pursue us?"

"Then we think of something else. I would also have Garth and Riderch take the Rheged warriors along the northern bank in case they do try to cross."

Garth nodded but Prince Ywain looked shocked. "A handful of our warriors against five thousand fresh and determined Saxons; it is suicide?"

"I told you, my prince, they cannot cross all of them at once; as we found when we fought the Hibernians all those years ago. It is boatload by boat load. And they would not know it was such a small number. If Garth lines them along the bank, double spaced in a single line they will assume that the whole army is behind them. Garth's task would be to slow them up and not to fight them. If they land in force then he has a fighting retreat. I will use the scouts to accompany him and then we can be kept informed. We will still have enough men here to slow them down. Adair said that it was a day's ride to their camp which means that it would take them two days, at least to march here."

"Unless they use their ships."

"In which case, Riderch, we have them for the bridge halts them and the river here is only wide enough for one ship at a time. I checked when we were digging the ditches." I paused to allow the ideas to sink in. "Any other plans or thoughts?"

They all shook their heads. "Then we leave tomorrow and Riderch will command the forces that are left here."

Chapter 9

Leaving all of the scouts but Adair with Garth and Riderch we set off to the Saxon encampment. The steep bluffs above the river were visible almost as soon as we rode over the ridge south of the bridge. It was a clear crisp day and visibility was good. Adair rode next to Prince Ywain and me, keen to add any further information he might have omitted.

"You are sure you saw no ditches and no walls?"

"No, my lord. Their camp was not as ours; it seemed to have no order."

"Good. And the ships were not beached?"

"No they were facing the northern shore."

I turned to the prince. "It means they are almost ready to attack. They will be waiting until the river is as high as possible and that will make loading and unloading easier as well as ensuring that they do not ground and damage their boats for they will want the security of knowing they have an escape route."

I noticed that Ywain was chewing his lip nervously. "What can two hundred men do against such a force?"

I shook my head, "I do not know but if we do nothing then King Morcant Bulc loses Bernicia and King Gwalliog loses Elmet. Your father's army is not mustered. We have to hold them up for as long as possible and disrupt their plans. This may not work but if it does not then we will think of something else." I sighed, "Prince Ywain, the Saxons have neither horses nor archers and we do. Not only that but we know that they are the finest soldiers of their kind anywhere. There may on be a few but we are mobile and we are better than the Saxons."

He looked at me with a look which I did not understand. "How can you be as you are Lann? I began fighting when younger than you and yet you seem to take everything in your stride. You can even send your men off to what may be their certain death without a care in the world."

"Then you do not know me at all. I care deeply about every one of those men and I believe they will live. I have trained Garth to be as I am and that means he will put the men's lives first and he will not risk a battle if he thinks he will lose. Had the Saxons possessed horses then I might not have used this tactic but they are slow and they are ponderous. When they try to move swiftly they have no order and my men can beat any other force which is not organised. No, I have sent them to do a job for me and I will see them all again, Prince Ywain."

He could tell by my tone that he had upset me. "I meant no offence Lann. I wish I could be like you but," he lowered his voice so that Adair would not overhear. "I do not want to die. I want to return to my castle and my wife."

"Nor do I wish to die and we will return to our wives and homes. It is those men who fear to die that are most likely to die. Believe that you will survive and you will increase your chances. You ask why we are different. I believe I can defeat anyone."

"That is because you are the best warrior with a sword."

"You forget that you trained me, Prince Ywain. Until I worked with you I was an archer. You taught me. You are a great swordsman. Believe that you can defeat every opponent and you shall."

A change came over Prince Ywain then; a change which lasted until the tragic events many months later. I think he needed someone to tell him that he could do it.

We did not stop for food. I wanted us in position and then we would eat. The valley of the Dunum was wide except for the place where Aella had camped. Across the river the land was flat and featureless. There was no obstacle before him. I had heard of a Roman Road which ran north and I knew he would make for that. If this plan failed then I would take our mounted men and try to ambush him there. I was not sure this would work but if we could kill some of his men and damage some of his ships then the confidence of those newer troops who had just joined him might be damaged.

We found a wooded area which Adair said was five miles from the Saxons. The men needed rest but I would go with Adair and see for myself the task which faced us. Prince Ywain seemed happy to remain with our pitiful force of archers and horsemen. The land was swampy and low in places with small woods and areas of tangled and unruly shrubs. It would not afford good cover. Night was falling as we approached the camp which was lit by a thousand fires. We dismounted in a small copse and I took my bow with me. Adair still used a sling and he was deadly accurate.

My cloak made me almost invisible as we hurried towards the first of the fires. I could see that they had hunted and fished by the smells which emanated from the camp fires. The noise and banter seemed to indicate that they were in good spirits. I also saw that they were drinking which meant their reactions would not be as they should be. We headed towards the river. As soon as we reached it I could see why Aella had chosen this as his camp. The river had a huge loop which meant he could anchor all of his ships and yet provide them with protection. The water surrounded three sides of the camp and it was just the place Adair had brought me that had neither water nor ditch. I estimated that the nearest ships were just forty paces from the shore. They were easily in range of my archers. This would be where we would attack. His sentries would be complacent and not expecting an attack. They would get a surprise when we did attack.

I led us along the river for I wanted to scout out a retreat. The ground rose slightly and seemed quite firm and that gave me hope; it meant that we could move swiftly and safely. Suddenly I spied something which gave me even more hope. There was a small oared boat moored close to the bank. It was either a Saxon one or one left by the inhabitants who had once lived here. It gave me the last piece of information I needed. We returned to the horses and then headed back to the camp.

I was starving when we returned and I quickly wolfed down some food and washed it down with warm beer. "We can do this Prince Ywain." Turning to the archers I said, "Gather kindling. I want dry material. Miach find an empty beer jug. Dry it and put kindling inside. We need to light it for the fire arrows."He had used this before and he nodded before finding one of the many empty jugs.

Prince Ywain seemed ready for the fight. "Well Lann. What do we do?"

"There is a low ridge close to the river; about four hundred paces from it. There are trees and shrubs at the top and it will hide your numbers. You and the horsemen will wait there. We will fire the ships and the camp and retreat. They will only have eyes for me and my men and it will be dark. They are drinking." I allowed the significance of that to sink in. "You fall upon the flanks of the warriors who chase us; no cheering just kill as many as you can and then join us. They will be their best warriors and they will have their backs to you. Kill, kill and then kill some more but do not risk our men. I will halt my archers a mile down river and when you come we will cover your retreat. "

I saw his smile in the dark. "It sounds as though we do have a chance."

We reached the ridge and the horsemen could see the camp less than a mile away. "You were right Lann. This will afford us both cover and height." He grasped my arm. "Be safe. We need the Wolf Warrior."

At the river we tied the horses to the scrubby bushes. The horses had grazing and they were tired; they would not move. We found the boat. "Fill it with kindling. Adair I want you to stay here and count to five hundred. Then light the kindling and push the boat off. It will float down river."

"Excellent my lord but if I pull it further downstream then we have more chance of it hitting the other ships. That way I can watch for your arrows and we will be certain."

"Very well. Miach, detail an archer to help Adair."

We moved like wraiths though the night. It was long after midnight and I hoped that they would all be asleep. We had identified the best ten archers and we would kill any sentries and then the archers would rain fire down on the camp. Half of the archers were detailed to fire the boats. As we halted I whispered my last command. "I want no heroes. When I say leave then we leave and Miach, if I am dead, then you command."

His serious, "Yes my lord," had the desired effect on the men. They would not take risks. We crept to within forty paces of the Saxon camp. Our eyes were accustomed to the night and we could see the sentries outlined by the fading fires. They made our life easy for they congregated in small groups. My archers and Raibeart's could release three arrows in the blink of an eye and twenty sentries fell to their silent deaths. Without a pause the fire arrows began to soar into the air. There was no one to watch them and I saw the flames flicker and grow as they struck tents, wagons and, from the screams within, men. The archers who had been detailed to the boats had done a good job and I could see many ablaze and, even better, the ghostly shape of the small fire boat sneaking down the river to engulf other ships with flames.

"Use ordinary arrows!" I did not want our position identified and we could now see our targets quite clearly as the Saxons ran from their tents to seek this hidden enemy. Many ran to save their boats and they were slaughtered by my marksmen. I knew that this could not last and someone would take charge. I saw a helmeted warrior point over to us although I knew he could not see us. "One more arrow each and then back to the horses!" We all released and then we ran, like foxes pursued by hounds.

They were forty paces behind us and their eyes were not attuned to the dark. I almost laughed as I heard them trip and fall over dead men, tufts of wild grass, mounds and small bushes. As I ran I notched an arrow and then I suddenly stopped, turned around and released it at the nearest warrior. It was the helmeted leader and the arrow struck him in the stomach. I did not stop to see how he fared, I ran, knowing that they would be warier now.

I heard Adair yell, "Here my lord!" And I ran in the direction of his voice. He had my horse and, as I mounted, I heard the whirr of his slingshot as he killed the warrior who was but twenty paces behind me.

Those who had mounted first also sent arrows at the enemy. "Retreat!"

I glanced over my shoulder. It was as though we had kicked over a wasp's nest. They angrily buzzed after us. They could now see us and they veered towards the river. This was as I had hoped. "Do not tire your horses. Keep a steady pace!" I had to remember that these were not horsemen; these were archers who had been taught to ride. I knew that we could outrun them. I also knew that the surprise of a hundred horsemen falling among them would be even more devastating if they thought that they were about to catch us.

The angry buzz became louder as they came within thirty paces. Then I turned in my saddle as I heard a wail of anguish and Prince Ywain and his equites hacked and slashed at the unprotected backs of the Saxons. The pursuit stopped and I kicked on. After a half mile I shouted. "Halt! Turn and ready an arrow." Their eager faces told me that they knew what we were doing. I could see swords rising and falling and hear the clash of steel on steel and wood and then the line of horsemen came galloping towards us.

"Leave a gap in the middle. Rheged to me!" Those at the front veered towards the line of horsemen and gratefully galloped through. Their horses carried armour and they were more tired than we. I knew that we needed to hold the Saxons for a while longer or they would catch horsemen on blown horses. I saw Prince Ywain grimace as he nodded to me and galloped through and then all I saw was a broken wall of Saxons. "Release!" A hundred arrows and then a hundred more punched the line of Saxons back as though they had been struck by a stick. By the third volley they had halted.

I deemed that we had given Ywain long enough and I shouted, "Retreat!" I notched an arrow and waited as my men thundered away behind me. I could see that they were watching me and I also knew that they knew who I was. My cloak and my helmet let them know who I was. I saw a war chief begin to rally the flagging men and I took aim. The arrow went straight through his throat and his stunned warriors stood in awe. I slung my bow, turned around and slowly rode off. Had any of my men done the same they would have had the sharp edge of my tongue but I was making a point; the Wolf Warrior did not fear the Saxons.

Miach was waiting for me and I saw the look of disapproval in his eyes and his tone. "A bit unnecessary my lord. What would Lady Aideen do to me if I returned with just your body?"

"I just wanted them to know who we are and what we are about. They will now fear us a little more and hate us but the fear will give us the edge."

Dawn was breaking when we halted at the narrow part of the Dunum. It gave us the chance to see to the wounded. Two of the prince's men had died and others were wounded. He had taken a cut to the leg but it was not serious. I think he was relieved to have been struck and survived. I wondered how my healer was doing. He was probably being more usefully employed in the Saxon camp. We might have even been close enough to see him and the unpleasant thought crossed my mind that one of our arrows could have accidentally killed him. Then the memory of his vision flashed into my head and I knew that he was safe.

I tended to the prince's wound myself. I had learned much from Myrddyn. "You were right Lann. That felt good. I was unlucky to be struck by the axe, it was meant for another." I smiled. He was becoming his old self again. "What now?"

I had been considering that for some time now. "I think we will cross the river here and join Garth."

"What of the Roman Bridge?"

"I think our men can hold them there but I think they will try to cross the river. We must be ready. Your father should have the news by now and he will let us know what he is to do. If King Morcant Bulc does not rush south to defend his borders then he has no right to be king. With the army of Bernicia behind us we could hold the Saxons off until the rest arrive."

"I am in agreement with that but I am not sure about crossing the river."

"It is easy. I will lead my archers first. You swim upriver and the current will take us there." I pointed to a shallow beach with a gentle slope behind it. I turned in my saddle. "Archers, which of you fancies a little swim before we eat?" Their cheers told me that they were in good spirits and I jumped my mount into the water. It was icy but, in a strange way, enjoyable and I urged him on. It was only in the middle of the channel where he had to swim and I hung on to the saddle. Our bow strings were safely wrapped in an oiled bag and we would soon dry out. The archers fared better than the armoured horsemen but only one equite fell; into the water and a laughing Miach pulled him out. The cheers, jeers and banter told me that I had no need to worry about my men's morale.

By the time we had eaten, my archers had dried off. I sent Adair to scout ahead. We would need to rest but I wanted to be with my warriors and Garth when that happened. We would be too exhausted to defend ourselves. We needed at least one day of rest and I was hoping that the Saxons, too, would need time to repair their camp and their boats. It was late morning when Adair returned to say he had found them and, two miles later, we entered their camp complete with ditch, wall and warm food. We were safe, at least for a short time.

When I awoke I saw the smiling face of Garth and behind him Riderch shaking his head. "I understand from Miach that you were a little foolhardy last night, my lord?"

I grinned, "Even an old wolf can behave like a cub now and again." As I rubbed the sleep from my eyes and took the proffered ale I asked, "Any sign of the Saxons?"

"The scouts say they are still at their camp. You managed to destroy over thirty ships. Their blackened timbers line the banks and, from the funeral pyres, you killed many of their men."

I shook my head. "I need to know if Aella has moved."

Patiently Garth said, "No my lord. He is still there."

"Good for we need time to recover our strength. I believe he will come across the river in the next two or three days."

"Before the tide?"

"Before the tide. He does not know where we are. The sooner he can invade Bernicia then the sooner he can reward his new allies. Send some scouts to find the Roman Road which goes north. We can ambush him there."

"He still outnumbers us."

"And he still has neither horsemen nor bows."

Prince Ywain limped over to me. He pointed behind him to the south; it was hidden by a levee, bushes and high grass. "They are busy as bees over there. They have had to clear away the remains of the burned ships but I think you are correct. They are making preparations to cross." I could see that he looked worried but I was not.

Garth returned with some stale bread, ale and a hunk of two day old meat. He gave an apologetic glance at the food. "We will have to ration soon. There is little but rabbits here and I did not wish the men to fish."

"No! I want us hidden. Aella may suspect we are here but if we can keep him guessing and uncertain then it works in our favour. I want no fires or smoke to alert him. The men only have a few days to suffer. They were well fed over the winter it will do them no harm."

Garth nodded. "Riderch and I have the scouts lying next to the river, they are small and in clothes which blend in. I do not think they will be seen."

I relaxed. It was now in the hands of the Saxons and we had done all that we could to delay them. "Do we just wait then?"

I smiled at the suddenly belligerent and impatient prince. "We will not have to wait long and our next move is determined by Aella's. If he chooses not to cross but to attack the Roman Bridge then we reinforce the bridge. If he attacks here then we contest the crossing."

"We cannot hold off that mighty host. We would be defeated."

"True but when a boat lands then we can hurt those who are trying to get ashore. They cannot fight back. True, they will overrun us if we allow that but their bravest warriors will be dead. This is a war of attrition. We grind them down little by little until they are small enough for your father to defeat. We will not fight long here; just enough to make them pay and then we retreat. Find an ambush site and keep doing that until someone comes to pour aid."

"He could defeat us now for he still outnumbers us."

I looked at Garth who understood my argument. "No he could not. The army he faces are not the farmers who make up the bulk of our army. They are raiders from across the seas. They are warriors who fight and take what they want. They produce nothing. Apart from our nine hundred men your father can count on another seven hundred or so who are the equal of those we face. We have to cull the best and then defeat the rest."

I could see the thoughts filling his head and the doubt entering as he said. "Will they ever stop coming?"

"Only when we make it so difficult that they choose to go elsewhere and find easier pickings."

We watched for two days. I occasionally bellied up the bank to see their preparations. It became increasingly obvious that they would either attack or return home, for they were preparing their ships. I thought a return home to be unlikely. We had bloodied their nose and that was all.

A rider returned from King Urien. The message was unequivocal. Hold them. The rider returned from Morcant Bulc with no message. I asked if he thought the Bernician king was preparing for war and he shrugged. "He had many men in his castle but they were not preparing."

It looked as though Bulc's indolence would kill more warriors of Rheged. The time we spent by the Dunum was not wasted. The injured horsemen and horses recovered and we spent each night burying stakes below the waterline and digging pits along the banks of the sluggish moving river. It was only two hundred paces wide at the closest point to the Saxon camp and, although it was narrower nearer to the bluffs we had used for cover, Aella would need to use this shore to land on. Further east the scouts reported shallows, marsh flats, bogs sinking sands and sand dunes. Our left flank was secure. Aelle could either land where we were or he could risk moving west where the channel was narrower. We prepared our traps extensively along the river and we scouted further inland for an escape route. It was time well used. As we counted each day with pangs of hunger I was delighted. Each day's delay meant we had more chance of success. But I knew it could not last.

The sentries awoke me before dawn. "My lord, the Saxon camp is moving." I knew it was one of my own men. It was a confident and succinct report and told me all that I needed to know. "Wake the camp but do it quietly."

We had discussed at length what we would do and I saw Prince Ywain moving with his men to the horse lines we had created some way back from the river. Miach was already spreading his archers out to cover as much of the bank as possible while Garth had the warriors in a single line. The scouts were lying by the river side, some of them half in the water to enable them to see as much as possible and remain hidden. I armed myself and made sure that Saxon Slayer slid in and out of its sheath easily. I also had my bow on the ground but I would only use it briefly. My position was in the centre of the warriors with Garth and my Wolf Warriors with their standard. We had deliberately placed ourselves in the centre to attract attention to ourselves. We wanted to goad Aella and his men into a premature attack. For the moment all of our archers and warriors were lying down and eating their meagre rations.

I summoned a despatch rider. I would only use one. "Ride to the king and tell him the Saxons are crossing. We will lead them north west towards the Roman Road." Nodding, the boy ran to the horse lines. I wondered if I would ever see him again or would our bones and bodies be found when the Saxons had won. I dismissed those thoughts. I was becoming like Prince Ywain.

One of the scouts crawled back to me. "The first ships have pushed off my lord."

"Tell Prince Ywain and then join the slingers." The scouts were not in enough numbers to cause damage to the enemy but I knew how annoying a few sling shots could be. I made my way to Garth. "Ready?"

"Aye my lord."

"Then let us tell Aella that we are here!"

My men all stood and we climbed the bank to stand with banner unfurled at the top of the levee. I could see the first ships and they were fifty paces away. I drew my bow and knew that Miach was ordering the rest to do the same. I released the first arrow and then began to notch draw and loose as quickly as I could. The sky ahead of me was black with arrows and the enemy were unprepared. Inevitably many of the arrows found steersmen who died and caused their ship to turn and crash into the next ship. There were so many ships that collisions were unavoidable. I hoped that the sheared oars would wound and maim the rowers who would have been the warriors we faced. Many of the ships struck the buried stakes and began to sink as they filled with water. The Dunum was filled with chaos but I could see organisation at the rear and the next sixty boats began to head upstream. "Signal Prince Ywain that they are heading west."

My standard moved and waved. After a few moments the standard bearer said, "Acknowledged, my lord, they are moving west towards the enemy."

Our only reserve was committed and now the survival of my men depended on my judgement. We were one thin line of warriors with a slightly longer line of archers. Soon the archers would get their horses to cover us while we had a fighting retreat but first we had to make them pay for their landing. While the archers poured arrows into the fleet we locked shields as the first warriors leapt from their boats to reach the unexpected warriors. Even as they landed they were attacked by the slingers who crouched before our shields. They were forced to raise their own shields and protect their faces and they stumbled blindly towards us. The bank caused some to stumble while others fell to be spiked by the pits and hidden stakes in our beach traps. The greatest danger we had was to our legs for we were above them but they were forced to swing blindly and it was easy enough to use our swords to stab down on their unprotected necks.

Eventually, after over a hundred warriors had died needlessly someone took charge and organised the men into a shield wall. They advanced towards us ominously outnumbering us. "Miach. Bring the archers forwards. I want you to thin these out with five flights and then get to your horses."

"Yes my lord."

"Garth, as soon as the archers have gone I want the line a hundred paces back. We start our retreat."

Already our plans had gone awry for, originally, Prince Ywain would have attacked the warriors to allow us to escape. He was now committed and we would need to adjust our plans. I knew that five miles away was a thickly wooded valley filled with shrubs. If we could make it there then we had a chance for the Roman Road was but two miles north of that. I smiled. If I said it quickly then seven miles did not seem so bad but I knew that the Saxons would be hot on our trail and after blood.

Miach and my archers cut the Saxons to ribbons. As they turned he gave me a satisfied look. "Like killing fish in a barrel."

I walked to the top of the levee to see how close they were. Miach had done well and there were but a hundred men who still stood but I could see hundreds more climbing from the boats into the river. "Garth, Riderch! Time to move."

We ran down the bank and headed after the departing archers. We had done little and were not tired. It would be a different story later. I was relieved to see Miach and his men mounted. "We can try one flight from horseback my lord."

"Just one and then send a despatch rider to Prince Ywain to let him know what we are about." I saw that the slingers were still gathered about the standard. This was no place for boys without armour. "You have done well boys, now get mounted and follow Miach."

After a mile I halted my men to catch their breath. We could see odd Saxons but they appeared to be scouts. "We have bought some time. Now we need to know about Prince Ywain."

"He will either come to our aid or he will be dead. Tuathal would have seen to that."

Miach suddenly appeared behind me. "My lord, there are Saxons ahead."

It was my worst fear. They had come between me and my horses. Now we were two isolated bands of warriors. "Use the archers to discourage them. We will head north for a while and then east. We will meet at the valley we scouted."

Garth had anticipated my next command. "Right lads, we are going to see if we can run faster than a bunch of hairy arsed Saxons. And the ones at the back will find out if the Saxons prefer men or women." The men dutifully laughed and we all strapped our shields to our backs. As we started running I felt the first drop of rain. Vindonnus was on our side and the rain began pelting down. Soon their landing site would become a morass of mud and their pursuit and invasion would be slower. On the other hand it made our job much harder as we began to slosh through the sticky soil. At least my Wolf Warriors had some protection from the rain.

I was relieved when I saw the ground dip towards the wooded valley. There had been no sign of the enemy for a while but that was partly because of the rain and the mist which made it impossible to see more than a hundred paces. The Saxons would easily be able to follow our tracks for a hundred men in armour leave unmistakeable signs.

Miach and his archers were already there and formed a thin screen in the edge of the shrubs. It was perfect cover for them as it was made up of blackthorn, hawthorn and elder. You had to be at the hedge to be able to see the archers. We would be hidden. My men used their wolf cloaks to make temporary shelter beneath which they cowered and ate the last of their dried rations. It was becoming dark when the horsemen rode in. It was obvious that they had had casualties. Garth peered into the murk and then he shook his head. "No sign of Prince Ywain my lord."

When Tuanthal, bleeding from a wound on his arm, dismounted, it was confirmed. "Prince Ywain has been captured my lord. His horse was killed and the Saxons have him."

I did not want any of my men in Aella's hands but Prince Ywain's capture was a disaster. What would I do now?

Chapter 10

"It was going really well, my lord. We charged them on the river bank and drove them back. Then they suddenly came at us from our flanks. They had landed men further up and we did not see them. We lost half a dozen before we extricated ourselves. The prince knew that we had to get through them and he led us west and around in a loop. We just didn't see the warband who were waiting for us a mile away from here. There was so much confusion in the scrubland that we didn't even know that the prince had fallen until it was too late and they had a shield wall around him."

"But he lives?"

"Aye my lord; we saw him struggling with two of his captors and then he was struck on the head and he came still."

"Where are they?"

He pointed to the south east. "They are two miles in that direction."

"Garth, get the scouts to find out where the Saxons are but I don't want them seen."

Garth, Riderch, Tuathal and Miach looked to me; I knew that they wanted a decision but I was in a dilemma. Had it been any other warrior I would have left them to the Saxons and that included Garth but Prince Ywain was the heir to Rheged and I would not face the queen with news that another of her sons had died. What was galling was that we had achieved what had intended. We had inflicted casualties, made their retreat more difficult and avoided too many casualties ourselves.

"I will have to find him." The looks they exchanged told me that they did not think much of that.

Garth was the one who took me to task. "My lord, you were charged by the king with leading this force. Who will lead it if you are not here?"

"You will. I have total confidence in you. I will just take two men and you can continue north to the Roman Road."

"I think you are wrong my lord."

It was a brave thing to stand up to me but I knew that Garth was both loyal and honest. "I may be, Garth, but Aella will have a bargaining chip if he remains in his hands. We have a short time to rescue him. If this happened just now then they will keep him with the warband and then tell Aella."

"Then let us all go to rescue him."

"No, Tuanthal, we still need to slow down the Saxons. I will take Ridwyn and Adair. They have both shown that they keep their wits about them." They could see that I was not to be dissuaded. "Garth, keep the army going north until you reach the Roman Road and ambush Aella there, should I not return."

The scouts returned and reported. "The Saxons have halted and are making camp my lord."

I nodded to Riderch, "Good that means you should be able to get away unseen." Adair and Ridwyn looked to be excited about the rescue attempt. "I will not order you two to follow me for if you fall into the Saxons hands then your death will be painful. Are you aware of that?"

"Yes my lord," they chorused. I could see a mixture of pride and concern on the face of Riderch as his little brother bravely volunteered. I would have felt the same about either Raibeart or Aelle.

Shaking my head I mounted my horse and led my two companions through the driving rain. We had a spare horse in the optimistic hope that we might actually succeed. Our only hope was that there were only forty men in the warband which had captured the prince. They still outnumbered us but it was not the whole army. Night had fallen early but we could follow the muddy tracks left by Tuanthal and his remaining one hundred and fifty tired and exhausted horsemen as they had retreated. The woods he had mentioned loomed up in the distance. We dismounted and walked the last hundred paces to the shelter of the elm trees. I left my shield with the horse and removed my helmet. They would not aid us now. It was not my arms which would save the prince but my mind. I strung my bow and led the other two into the woods. I could see a faint glow in the distance and I assumed that they had a fire going.

We used no words as we moved through the darkness. It was not thickly wooded but the trees were thick and provided us with cover so that we could move from tree to tree. The soft ground helped us too as nothing crunched underfoot and the occasional squelch was not loud. The Saxons were making much more noise and there appeared to be an argument raging. We drew inexorably closer and I halted us twenty paces from the outer edge of the rudimentary camp. They had used some cloaks to rig up crude tents and shelters. They had used the trees as stanchions and it meant they were spread out over a larger area than was wise. We now had a chance. The majority of the warriors were around the fire in the middle of the camp but I could see a knot of men on the far side of the camp beneath a shelter. Two looked like guards and it seemed likely that, if the prince were still in the camp then that is where he would be. I decided we would make for the knot of men as I could not see prince Ywain near to the fire. Before I did so I spent some time listening to their conversation. Although I did not pick out all the words, for some spoke with a Frisian dialect, while others sounded distinctly Frankish it seemed that the newcomers were not happy with King Aella's plans. It made me feel better about the day. If we had sown dissention within their ranks then that would make King Urien's task much easier.

I signalled my companions and we slowly made our way around the perimeter. We had to keep hiding and we occasionally lost sight of the men we sought but I glanced over and saw Ywain's helmet close by. It seemed increasingly likely that he would be with them and I notched an arrow in anticipation of action soon. We were moving almost imperceptibly the closer we came to the men. One of the three who were standing laughed and left to join the men in the middle. There were just two men standing over the man who was lying on the ground. I recognised the armour and knew that it was Ywain. One of the men knelt down next to Ywain and took out a knife. I took a sharp intake of breath. Would the heir to Rheged be killed when I was but a few paces away? Then I saw that the knife did not plunge into his body but cut away some material from the tunic which was worn beneath the armour. The man was a healer and then, as he half turned and the fire light caught his face I saw that it was Myrddyn. My acolyte lived and, he was in a position to help us. The problem would be getting by the rest of the warband for we had travelled all the way around the camp. Our mounts were even further away now than when we had started.

We moved around until we were as close as we could be and yet remain hidden. The warrior with Myrddyn was obviously a leader from his torc and his warrior bracelets. He had a long scar running down his face which showed he had been in battles and suffered serious wounds. I absent mindedly ran my finger down my scar. We had much in common. Myrddyn did not look unhappy and was smiling as he tended the prince. I could see that the prince was not awake. If we did manage to affect a rescue then that might be a problem but I was getting ahead of myself. We had not even got him in our hands yet.

I motioned for the other two to make themselves comfortable; it looked like we were in for a long wait. I had tuned out the noise and arguments from the fire and I could hear the occasional words.

"Healer, will he live? You have been working on him for some time."

"As I told you, Lord Ida, the draught I gave him made him sleep. You could hear him raving and thrashing about. I had to get him quiet and then tend to the wound. The wound is a bad one but it is not serious. He has a broken leg and I must stitch his shoulder where the spear went through. When I have done that I will splint his leg and by then it may well be dawn!"

"I know that our king has much faith in you. If you can save this warrior and return him to King Aella then you will be rewarded. It is the son of the King of Rheged and he is a worthy prize. I will set some guards and then get this rabble to get some rest. Those warriors we pursued cannot be far away and I hear that one of them was the mighty Wolf Warrior. There is a chest of gold waiting for the man who kills or captures him. I would do it just for the honour of killing the man who maimed my brother."

He walked across to the middle and shouted to get their attention. He had some arguments from two men and he brought their heads together with such a crack that they both fell to the ground and lay still. The rest became silent and more compliant. Four men were selected to become guards and, to my horror, one marched straight towards us. I saw my comrade's hands go to their weapons but I shook my head and gestured for them to hide. He strode towards us, pausing only to pick up a sword and then he walked next to Myrddyn glancing down as he passed. His foot almost stood on my hand as he left the light of the camp and entered the wood. He did not see any of us. I pointed to him and then to Ridwyn and drew my hand across my throat. He nodded and followed. That would be one less guard to deal with. A short while later I saw Ridwyn appear, wiping the blood from his dagger. Our only problem would appear if they decided to check on the guards before we had escaped. That was in *wyrd's* hands.

It seemed hours until the camp was quiet but in reality it was a short time. The warriors had been fighting and running all day, they would be tired. I moved forwards slightly and murmured, "Myrddyn." I was still hidden by the bush and I spoke quietly.

"I saw you when you first came. Are they asleep behind me?"

"They look to be."

"Then let us move swiftly. I will need some help to lift the prince, he is sleeping."

"Ridwyn. Pick up the prince and put him over your shoulder." Ridwyn was as strong as an ox and could easily manage the prince. The Bernician stepped forwards and lifted the prince as though he was a sack of grain.

"Do not be rough with him, he is badly wounded." Myrddyn and Ridwyn stepped out of the light and into the woods.

"Adair get to the other side of the camp. Close to the next guard. Kill him with your sling and then close with the other." I held my breath as I watched the unconscious prince and my men slipped from the firelight. I walked backwards with my bow notched just watching for any movement. There was none. All it took was one warrior to wake and see us and we would all be dead. When we reached Adair he had killed the first guard. "Ridwyn take the prince and Myrddyn back to the horses and we will cover you."

Adair and I slipped quietly towards the place we had seen the third guard go. I saw him leaning against a tree and I drew my bow. Suddenly a fox bolted from behind me and he looked directly at me. Before he could utter a sound I had sent an arrow through his throat to pin him to the tree. "Let us back out slowly. We should be safe now."

By the time we reached the horses the prince was slung like a piece of dead meat over the saddle and Myrddyn was sitting uncomfortably behind him. "Myrddyn, ride double with Adair, he is lighter than the prince. You two take the reins of the prince's horse. Ridwyn and I will protect the rear." We walked the horses away from the woods to avoid making a noise. Once we had travelled a mile we were able to kick them on. Adair held the reins of the pack horse while Myrddyn kept his arm on the prince's back.

By the time dawn was breaking on a cold and damp morning we had passed the valley where we had hidden the previous afternoon. Adair had taken us further west than we had travelled to avoid the enemy but now we had to risk their patrols if we were to make the Roman Road. A murmur from Prince Ywain told us that he was waking. We had, however, no time to stop and Myrddyn just spoke some quiet words to him. We had but two miles to go before we struck the Roman Road and then we would have to find where Garth and Miach had taken the men. I hoped that it was not too far.

Although the road was straight it dipped down small hollows and climbed low ridges. The Roman legionaries who had built it had cleared the trees from both sides but it had been neglected for over a century and bushes had colonised it. It was a nerve wracking two miles for we knew not where the Saxons were. It would have been tragic to be captured so close to safety. The first of the scouts suddenly stepped out from one of the bushes, his face filled with delight at our arrival. "My lord you made it!"

"Where is Captain Garth?"

"He has made a camp a mile up the road."

"Good keep watch here and well done." He beamed with pride at the praise from the Wolf Warrior.

When we reached the camp Garth shook his head as he approached us but a smile creased his tanned face. "Someone watches over you my lord. You get into their camp and not only rescue the prince but bring back our healer."

Myrddyn ignored the words and ordered the nearest warriors. "Get the prince down from his horse and make a shelter. I had not finished with him when we left the camp." I saw Riderch come over and embrace his brother. I suddenly missed my own brothers.

I dismounted stiffly. My leg had hurt me for two days; I blamed the rain but I suspected I had done too much. It was a good thing Brother Patrick was not around to chastise me. "We saw no sign of them but that doesn't mean they will not be chasing us; although if they do not chase us then our mission has failed. I take it you have prepared an ambush?"

"We have dug some pits and laid ropes to trip them if they try to flank us." He looked at Prince Ywain. "We do not have enough fit horses and horsemen to be a threat and Tuanthal will have to annoy them. The archers are running short of arrows but we can cope with one more attack."

I put my arm around his shoulder; I could see that he felt as though he had not done enough. "You have done well. When your scouts have rested, send them south to find the Saxons."

Miach wandered over with a bowl in his hand. "We found some game and made a stew. I'm thinking you will be ready for this."

"I am indeed. Thank you." As I ate they watched me. Between mouthfuls I spoke. "We are still better off than either King Urien or me expected. It is Aella's early attack which has thwarted our plans but we have only lost horsemen and the rest are still in fine mettle. I suspect that Aella will be livid when he discovers we have rescued Prince Ywain but he will probably now take the time to organise his men and follow us with a plan in mind rather than a reckless pursuit. When we were at their camp I heard arguments between the different tribes. They are not as unified as they would have us believe."

Myrddyn wandered over. "I have given him a draught and checked the wound in his shoulder. It is knitting."

"And his broken leg?"

"I lied. He had a slight wound to the leg but I was playing for time until I could get him away." He smiled. "And then, as it was ordained, you turned up."

"Get some food and tell us your tale."

"I took the long way to Aella. I approached from the south, from the land of Elmet. I was lucky or, perhaps *wyrd* intervened, for there was a chief who had an illness and they were blaming witchcraft. I was able to cure him and King Aella said it was a sign that they would win and he took me into his household as his healer. That was why I was at the camp. The king sent me for he did not want Ywain to die. He intended to trade his life for the neutrality of Rheged."

"King Urien would never have agreed to that."

Myrddyn shrugged, "I know but it gave me my chance. I had a draught ready to make him sleep for I did not want him to recognise me. He nearly gave the game away but I saw it in his eyes and I had the men hold him and open his mouth so that I could give him the draught. It worked quickly and my identity was hidden. I knew that you and your men would not be far away and I played for time. I told the chief that we needed a fire and he obeyed me. I thought it might make a beacon for you and so it turned out. You were lucky that the chief had sent two hundred of his men to Aella to continue their pursuit of you. They did not know of the Roman Road and they headed west. They will soon realise their mistake."

"What did you discover then?"

"He has six thousand men and they have come from all over the lands in the east. He also has another two thousand men who are on their way from the south, from the land of the Eastern Angles. They will arrive within the next four weeks. His plan is to march north and defeat King Morcant Bulc. He knows that with the fortresses in his hands he can withstand the horsemen and archers of Rheged. It is Rheged he fears. He has also sent bribes to the Irish to begin raiding the west coast. He hopes to distract Strathclyde and Rheged."

"You have done well. It is a pity that you could not have remained there."

He shook his head forcefully, "No, my lord. How would I have got information to you? The aim was for me to learn their plans and I did. I also discovered that the alliance is fragile but then so is ours." Garth looked shocked as though the healer had blasphemed but I knew he spoke the truth. King Urien alone held the alliance together. Myrddyn looked at me, his green eyes piercing and sharp. "He hates you and has sworn vengeance for all that you have done. He sees it as a blood feud between you until you are dead. There is a price on your head."

"I know I heard the chief."

"It is more than the chief. Every warrior who fancies himself with a sword will be hunting you."

"Good!"

All of my leaders looked at me in shock. "Good? Are you mad my lord?"

"No, Garth for if they all come to me then they will be weaker elsewhere. We now know where the point of their attack will be; wherever I am. Now we know that the scouts will return soon and tell us that the Saxons are five miles down the road."

The words were no sooner out of my mouth when two boys rode in. "The Saxons are four miles from here my lord; their whole army."

The boys could not have expected the reaction they got. Garth, Miach and Tuanthal; looked at me as though I was a witch. Before they had chance to comment one of the guards to the north shouted, "Stand to. Horseman!"

Every warrior grabbed a weapon and stood fearing the worst until one of King Urien's equites rode into the camp. "My lord, King Urien tells you that he has started bringing over the warriors he has available. He wants you to draw the Saxons to Dunelm and he will meet you there."

I felt a huge sense of relief. "And the other kings?"

There was a pause. "King Gwalliog has left Elmet and King Morcant Bulc is also heading for Dunelm. The king of Strathclyde will bring his army and the rest of ours in fourteen days." I wondered if this was another ploy from the king of Bernicia but we had no choice but to follow orders. "The king said to tell you not to take risks."

Garth snorted. "A bit bloody late for that!"

For some reason that made all my men laugh. "Myrddyn take the equites and the prince. Get to Dunelm. Tuanthal begin to fortify it when you get there. Find any men you can and build walls and ditches." They both looked to argue. "Go!" I turned to Miach. "You are now the rearguard. Mount your men and keep attacking the Saxons. Slow them up and give us time to get down the road. We have twenty miles to go. We will try to do it in one. All I want you to do is make them look at every bush and think it contains an archer. When your arrows are finished then return to us. Do not lose any men; you are the only ones who can delay the Saxons now. When you reach me that will tell me how much time we have before they attack." Nothing ever worried Miach and he ordered his archers to mount immediately. "Riderch, Garth, get the men moving. We march and we march hard. We have a four mile lead and I do not intend to lose it."

We were now used to moving quickly but I felt slightly naked as the archers left us to harass the enemy. We were reduced to a small warband; an efficient and dangerous warband but one without any aid. The road we travelled had not been the main one, the one we called Dere Street. This was a subsidiary connecting the Dunum with Dunelm, Dere Street and the coast; as such it had little traffic and was slippery with moss in places. Our pace was slower than on a normal Roman Road but I was determined to make Dunelm by nightfall. I wanted a river to defend and some sort of shelter, however rudimentary.

I had two men half a mile ahead as scouts. They could give us some warning of an ambush but that was all. Suddenly they came hurtling down the road. As soon as they were in sight they yelled. "Armed men ahead!"

Garth and Riderch quickly took their places on either side of me and the rest went into our wedge formation. A shield wall could be outflanked, a wedge was more flexible. We had our swords in our hands as the scouts took their places at the rear of the wedge. I wondered how Saxons had got ahead of us although it was possible that some of their army had been sent to secure the road as I had done.

We heard the hooves of at least one horse and the tramp of men. There was a slight hollow before us which meant we had a slight advantage. "Forward!" We marched resolutely to meet this unseen foe. "Unfurl the banner!" We carried the banner furled in an oiled bag when marching but if we were to fight it was worth another ten or twenty men. I felt the wedge surge as my standard bearer, striding behind me, raised the Wolf Banner.

I saw a helmet appear over the rise in the road and a shaft of lonely sunlight lit up the armour and then I heard the familiar voice. "Brother, would you fight the whole world? I bring aid!" A visible ripple of relief ran down the wedge as they recognised Raibeart, his archers and his small band of equites. I held up my hand to halt the men as Raibeart and his warriors approached. "The king sent me ahead. My crops were sown and the lambs were born early this year so we left a few days before the king. I passed Tuanthal and he told me of your plight."He leaned forwards. "And your reckless bravery! And so we came." He looked at my men. "They look tired and weary."

"Aye they are but it has been tough marching and not fighting. We had but a skirmish. Aella has many warriors brother. More than the last time. This will not be an easy fight."

"With two of Hogan's sons fighting then they stand no chance. Where do you want us?"

"If the road ahead is clear then your equites a mile back from us and your archers guarding our rear."

Garth grinned. "Are we safe from this sheep shagging bum bandits from the north my lord?"

Raibeart just grinned back, "Believe me Garth our sheep are more attractive than you will ever be!"

I knew then that we would make it. Raibeart gave his orders and then dismounted to walk beside me. I told him what had happened and he nodded when I told him something which he knew. "The king moved heaven and earth to muster the army." He dropped his voice, "We have no idea what the Bernicians are doing. They receive messages but they do not send them. I am sorry that the prince's father in law was so tardy but he had problems with early raiding Hibernians. It is almost as though the Saxons had planned it."

"They have. Myrddyn discovered that Aella has bribed the Irish. I fear Rheged will suffer the same attacks."

"It is a good job then that the princes did not bring all their warriors and they have left defenders for their strongholds. The sooner we rid the world of Aella the better."

"And what of the defences in the west? If we lose then they will need to hold out."

Raibeart's concerned expression spoke more than his words. "This is not like you brother. You were always the confident one. The one who knew we could win."

"That was before I knew that the Irish would be raiding Rheged. Perhaps we should leave the Saxons to the king they threaten, Morcant Bulc."

"You are tired and it is tiredness talking. You know as well as I that we have to rid the land of the Saxons or we will have no peace."

I became silent as I mulled over his words. What peace would we have? Perhaps we could come to an arrangement with the Saxons and live side by side? As soon as the thought erupted in my mind it was extinguished; they wanted the whole land and, as Aella's army showed, he had endless numbers of warriors to help him.

We trudged over the bridge at Dunelm and we could march no further. Had Raibeart and his men not come to our aid we might have lain down in the woods and slept but they jollied us along and demanded that we tell them of our deeds. A man, who sings or talks when marching, marches further than a silent one who feels every pain and every inch of his march.

Tuanthal and, I suspect, Myrddyn had transformed the small settlement overlooking the river. The bridge was now bristling with warriors and I could see log barriers ready to be erected when we all arrived. There were shelters already made and I could smell the food that the villagers were preparing. As Tuanthal told me, once they knew that the Saxons were coming they were willing to provide anything the army needed. There were only twenty men in the village but that was twenty more than we had when we arrived and were welcome for that. This was the only point an army could cross the river for some miles and there was nowhere closer to the coast than this. If this could be held then the Saxons would be forced west, towards King Urien.

Raibeart had left his wagons of arrows with Tuanthal. When my archers rejoined us then we would be in a much healthier position. Raibaert's equites and Miach and his archers arrived an hour or so after we did. I could see a few empty saddles amongst the archers but the cost of delay had not been high. While Garth and Riderch saw to the men, Miach reported to my brother and me. "They are keen to get you my lord, we had to keep attacking them and they had slingers. We lost four men to them but we still had the horses. We only stopped when our quivers were empty."

"I brought more you can refill them when you have eaten." Raibeart and Miach, as fellow archers, had the same priorities.

"Where are they?"

"Less than a mile yonder. If I was to make a guess I would say that they will camp on that rise. That way they can see our defences below them."

"You have done well. Get some food." I led Raibeart up the hill a little where we could see down towards the bridge and the river. "We have almost the same number of men now as when we began. With your horsemen we are a hundred and ten down but your archers have increased our advantage there. We could destroy the bridge and deny him the crossing or we could contest it."

"Destroying the bridge sounds a good idea to me. He would have no choice but to go west."

"You forget his fleet. If there are no bridges between here and the sea then he could send a messenger and bring his fleet up. He could cross the river anywhere. I agree that the destruction of the bridge would enable the king and the reinforcements to arrive but we would then be stuck here. We could not pursue him easily. We destroyed many of his ships but he has more than enough to ferry them across this river." I pointed to it. It was barely forty paces wide. It was flowing swiftly but that was because of the weir. Nearer to the sea and it would be like the Dunum and more sluggish. I grinned at Raibeart and clapped my arm around his shoulder. "It is good to talk to you brother. It clarifies my thoughts. We will defend the bridge and make him take it. If the king is but a week away then we only need to hold him for seven days and we will have him."

My men had found an old church from Roman times. There was no roof but they had rigged up some tents as a temporary shelter. We gathered there. Prince Ywain was awake and had insisted upon his inclusion. He looked pale but determined. Apart from the leaders Myrddyn took his place beside me. He had earned that right and I knew that he had knowledge which we did not. After we had eaten our first hot meal in a while I went through the plans. "Prince Ywain's wounds have meant I have not been able to confide my thoughts to him. If you disagree my prince, with anything I say then please speak."

He gave me a wry look. "The day that my tactics and planning is better than yours is unlikely to be today Lord Lann. Continue and, may I say before the warriors here, that I am grateful to you for my life. I would not be here if it were not for your reckless bravery. I will reward you when the time is right."

I gave an embarrassed nod and continued. "We must hold the bridge and entice the Saxons over. They can only bring ten men at a time for it is a narrow bridge and this plays into our hands. Ten of our men can defeat any ten Saxons. We will use the superiority in archers to thin them out. I am afraid that the horse will not be needed but, as we have lost a large number already, that is no bad thing. King Urien will need every horseman he can get if he is to defeat this horde." There were satisfying nods of agreement.

"My lord?"

Every eye turned to Myrddyn. None doubted that he had the right to speak but I saw a sceptical look on Raibeart's face. He knew the young healer less well than any. "Speak for you have earned the right."

"Brother Osric told me of the Romans and how they fought. They knew that they could only fight for a short time and to freshen up the fighters they rotated fresh men to fight at the front."

Riderch frowned. "How could they do that? As soon as you stopped to turn you would be killed."

"I am not sure but I have thought of a way we could do it. If the new warriors had a line of spearmen behind them then the spearmen could thrust the spears between the heads of the warriors at the front and that would make the enemy recoil. At that point the warriors exchange places."

Garth nodded his approval. Of all of the officers he knew Myrddyn best. "It would need a precise command."

"How about, 'Front rank prepare, third ranks stab, second rank rotate.'?"

The two warriors nodded and I said. That would work. Teach the men the command tomorrow. Thank you Myrddyn."

"I would teach at least fifty tonight for you will be fighting tomorrow early I think."

As we went to bed I wondered how accurate my healer was and the answer was, very!

Chapter 11

I was awoken before dawn by Garth; he was fully armed and armoured. "My lord, there is movement across the river. The sentries have reported warriors heading towards the bridge."

"Call everyone to arms."

He grinned, "Already done my lord!"

I felt the stiffness in my leg as I struggled into my armour. Summer would mean some respite from my wound but the winter and spring dampness had made me acutely aware of my injury. As I strapped on Saxon Slayer I remembered that it had not been sharpened lately. I would have to remedy that. I put my shield over my back and carried my helmet. I needed to see clearly if I was to make the right decisions. As I walked down to the bridge I saw that Riderch and Garth had organised the first thirty warriors who would face any foe who came to the bridge. We would meet them at the far side although I suspected that I would have to give that up at some point as my warriors could be attacked from the flanks there and we had to minimise casualties. Our side, the northern bank, of the river was much easier to defend but we intended them to buy the bridge crossing at the cost of their warriors.

Raibeart was already there as was Myrddyn. My healer thrust a hunk of bread and a piece of cheese into my hand. I did not feel like eating but he glared at me. "Brother Oswald stressed that you must eat before battle and, as the Lady Aideen backed him up I would rather face your wrath than theirs. So eat." He walked back to the area we had set aside for the injured.

"Bossy little bugger isn't he?"

"Yes brother but he is as valuable to us as another twenty archers."

"From what I gleaned last night he is."

I could see that the warriors, with Riderch at their head and Ridwyn next to him, were at the far side of the bridge. The spearmen at the rear had hidden their spears and behind them were forty archers. We had more archers waiting on our side of the bridge but they would give a concentrated and withering rain of arrows to deter attacks. I was confident that we would hold them this day but as for the next, I was not so sure. The rest of the warriors waited patiently in three huge lines on the steeply sloping banks of the river. The terracing made them look to be a larger force than we actually were. The twenty men from the village formed a small fourth rank. The warriors who would replace those on the bridge had all been assigned a number so that they would reinforce the others in groups of tens. It was another Brother Osric idea stolen from the practical and ingenious Romans. All of the rest of our archers and slingers were on either side of the bridge.

As we waited a huge warrior from Strathclyde approached us. "My lord, I am Angus and I lead the warriors from Strathclyde."

I nodded, "And we are pleased to fight alongside you again."

"Aye, well we know yon laddies are very useful with swords and very organised." He gave me a shrewd look. "I ken that ye think we are mad buggers and we are but we do have a weapon that you do not. This."

He pulled out a huge metal ball held by a thick rope. "What in Belenus' name is that? And how do you use it?"

"It's like a war hammer but you whirl it around your head and you throw it."

I picked it up, but only just, it was incredibly heavy. "What does it do?"

He grinned and I noticed that he had no front teeth; he would be a frightening warrior to fight. "It will smash through a shield and armour. Even a helmet and shield will not stop it."

"What is to stop them throwing it back?"

"That is why we stopped using the hammer; our enemies could use that against us but this takes years of practise to perfect. We only have ten warriors who can use it really well. If the Saxons try to throw if back they will hurt their own men more than us."

"Send your ten warriors to me and I will use them when it is right."

"So that'll be nine others and me then eh?"

He picked it up with one hand as though it was a turnip and wandered over to his men. "That might be useful; especially if they mass against us."

Dawn broke behind the Saxons and we began to see them as they marched down the slope towards the river. Their shields were locked and they looked determined. Aella had many fresh warriors to throw against us and he would have chosen his assault troops carefully. They would have seen our camp fires and estimated our forces. It would have been obvious to Aella that it was not the full army which faced him and that would have given him some hope that he could destroy us and then rampage through Bernicia. We were relying on our training and our archers to withstand this first assault. This was the first battle I had watched rather than fought in and it was a strange experience. Men would be dying and I would just stand by.

"Look Lann, there are flames!"

I could see torches coming towards us; they were ahead of the wall of shields. There were too many just to light up their attack and I wondered what Aella's plan was. It became clear when they hurled them at the log barricade erected across the bridge. They would burn it and force the warriors back. Miach would have to deal with that. I yelled, "Miach take out the men with the torches."

The answer came quickly and I saw the torches drop but they were brave men and others took their paces to be dropped again but they came inexorably on. I was about to change the order when Miach read my mind. He rained arrow after arrow on a twenty pace section and there were no more warriors to throw the torches. Myrddyn sent the slingers forward with buckets and they hauled river water to douse the flames. Even after they were out they continued to wet the logs to prevent a second attempt.

The sun was fully up and I could see the wall of bodies which littered the road on the other side of the bridge. The men had been unarmoured and I suspect they were little more than boys but they had died for Aella and they had failed. What would his next strategy be?

Aella was forced to resort to brute force. He sent his warriors down in a ten wide, one hundred deep column of heavily armed and armoured men. The barrier would delay them and they would lose warriors but it could be demolished. Miach needed no orders from me and he and his archers began to release arrow after arrow, continuously so that the Saxons had to hide beneath their shields. Warriors fell but they were quickly replaced and, when they reached the barrier they began to demolish it. That was when they began to lose larger numbers of men. They had not trained sufficiently and there were gaps in the shields. Warriors died. They were not large numbers but they were whittled down as the men at the front tore down the logs with their axes and, in some cases, their bare hands. The first few logs were easy but then they came within the range of Riderch and his men. The warrior's swords chopped off hands and arms as they appeared. Still they came on and still they died. Eventually the barrier was down and warrior faced warrior.

It was hard to see who was winning but when I saw a ripple at the front then I knew we had changed for the first time. I could see that, had we wanted to, we could have pushed them back but Riderch and his men were under strict orders to hold at the bridge. Beyond the edge of the bridge we could be outflanked. Eventually I heard a horn sound and the Saxons pulled back. Garth immediately sent down the next thirty warriors as the Saxons move back up the hill.

Riderch and Ridwyn came to me as soon as they had crossed the bridge. "Myrddyn's idea worked well my lord. We lost but four warriors and they lost many more."

"Good, get some rest for this is not over."

This time the warriors who held the southern end of the bridge were led by men from Elmet. They all shouted Wolf Warrior and saluted me as they marched down to the bridge. They held me in high esteem for my efforts against Wach. They were good men. It was noon and I had ensured that all my men were fed. Raibeart had replaced Miach to give him and his men a rest. Pulling a bow as often as they did tired a man, no matter how fit he was.

The next attack did not come until late afternoon. Their warriors had remained close to the bridge. I would have replaced the logs but it risked the men replacing them being attacked. We still had the second barrier at the northern end of the bridge and that was more important; the narrow bridge would be a bottleneck for the attacking Saxons. Their next attack was cleverly thought out and took all of us by surprise, including the thirty warriors from Elmet who guarded the end of the bridge. They had cut down some mighty trees and attached ropes. Their warriors pulled them down the hill and then, when they were but thirty paces from the bridge they released them. Raibeart had his wits about him. He ordered his archers to kill the men who were pulling the third and fourth logs so that the logs slewed to the side and did no damage. That did not matter for the first two struck the charging warriors in quick succession. It was carnage. There were just the dead and dying. The Saxons rushed down to take advantage of the disaster. I saw Raibeart look around and I said to the standard bearer."Signal retreat."

He did so and I was relieved to see Raibeart order his men back. He also ordered a handful of men to find those wounded Elmet warriors and drag them to safety. "Miach, cover Raibeart!"

The Saxons were rushing towards the bridge. Garth had the next thirty warriors ready at the barricade and Miach's men and the slingers were doing all that they could to slow down the enemy but it was a disaster. Raibeart loosed arrow after arrow to protect his men and soon they were heading back across the bridge with eight injured and wounded men with them. Myrddyn would be busy that night. The archers struggled over the barricade, helped by the remaining Elmet men who had seen the cream of their fellows slaughtered by logs. It was not a warrior's death.

I went down to the bridge. "I want them clearing from the end of the bridge. Do not use volleys Miach but use your best archers to kill any who stand there."

"What if they rebuild the barricade?"

"Then let them. They will have to take it down if they wish to attack us."

He grinned. "Excellent my lord."

After they had lost twenty men Aella realised the futility of trying to get across the bridge piecemeal and his men retired. He would be back but we had bought King Urien another day. I felt like a cheat for all I had done was stand and give orders. It was others who had bled and died. I now began to understand King Urien. He too had pressures and problems which ordinary warriors could not begin to comprehend.

I left Garth in charge and headed for Myrddyn and Raibeart who were with the wounded. "That was well done brother."

He inclined his head and said, "That was a clever move. Will he try that again tomorrow?"

"I think not. The logs would have more chance of striking the side of the bridge and jamming. No I think that tomorrow he will try his frontal assault again but he may try something different with the logs on our barricade. Have the men pour oil on them. Make them slippery and hard to grasp it will only slow them up but..."

"Excellent idea, brother." Raibeart patted me on the back and went to give the orders.

I walked up to Myrddyn. "How goes it with you healer?"

"We have lost two."

"Which means you have saved more. If you were not here then all would have died."

He looked at me and understanding flooded his face. "I think that this was also intended my lord but I think that I am destined to help you defeat Aella."

"Of that I am certain, my young friend. He is a clever opponent all right."

The men were in good spirits that night despite the loss of the bridge. We built a pyre and burned the bodies of the Elmet warriors and placed their remains in an urn to return to their homeland. The survivors were sombre but desperate for revenge. I knew that the next day would be much harder; the enemy would press us until we burst and then they would be free to ravage the land to the north.

I awoke early the next day and smelled the air. The wind was from the east and something did not seem right. I saw Myrddyn already up and he too was looking east. "What do you see healer?"

"There is a strange feel to the air this morning and I sense danger."

That confirmed my feelings too. "I think Aella may be up to something." I summoned the nearest sentry. "Go and wake Lord Garth and tell him to come to me." He trotted off down the hill to the sleeping warriors. I could see the pinpricks of fires across the river but that did not concern me. We had warriors at the barrier and they were alert but the river was another matter. It flowed through a steep sided valley creating shadows and darkness in which anything could hide. We had placed sentries all along its banks but I knew from our own endeavours that men could hide if they chose.

"My lord?"

"Myrddyn and I feel there is danger along the river. Wake and feed the men and then send Miach and my archers to the east to watch the river. If my brother is awake then ask him to join me."

We watched in silence as the false dawn broke. It did not aid us and we still peered into the blackness when Raibeart joined me. "Raibeart I think there may be danger along the river and I am sending Miach and my archers to watch it. Your men will need to cover the bridge."

He nodded solemnly. "It will be at least five days before the king can reach us."

"I know. I am not worried about food and water nor do I fear an attack across the bridge but the river is something different. We have no ships and we cannot control it."

"We can my lord."

We both stared at the young healer who was peering a little close to the bridge. "How?"

"We make a floating barrier. The river flows to the sea. If we tie barrels and logs together and feed them out across the river there," he pointed at a wide loop of the river, "then when they reach the narrow part they will form a barrier. If Aella attempts to come with his ships they would have to negotiate that obstacle. Our archers could make that an expensive task." He shrugged. "It would buy us a day and cost but a few bits of wood and rope."

I slapped him on the back. "I think it is an excellent idea. Brother, go and prepare your archers and I will get Riderch to organise the barrier."

By the time dawn broke the river was clear, our fears appeared to have been groundless but we put Myrddyn's plan into operation anyway. The huge warriors from Strathclyde cut the logs and found the timber which Myrddyn tied together. The Saxons from the other bank watched from behind their shields as the first log was lowered into the water. It may have been coincidental but Aella chose that moment to launch his first attack of the day.

I heard the shout from the bridge as Garth ordered the men to prepare and I ran back to the bridge, Riderch and Myrddyn could complete their task unaided. By the time I reached the bridge I could see the wedge heading towards the demolished barricade. They had cleared the bodies and the debris during the night and the warriors had a clear run. I knew that they would run, it was how a wedge worked and I saw Garth already adding more warriors behind the existing three ranks to absorb the pressure. I suddenly remembered the caltrops we had brought with us. They would have disrupted the enemy but it was too late for that. We would have to wait until we had defeated this attack first.

There were ten ranks in the wedge, fifty men in all. That was as many as would fit on the bridge and any more would have been unnecessary. They intended not to break through but to weaken our warriors and allow the next wedge which was already forming up, to complete their attack. Raibeart's archers were already peppering the wedge with arrows which were released from very flat trajectory. It needed accuracy to strike home but the power of the arrows penetrated the shields and armour of the advancing Saxons. They came relentlessly on and I saw them begin to speed up. I could hear Garth and Riderch ordering those at the rear to brace and then with a crash of metal and wood the two lines came together. There was no opportunity to use swords for the men at the front were tightly pressed hard against each other. The third row of spearmen kept their spears for the rotation which would come once they had begun to fight; instead they added their weight to the wall of men who pushed and heaved. Being taller spear men they had more weight and, with the reserves Garth was able to call upon the Saxons were slowly pushed back. It was a stalemate but that suited me more than Aella for we had to buy time but Aella needed to buy land!

Angus returned. "Yon barrier is erected my lord! It goes from bank to bank and it tangled up nicely in the bushes at the other side."

"Well done Angus. Now line your men up behind the warriors and have your hammers or whatever you call them ready." He gave me another grin and his mouth reminded me of gravestones. He would not be a pleasant man to face in a fight.

The Saxon war chief had had enough of the stalemate and he somehow wriggled his sword above his head and brought it crashing down on the warrior before him. The blade slid down the side of his helmet and caught him at the top of the shoulders. Perhaps he cracked his collar bone or penetrated the mail but whatever the cause the man fell and suddenly there was room to swing axes and swords. The front ranks were filled with individual combats from men who had been, impotently, face to face for a long time. It was a vicious fight with every tactic possible being employed. Daggers were stabbed under shields, heads were butted, noses were bitten and men died. I heard Riderch order a rotation as most of the front rank was already dead. The spearmen stabbed and the Saxons recoiled. The survivors from the front rank dragged their bloody bodies to the rear and a second ten took the place of the ones who now faced the Saxons. The fresh warriors pushed the Saxons back a little. I knew that the warriors at the front were suffering and only the war chief remained. This was where we need a warrior like me or Garth or Riderch at the point for the war chief was superior to those he faced.

"Raibeart, the next time we rotate see if you can put an arrow into the war chief; it may discourage the others." He nodded and selected his straightest arrow. I saw him smoothing the goose feathers with his lips and he notched the missile.

The front rank had suffered almost as many casualties as the first one and Riderch called rotation. I noticed that Garth had placed himself in the second rank which would stiffen the line. As the spears stabbed and the survivors retreated I could see the war chief clearly; Raibeart saw him too and his arrow flew true striking him in the eye. The barb must have entered the warrior's brain for he fell to the floor like a sack of turnips and my front rank pushed and stabbed the surviving Saxon front rank. All semblance of order went from the Saxon formation and they began to be pushed back. There were less than thirty remaining and they broke and ran. Raibeart's archers took care of another fifteen before they made the safety of the other end of the bridge where Aella had built walls of wood behind which his men could shelter from our arrows.

Garth marshalled the men back to the bridge and, waving a hand at me, took his place in the middle. When the next attack came we would have a champion facing the war chief and it would have a different outcome.

Aella wasted no time and the second wedge lurched forwards. This time the rear ranks were stiffened by another forty five men. This formation would last longer and I could see the Saxon king's reasoning. He knew his men had killed my warriors and he knew we had a limited supply; he had a seemingly inexhaustible number of fresh warriors. It would be a matter of when, not if, he defeated the defenders of Dunelm. Once again there was a crash of arms and metal but, even though they outnumbered us Garth and his men held the line and it barely moved. The Saxons had attacked this time with weapons raised although that cost some of them wounds from Raibeart's arrows and this was fight to the death from the start. Garth was more than holding his own and their champion died quickly. I could see others in the front rank falling and heard Riderch's command to rotate. Once again it was flawless but only three warriors stepped back with Garth.

I turned to Angus. "This looks to be a good time to try your weapon out. How many have you?"

"We have three each." He looked at the press of men. "If we try it here they will not be able to use these against us." His tombstone grin told me he was happy. "We'll collect them when they are all dead!"

"I look forward to this demonstration." He took his nine companions forward. "Riderch give these men some space." He obeyed me but looked curiously at the ten giants who stood in a line. Angus stepped to the front and began whirling the piece of iron and stone above his head. It seemed effortless. Suddenly he released it and it flew over the heads of those fighting and smashed down in the middle of the mass of men pressing forwards. The splash of red and the sudden gap told me he had struck well. The second man quickly took his place and repeated the action with the same success. "Garth, push the men forwards the Saxons are weakening!"

The next eight missiles totally demoralised the Saxons. They looked up to see the terrifying weapons descending and Raibeart's archers struck the upturned faces. Others threw themselves in the river and most were drowned by the weight of their armour. It was too much for the ones at the rear and they fled for the safety of their own lines. Soon the bridge was empty of the living.

I summoned Angus. "That was well done. Riderch, have some men with shields protect these warriors while they reclaim their hammers. Retrieve any arrows or weapons that you can."

As the warriors moved forwards there was the clatter and bang of stones striking their shields but they suffered no casualties. Raibeart and Garth joined me. "That was a fearsome weapon brother. When I saw it in his hands I thought it would not hurt a fly."

"They are deceptively heavy. I could barely lift it never mind swing it around my head. Those ten warriors are valuable and need to be protected; the Saxons appear to have no answer to it."

"The bridge helped my lord."

"Aye it did."

Just then an archer ran up. "My lord, there are Saxon ships approaching up the river. Captain Miach is engaging them."

"Good. Garth, take thirty warriors and see if he needs help." I wandered down to Myrddyn to see how the wounded were faring. The Saxons did not look to be readying another attack just yet but when they knew their fleet was there then they would.

The healer had just finished stitching a warrior's scalp which had been laid open to the bone. He looked up at me as he stood. "It looks dangerous but he will live and fight again in a few days."

The warrior gave a weak smile and I patted his shoulder. "You did well today." I led Myrddyn some way away so that we would not be overheard. "The Saxons have sent ships here what do you think? You were in their camp and know the mind of their king."

"They will not be the big warships for this river is narrower than the Dunum; they will be the smaller ships. They will be perfect for transporting groups of warriors across the river."

"He would outflank us."

"He has enough men but so long as we hold the bridge he can only attack form one side." He gave me a cunning look. "When you attacked their camp the most effective weapon you used was the fire ship."

"It was but one ship."

"Ships are made of wood and caulked with tar and grease; they burn well. Many ships tried to flee the fire and struck each other. You could do the same here where the river is narrower."

"Thank you Myrddyn. Once again your ideas are our salvation."

I sought Tuanthal; he and the horsemen were unemployed at the moment. "We need some boats. Have some of your men find as many as they can. So long as they can float they will do. You need to take them beyond our boom. Fill them with wood and other things which will burn. We will try to burn the Saxon fleet. My captain of horse was glad to be doing something. It must have galled him to see the warriors and the archers having so much success and the elite of the army being idle.

I heard a roar and saw that the Saxons had launched another attack. Aella must have been informed of the arrival of his ships. Another messenger found me. "They are trying to demolish the boom, my lord."

I knew that they would not be able to totally destroy it as one end was secured on the bank near us but they must be made to pay. "Order Captain Miach to discourage them."

Riderch in the absence of Garth had taken his place in the middle of the second rank. I went to my quarters and donned my armour. It was time that the Wolf Warrior went to war. I sought Scean, my standard bearer. "Come Scean, it is time the wolf bit."

He grinned, "Yes my lord, I was beginning to feel like a one legged man at an arse kicking contest!"

I went to the reserves that were ready for the next rotation. I chose the smallest warrior. "I am sorry but I will be taking your place. Join the next ten." Scean stood behind me and unfurled the Wolf standard. Some of the men I would be fighting alongside were wolf warriors but all nine of them swelled with pride that they would be defending the banner. I turned to Angus. "Time for your weapon again I think."

I watched as they strode forwards. Aella had stiffened his men with better shields and those in the middle held them above their head like the roof of a house. It might have saved a few lives but each missile injured the man with the shield and weakened the formation. I heard Riderch order rotation and we stepped forwards. As he passed me, with blood dripping from his sword he looked in surprise at me. "I need the practice," was all I said.

I stood with my men behind the front rank. I could see the anger in the faces of the Saxons as they faced the warrior they hated above all others. The warrior in the middle of the front rank fell and I stepped in quickly, Saxon Slayer stabbing forwards to catch the war chief, who had been a little too eager to kill me, in the mouth. The sword went through his head and into the face of the man behind. I quickly punched with my shield and we moved forwards. The men took heart from the presence of the banner and fought harder. The loss of their chief and my sword also seemed to dishearten them. When Angus and his men threw their second weapons we were able to move forwards again. By the third attack we had reached the halfway point in the bridge. Raibeart's arrows finally drove this third wedge back to the safety of the Saxon side.

"Second and third ranks pick up arrows, hammers and any other weapons. Front rank, protect them with you shields." This time they all seemed to target me and stones pinged off my helmet and shield. It sounded like someone banging on a metal cauldron but I was quite safe.

Eventually I heard Scean say. "That is it my lord we are done. Let us get back before one of those buggers gets lucky with a stone."

We walked back to the cheers of my whole army filling my already ringing ears. It was as though we had won a great victory but we had killed but forty of their warriors. Angus was grinning and cheering with the best of them. "Very good of you to collect our hammers, we thought we had lost them."

"You keep tight hold of them Angus they saved many a warrior today."

One of my equites came running towards me. "My lord, Captain Tuanthal has the boats and they are filled."

He looked at me in anticipation. "Raibeart take charge here. They may come again but somehow I think they may try something tonight."

"We still have warriors who have not fought and they are keen to copy the deeds they have seen this day."

When I reached the far end of the defences I could see Miach and his archers raining arrows on the boat. Although it looked haphazard I could see that they were aiming for the rowers and steersmen. They were measuring their flights and conserving their energy. Miach was an old hand at this. On the far side of the river I could see the Saxons who were trying to disentangle the boom. Ten of my archers were making their life difficult; from their laughter my men obviously though this to be a good game. Tuanthal and thirty of his men had gathered ten small boats and rafts. He gave me an apologetic glance. We only found six boats so the lads made four rafts."

"So long as they float that is all that I care." I could see that they were all filled with wood and kindling and other flammable material."Light the first one and push it off; the second a count of forty later and so on. We will let the current do its work and pray that Icaunus favours us. We will make an offering to him later."

We all watched eagerly as the flames began to erupt from the dry wood and two men went into the shallows and gave the fireboat a good push. The current took it towards the Saxons and I could hear their panic as they saw the small inferno lurching towards them. The second one took a slightly different course, towards the ones in the middle, and the panic spread. Soon all ten were heading downstream. Three of the Saxon ships had managed to get under way and were heading away from the danger. The others had oars out to fend them off but that made them susceptible to Miach and his arrows. One of the ships on the end of the fleet caught fire and it was frightening how swiftly the flames took hold and engulfed it. Soon every Saxon ship was heading downstream. Some of them had fires burning and the crews were busily trying to save their ships. Three of the fire boats followed like malevolent hunters just waiting for a mistake. Had we done this at night we would have had more success but I was pleased with the outcome. The threat had not been eliminated but they would need to cross the river further downstream. The Saxons who had been attempting to get rid of the boom had given up when the ships left.

"Well done Captains Miach and Tuanthal. Your men did well. Miach, take your men back to the bridge. Tuanthal, take your twenty horsemen and follow the ships until they are at least ten miles away. I want no surprises and then send for the rest of your equites and have them here ready to repulse any repeat of today."

We had survived a second day. Tuanthal and his men were fresh and eager to emulate the rest of my force and this would be a good opportunity for the remainder of my men, I would have to put them into shifts- it would be a long night.

Chapter 12

After we had eaten I summoned the officers and we met in Prince Ywain's quarters. He had been pining to be part of the action but Myrddyn would hear no more about it for his wounds had been serious. The young healer, reluctantly, allowed the prince to be part of the briefing but was adamant that he was some days away from moving. "We did well today but we have barely touched their army. They lost but four ships."

Myrddyn was busy grinding a paste in a bowl and he muttered, "Just a drop in the ocean really." I threw him an irritated look and he gave a half smile, "Sorry!"

"We have made them warier but they will try that trick again. I also think they will attack tonight. I would if I were the Saxon leader."

Riderch laughed, "If they didn't do it in daylight what makes you think they could do it at night?"

"They could make rafts and ship their men over. The darkness would hide them from our archers but in daylight they would be slaughtered. I want half of the warriors and half of the archers asleep within the hour. The rest will be on guard until well after midnight and then we will swap. I will wake with the second shift and Raibeart will be in charge until then. Miach and Angus you too will sleep. Riderch and Garth you will be with my brother."

"Fire arrows." This time there was no levity from Myrddyn.

"Fire arrows Myrddyn?" I knew he would have a good reason for his statement but I merely voiced the thoughts of the others.

"Your archers could loose a fire arrow into the air, to land on the other bank. If you had the archers counting to a thousand between each arrow it would illuminate the other bank consistently."

"And what makes you think my men can count at all, let alone to a thousand?"

Everyone laughed but it was a serious concern. Myrddyn's face was all seriousness. "I am sure we have two warriors who can count. We put one in each shift and they do the counting." He shook his head and mumbled, "Who knows the rest might learn to count just by listening."

Raibeart clapped his arm around Myrddyn. "That will work healer. It will eat into our supply of arrows but we can use the ones with damaged barbs we recovered and the pathetic ones the Saxons send at us." He stroked his beard. "Of course it doesn't stop the Saxons building boats or rafts up stream and floating down with the current."

"No but that entails more risks for them. We could always have two archers, one upstream of the bridge and one downstream. We also need everyone who is on guard to be alert. If you have watched at night then you know how shadows can make you see something which is not there." They all seemed happy and, as we would all be losing sleep, we headed off to our duties or our beds.

As I was heading for my quarters Adair was waiting for me. The slingers had been given the freedom to attack where they chose. They were not a large enough force to make a difference but they could annoy and they knew how to do that well. Adair led them well and, as chief scout, he often spoke with me. "My lord one of the slingers has a request."

"Yes who is it?"

"Pol, son of Tadgh."

"His father died today did he not?"

"He did and his mother fell ill and died this winter. He wants to serve you. He believes that he will be a better warrior if he serves you."

"I don't know." I had never liked the idea of someone serving me. I liked my independence.

"My lord many of the men feel that you need someone to look after your weapons." He pointed at Saxon Slayer. "I would bet that you have not sharpened that since before the Dunum and that you have barely eaten. Pol is a good lad sir and it will help both of you. He will not feel so alone and you will not have to worry about mundane things like eating and keeping your weapons sharp." He took a deep breath, "I know that many of the warriors worry about you my lord. They do not want to lose the Wolf Warrior because he does not eat and forgets to sharpen his blade."

There was an air of admonition which reminded me of Brother Oswald and Myrddyn. But I could not argue against it. "You are right and Tadgh was a loyal warrior. If his son is half the man his father was then I will have the better of the bargain. Very well send him to me tomorrow."

Adair grinned and opened the door. "Why not now as he is already here?"

I threw an irritated look at Adair and then laughed. How could I criticise someone for having the wit and guile to do what he had. It was what I wanted in my scouts. "Bring him in."

Pol was older and taller than the other scouts and his eyes were filled with a mixture of eagerness and hero worship. "You wish to serve me?"

"Yes my lord."

"You know I am bad tempered and cantankerous and I shout a lot."

"Yes my lord."

"And you still wish to serve me?"

"Yes my lord. I would be a warrior like you, and until I am strong enough I will learn by watching over you and your weapons. I will stand behind you in the shield wall with Scean and watch your back." He was so earnest it took my breath away.

"You had better get some sleep then for we will be up in the middle of the night. Where will you sleep?"

He pointed to the doorway. "Why there of course my lord then no-one gets in and if you leave I will wake and serve you."

I was nonplussed and had no answer. Adair grinned, "Goodnight my lord, see you in the small hours."

When I was woken by Garth I was amazed to see Pol standing there with a highly polished and recently sharpened Saxon Slayer and an oiled and polished mail shirt. "Did you sleep Pol?"

"A little, it was enough." He went outside with the pot we used for night water. He had taken to his job like a duck to water.

Garth smiled at the boy's departing back. "No sign of the Saxons, my lord, although I think that the flame arrows are upsetting them."

"Good, that is their purpose. Get some sleep, Garth, we will need our energy in the morning."

I fixed Pol with what I thought was my most intimidating stare, "I will not have you losing sleep just to look after me."

He grinned back cheerfully, "Do not worry my lord, I am young and do not need sleep. Come, you need readying for war. Your food is outside."

I could see that it was useless to argue and, after I had dressed and eaten my food, I did feel better. It was cold outside and I wrapped my cloak tightly about me as I joined Angus and Miach at the bridge. The flame arrows went off regularly and it was a satisfying sight and sound as they whooshed into the air.

Angus yawned, "I think we have lost sleep for nought. They will not come."

Miach scratched his beard. "I think had we not done this then they would have come."

We watched the opposite bank which was illuminated for an instant and then plunged into darkness. Suddenly Pol said, "My lord. There is movement in the water there!"

He pointed to the bank close to the bridge and I could see the movement he meant. It was too dark and the bank too entangled with bushes to see clearly but I grabbed Miach's arm. "Fire arrows there! Now!"

He knew me too well to hesitate and within a heartbeat five fire arrows were loosed at the bank. One of them struck the Saxon who was standing on the bank but more importantly they showed the Saxons and how close they had come. Angus roared, "Saxons! Kill the bastards!" which effectively woke up the camp.

It looked like more than a hundred Saxons had drifted on rough rafts close to our bank of the river, hidden from the light, and they erupted up the slippery bank. But for Pol's warning we would have died however my men, refreshed by sleep, formed a shield wall around us while the archers stood behind us striking bare faces and bodies as they appeared from the dark. Saxon Slayer swept all before it and Angus stood by my side with his mighty war axe. We were aided by the sure footing we had and the slippery muddy morass they had to climb. Soon the only Saxons left on our shore were dead and the rest had fled, risking the river to reach safety. We had been saved by a boy who had joined me by chance… or was it?

When dawn broke we saw that it had been a warband of about fifty warriors who had died attempting to secure the bridge. I suspect others had been ready to join them but our illumination of the river had foiled them. We were tired but we had achieved our aim; we had held them off a little longer. The question, however, remained what would the wily king try next? King Urien and our reinforcements were still days away and we had heard nothing from King Morcant Bulc. Ironically my hope was that, as the Bernicians would have to travel towards Dunelm they would secure our left flank which was threatened by their fleet of small ships. Tuanthal had sent scouts north but, so far, they had seen no sign of the elusive king. Riderch was unhappy about the situation. He was Bernician and had sworn an oath to the king but he had watched as men from Elmet and Rheged had died for Bernicia and I could see that it did not sit well with him for he was an honourable and brave warrior who took oaths more seriously than his king.

Pol appeared at my side with some cheese and some bread, a jug of ale and a look which suggested that the Lord of Dunelm should eat. I could see the smirk on Myrddyn's face and I wondered just how much he had had to do with Pol's present employment. Raibeart joined me, yawning and stretching. "Losing half a night's sleep does not sit well with me, brother, but," he pointed at the bodies being piled up prior to burning, "I can see that you had even more exertions last night."

"Aye, they must have crossed further upstream and made it down the bank unseen. We may have to use some sentries there tonight."

"We are stretched thinly as it is. Now that the horse is on our left flank we have no reserves."

I chewed glumly on the slightly stale bread. "It is hard to see what else to do. We have plenty of provisions and water but we have barely dented the Saxons. When they were content merely to try to force the bridge we had a chance but if they attack on our flanks then…"

"We need to make a stronghold here my lord."

I looked around and saw that Myrddyn was by our side. "How?"

He pointed to the left and then the right. "The banks of the promontory are steep there. If we were to dig a ditch with stakes then any flank attack could be broken up. There is enough wood to make a wall behind the ditch and," he pointed to the top of the hill behind us, "that would make a last refuge if they should break in. We could dig another ditch. We could pay them pay a heavy price for this little piece of land. We would always be uphill of the enemy and archers could use their bows over the heads of your warriors."

"He is right Lann. You know how hard it is attacking uphill but my archers will need to make more arrows. We have the shafts, the heads and the flights but they must be made. I will let you have a third of my archers for digging if you need them."

"You think it is a good idea then?"

"It is the only idea. No matter how tired our warriors are it will slow down the enemy and buy us the time King Urien needs to reach us."

"You could use the villagers as well my lord. I am sure they would do everything in their power to prevent the Saxons taking this place."

"I am decided! Riderch, Garth." The two warriors joined us. "We are going to dig two ditches one there to the left and the other there to the right. Use the villagers and half of the warriors. The other half will be with me and Miach's archers at the bridge. Cut down trees and build a wall behind the ditch."

They both nodded. It took more than this to surprise my men. "How deep my lord?"

"As deep as you can make it and put some surprises in the bottom. When you finish you can try to do the same up there near to the top of the hill. We need defences behind which we can shelter. The kings are coming and we need to hold this crossing until they arrive."

I was down to a hundred and fifty warriors to guard the bridge. They were all tired and needed a longer rest than I could give them. The fifty archers I had was also the smallest number we had used against the Saxons. I hoped that our enemies were as tired as we were and would not attack. I was wrong.

They came soon after my men had begun work on the ditches. It was a huge wedge. The frontage was the same but I could see its tail trailing back up the hill. Aella could see into our defences from his lofty position and knew how few we were. I stood with the second rank of replacements. The men of Strathclyde formed the front three ranks while Angus and his hammers waited behind them. Our archers and slingers made little impression on the wedge as the Saxons had learned how to protect themselves. Our only advantage was that their measured approach meant they could not run at the Strathclyde warriors and strike them with their combined armour. The weight of men began to press the ranks back slowly and I nodded to Angus. He and his men began hurling their lethal weapons. Soon gaps appeared behind the point of the wedge and our line stabilised.

I could see the front rank taking casualties and I gave the order to change. Angus and his men threw their last hammers and the spearmen jabbed and I found myself in the second rank; this time with Pol and Scean behind me. Pol had armed himself with a seax we had found on the body of one of the Saxons from the night raid. It was shorter than a sword but longer than a dagger and perfect for the close fighting of a wedge. I hoped that he would not be needed.

The warrior who hurled himself at me, even though I was in the second rank, had no shield but he whirled a mighty two-handed war axe above his head. He detached himself from the wedge and threw himself at our line. I raised my shield as the long axe sliced and hacked down. The blade caught on my shield but, such was the force, it tore itself free and took off the head of the warrior who stood before me in our front rank. Saxon Slayer was at my side and, as soon as I saw the gap where the Strathclyde warrior had stood, I stabbed upwards. The blade entered his ribcage, ripped through his heart and emerged from his neck. Pol had sharpened it well. As I pulled it out his entrails dropped to the floor. The wedge struck our line but the dead had made the floor slippery and cost the first two warriors in the Saxon line, their lives as they rushed to get at me; they fell before they could swing their swords and were easily despatched. Their deaths allowed me the freedom to swing Saxon Slayer at head height and there are few warriors who will willingly walk into the scything death of a long sword. The pressure from the warriors behind pushed three warriors into the arc of death. Miach and his men now had targets as the gaps appeared and took a great toll on the warriors behind the front rank. Despite the numbers of men pushing forwards, it was obvious that the wedge had failed and I heard their trumpet sound and the Saxons retreated. They must have been given better instructions for they retired in good order with shields held high and Miach was unable to score many casualties but we had driven them back. My men moved forwards to clear the bodies and retrieve arrows and weapons.

"Hold! Just take the weapons and armour, leave the bodies there." They looked at me in surprise. Hitherto we had cleared the bridge of the bodies but I had just witnessed the benefits of leaving the bodies there. They would form a barrier which the Saxons would either have to clear or surmount. Whichever course they took would suit us.

I turned to Pol and Scean, "So Pol. You survived your first action."

His white face showed how terrifying it had been but he gave me a weak smile."I thought the man with the axe was going to kill us all."

"He was a brave man. He knew he would die and was willing to sacrifice himself by killing me. He thought to end this as they did in the old days by champions." I saw Angus who had just collected the bodies of his dead warriors. They had died well. "Angus. I want a wooden wall building here at the end of the bridge. I want it as high as a man, three paces wide with a step half way up to allow us to fight from the top."

He nodded his approval. "That'll slow the buggers up!"

"I have had enough of playing into Aella's hands. He thinks to wear us down man by man. Now we will let him bleed."

Aella saw what we were about but he was helpless to do anything about it. He tried two furious rushes of warriors to disrupt the building but they did not even make it half way for Miach's archers stopped them. By evening the ditches had been built and there was a wall around. We would need to lose sleep again but another day had gone by and that meant King Urien was but three days away. They would be three long days.

Our night of interrupted sleep was fruitless for they did not come and I wondered if they had given up but, as I peered across the river I saw their camp still standing and their warriors with their shields still facing us. Raibeart and Garth joined me. "Is it my imagination or are there fewer warriors there today?"

They both looked. "Perhaps, Lann the others are preparing an attack somewhere else."

"Perhaps. Garth put one third of our warriors behind the wall on the right and the other third behind the wall to our left. They may have a surprise yet for us."

Garth had no sooner put the warriors in position when Tuanthal and his horsemen came galloping up. "My lord. They have landed a large number of men downstream. We charged them but there are too many. They are coming this way."

"You have done well. Bring all our sentries in and get yourselves behind these new walls. Put your equites at the top of the hill behind the last ditch. You will be our reserve." I paused. "You will be fighting on foot."

Raibeart joined me. "Well at least we know what his surprise is."

"Aye. You and Miach need to spread your archers evenly; place a third around each side of our perimeter. They have crossed the river but so long as we stand they cannot move their army."

Aella then launched his second attack across the bridge. Angus had done well in the time available and the barrier was effective. I knew that they could build a ram as they had before but they would struggle to use it effectively on a bridge slippery with gore and filled with their dead. Aella showed his final cunning as a third attack materialised along our right flank. Like the ones in the night raid they must have floated over on crude rafts. Riderch estimated a thousand men and, added to the two thousand coming upstream we were well outnumbered. It would be a long day.

Myrddyn came up to me. "If you have men wet the slopes before the ditches then the Saxons will find it hard to climb." Myrddyn was the best of all worlds, he was a healer and yet he had a military mind as sharp as any warrior. "We have plenty of water from the river and it will give the villagers a part to play."

Soon there were two human chains carrying any kind of receptacle to the walls and pouring it down the slopes. The fact that some of the water went into the ditch did no harm, in fact it aided us by hiding the stakes. We stopped it when we saw the first Saxons on our flanks. Angus and the men at the bridge were busily engaged and one disadvantage of the barrier was that the men from Strathclyde could no longer reclaim their hammers and so they fought with their swords, supported by Raibeart and his men. Leaving Raibeart and Angus to defend our bridge I went to the greatest threat, our left flank; where the greatest numbers were attacking. Garth was there with the bulk of my men. Riderch had the survivors from Elmet and the Bernicians on the other side. As soon as my banner was unfurled my men began banging their shields and they chanted, "Wolf Warrior!" over and over. The Saxons now knew whom they faced.

They had formed a shield wall and they had many spearmen amongst their warriors but they struggled to keep a straight line as they approached us at an oblique angle. Miach's archers chose their targets carefully. We had used too many arrows lately and could not afford to be profligate. They came on steadily until they reached the wetted ground. As soon as a warrior slipped he was despatched by an arrow. The gaps were then exploited by other archers but still the Saxons came on. The first warriors who reached the ditch had their shields held up to protect themselves from the rain of arrows and stones. They crashed screaming into the muddy, stake filled bottom. Those who were able to tried to extricate themselves but they were quickly killed. Perhaps the warriors were lured on by the thought that, if they reached me, they would be rich men; whatever the reason they kept coming until the ditch could be negotiated for it was filled with the bodies of their dead.

When they reached the wall they tried to hack it down with their axes whilst protected by their spears but the archers and my own spearmen made that task difficult. Even so we began to lose men. They were winning the war of attrition. We fought through a long afternoon. Myrddyn found the time in his healing to send food and drink to the men at the walls and we rotated whenever possible. Inevitably it was the Saxons who tired, and as night fell they withdrew taking, wherever possible, their dead and wounded with them. Before we could rest I sent out my men to empty the ditches of the bodies and to have the villages pour as much water down the slopes as possible. By the time the hill was sodden and the ditches cleared everyone was exhausted. I gave the orders for the men to sleep at their posts and I ordered Tuanthal to use his horsemen as sentries. I hoped the enemy would not return but I could not be sure.

I met with Myrddyn and my officers to plan the next day and we hungrily grabbed bites of food as we talked. "Let us start with the bad news first and get that out of the way. How many dead and wounded?"

There was a pause then Myrddyn's calm voice listed what he knew. "There are fifty wounded warriors. All can fight again but only thirty will be ready tomorrow."

Raibeart chimed in, "We have lost fifteen archers but we are desperately short of arrows."

"We lost another thirty horsemen delaying the enemy; we are down to one hundred and twenty equites but we now have ten spare horses." I threw him a look. I knew what was behind his last comment; we could all have an escape route on a horse but I think Tuanthal knew me better than that. I would not ride away to leave my men to be slaughtered.

"Garth?"

"We have lost heavily today my lord. We have less than two hundred warriors left. If we add the wounded that will still only give us seventy men on each side of our defences. Another attack like the one today and we lose." He looked at Miach. "We may have to arm some of the archers and let them fight in the shield wall. We have the shields and the armour," he paused, "from the dead."

"Aye that might work. We could give our arrows to Lord Raibeart's men."

"Tomorrow we will send the villagers to the top of the hill where the equites will be. When I give the signal to retreat then everyone falls back there. Myrddyn has sent all our food there and we will have that as our last defence." I nodded to Prince Ywain. "You, my lord can organise the defenders for I shall stay outside until all hope is gone."

There was an ominous and sombre silence around the fire. All of us were exhausted but none had given up hope. The fact that they were still coming up with ideas spoke well of their morale. Pol came in with a gleaming Saxon Slayer."Here is your blade my lord, sharp enough to shave with!"

For some reason that cheerful comment made everyone laugh and in that laughter came release. We were still positive and we all thought we could still win, even a young squire. None of us knew how but there was a belief in the camp that King Urien would reach us in time and the sacrifice would be worthwhile when we defeated Aella.

When the next day dawned we could see that the forces on our flanks had been massively reinforced. They intended to finish it that day. "Raibeart take half the men from the bridge and reinforce the two flanks. I think the bridge will be a diversion and their real effort will be where their main forces are." I sought Riderch. "You take charge of the same flank you did yesterday but send me five of your warriors." "Garth, you are to defend the left flank. Send me five of your warriors."

When I had the ten men I sent Pol to Tuanthal for five of his warriors. Raibeart came over when he saw the small detachment. "What do you intend brother?"

I pointed up the hill. "That will be the last point of defence but I want to delay the enemy. When he breaks through I will take these fifteen men and we will attack the ones who break through." I shrugged. "I know it will only delay the inevitable but every hour we save might mean the king reaches us or at least reaches us in time to bury our bodies and defeat Aella."

No words were needed and I clasped my brother's arm. "Pol, get a shield and find a helmet." He cheerfully ran off. I wanted him protected and able to defend himself. "The rest of you arm yourself with a couple of spears. There are plenty. We will throw one and then use the other. We need to be mobile. We fight as a line of ten warriors with the equites watching the rear and the flank. We will be the last to retreat. We give the others time to get to the top of the hill." From the looks on their faces one would have thought I had given them a bag of gold rather than signing their death warrants.

Myrddyn trudged up the hill. "I will heal from the top of the hill. We may save more that way."

"Good and, Myrddyn..."

"Yes my lord?"

"Arm yourself. Aella will remember the spy who was in his camp and helped the prince to escape." He nodded and his face became serious as he understood the implications of my words. His service to me might be brief and cost him his life.

Aella tried to intimidate us by banging drums at the same time as his men banged their shields. I didn't mind. Any delay was welcome. When his horn sounded the whole Saxon line, on three sides, leapt forwards. They were relying on numbers and on speed. We had fewer archers but they could keep the arrows flying for longer as they had more shafts. The warriors at the front fell like wheat to a scythe but still they came on. They tried to leap the ditch but the water we had used had made the grass greasy and they slipped and fell on to the stakes which were covered in last night's shit. The men had particularly enjoyed that bowel movement. The dead bodies in the ditches meant that they soon closed with the walls. I glanced at the bridge. Raibeart and Angus had half the number of warriors they had had the previous day but the Saxons were making no impression on their barricade.

Suddenly part of the thin wooden wall on the left flank gave way and Saxons hurtled through overrunning the defenders. Adair and his slingers slowed them a little but it was time for my detachment. We raced forwards towards the fifty men who had broken through. Fifteen spears flew through the air and twelve men fell. We struck the disorganised mass with a solid line of spears and every spear struck home. I threw my spear at a warrior ten paces away and watched as he gurgled his bloody death. I drew Saxon Slayer and backhanded a warrior who was coming towards me with an axe. I heard a groan behind me and saw a Saxon, who was about to stab me on my unprotected side, fall to Pol's seax. I looked around for my next Saxon but the slingers and my men had ended the threat. Garth had fortified the gap in the wall but it was still a desperate fight.

Scean shouted, "My lord. Riderch is in trouble!"

I saw that the Saxons had now broken through on the other flank and Riderch's men were being attacked on all sides. "Follow me!" Grabbing a spear I led my men towards the Saxons who were oblivious to the danger in their rear. We threw our spears and then hacked into unprotected backs and legs. Soon we were standing side by side with Riderch who nodded his thanks but I could see that there were another thousand warriors massing before us. "Pol, tell my brother to retreat. Scean signal the retreat." I yelled as loudly as I could, "Retreat!" and we began to edge back up the hill. "Riderch take your men and form a defensive line just below the ditch." He looked as though he was going to disobey but then thought better of it.

We were a line of twelve warriors and we faced the Saxons who thought that they had won. They advanced towards us, each one of them anticipating being the one to kill the Wolf Warrior. That was their undoing for they forgot about the other eleven who were all skilled warriors. Nor did they anticipate my brother and Angus charging into their flank. It was a bitter battle as we edged backwards and the Saxons had to fight over their dead and dying to reach us and we were always just out of reach. And then we were in one line with Riderch and Garth. The last warriors left, standing in a circle before the ditch. Behind us were Miach and the last archers who had arrows. There was a hiatus as the Saxons paused. They had us surrounded and were eagerly waiting for the order to charge us.

"Miach, use your last arrows when I give you the order. Riderch and Garth, when I give the order, retreat to the prince and we will fight from the walls. Now!"

A number of things happened at once: the arrows flew, we ran back and then I heard the thunder of hooves. I stopped and I turned, The Saxons before me were now fleeing and I saw the standard of Elmet. King Gwalliog and his men had arrived. We had reinforcements! One of the kings had reached us in time.

Chapter 13

Although the king had only brought a thousand men, two hundred were horsemen and they had destroyed the men on the right flank. The one thousand men who had started the attack had paid heavily at the hands of my men and the sudden charge of the mounted men had been enough to send them fleeing back across the river. Although over three thousand still waited below us the sudden collapse of one of their wings had halted them. "Quickly, form a new line on me and the men of Elmet." Within minutes we had our left side anchored at the top of the hill defence and the right flank at the river. We were still outnumbered but at least we had fresh troops and, more importantly, hope.

I had not seen Aella until that moment but I saw him then. He stood at the rear of his line with his bodyguards around him. I risked a glance across the river and saw that he still had many more warriors ready to flood across the bridge once he secured it again. Our barrier had thwarted their attempt to rush through the middle and I could see that Aella would try to attack there. "Miach take your archers and the slingers. I want any Saxon going near to the bridge killing. Tuanthal, mount your equites and join the men of Elmet on our right flank."

Raibeart was next to me. "You are gambling that he will try to take the bridge?"

"Wouldn't you?"

"Of course but if you are wrong then we lose the hill and that will mean that we lose the battle."

"Our task was to defend the river crossing and that we will do. The king should be here in two days. With King Gwalliog's men we might just do it. Now join your father in law and tell him of our plight. I will stay here and defend the top of the hill."

Aella waved his warriors forward and they came at us in three enormous wedges. We still had the advantage that we were uphill of them and they were tired; so were we but we did not have to drag our armour up a slope steep which was slippery with gore. We had no archers now and they came on relentlessly without the annoyance of archers and slingers. They were able to watch us as they steadily trudged up the hill side of death. They had seen some of their men defeated, they were now swimming back across the river or fleeing to the west, but they still outnumbered us and their king was leading them this time.

"Lock your shields!" They would push us back. We were but two lines of warriors but they would find the slope hard. I took the first sword which hacked at me on my shield and gave it a slight turn so that it slid down and snagged on a nail. It only took the warrior a moment to free it but that was all I needed. I slashed down on his neck and almost severed his head. The next warrior had punched with his shield but Scean's sword appeared next to my head and pierced his eye. I ended his life swiftly but I was forced to step back. The Saxons took that to be a sign of weakness and pushed forwards but they only served to hamper the warriors on the front line who could not swing their swords. We had no such problem and I swung Saxon Slayer over my head to split the helmet and head of the unfortunate warrior who had lunged at me. There was no time for self congratulation for there were more enemies to kill. Had the Saxons been able to enjoy another hour of daylight they might have beaten us but as night fell Aella withdrew his men to our first ditch which he used as a defence against us.

Soon both sides had fires going, partly for defence but also to give warmth and to cook some food. We had fought all day and I knew that we would struggle to stay awake. I sought King Gwalliog and I embraced him. "You have saved the alliance this day."

He gave a shrug which almost appeared to be one of embarrassment. "I could not have my daughter widowed yet could I?" Raibeart too embraced his father in law. "I took a leaf out of your book Lord Lann. I brought the one thousand warriors who were ready. The others will leave in seven days when their tasks are complete. I came to the Roman Bridge and was told where you were. I could have waited for King Urien but now I see the state of your force then I am glad that I came earlier. Where is the king?"

"Still two days away and no sign yet of King Morcant Bulc but I expect him with King Urien. We have two more days of hard fighting if we are to hold this river crossing."

King Gwalliog looked at the fires which littered the hillside and across the river. "It is a mighty host. Can we hold them?"

"Had you not arrived then the answer would have been no but I now have hope. Let us join the prince for he will be pleased to see you."

While the king and the prince spoke I sought Myrddyn. "What is the cost?"

"It is a high one." He looked at me with sadness in his eyes. "Adair is dead." I felt my heart sink. Adair was brave and he was intelligent. I had high hopes for him he would have made a fine leader of horse to aid Tuanthal and now he was gone. "You have less than five of your oathsworn warriors left and that includes Garth. Two are wounded but may fight again. Rheged has paid a high price. I think you have less than a hundred warriors and a hundred archers left from the ones who left Rhege." I suddenly realised that I had not told the king of the loss of his contingent of warriors. There were just six of them left. Only Angus and his Strathclyde men seemed indestructible.

It was dark when Pol awoke me. "My lord you are sent for. There is something happening in the Saxon camp."

I threw my wolf cloak about me to take away the chill of the night. Garth and Raibeart were stood watching the Saxon camp. "What is amiss? Are they attacking?"

"No, my lord. We have sent Ridwyn to investigate but we think that they are leaving. They banked up their fires and there was noise but, for the past hour there has been silence and we can detect no movements."

"What about the bridge?"

"The fires still burn on the other side of the river but, as with this camp here there is no movement." Was this another of Aella's tricks? True we had been reinforced but we were still vastly outnumbered. "Should we wake the men?"

"No we can wait until Ridwyn returns. I can see that what you said was true there is no sign of sentries but I wonder where they have gone."

"Their ships are still downstream."

"True but, as we know, there are only enough to ferry them across the river not to go further afield."

Raibeart smacked his hand on the pommel of his sword."I would hazard a guess that he has taken all his troops north of the river and is heading for Bernicia."

"You may be right brother. I should have thought of that before and put scouts to the north."

Garth laughed. "With the small number of warriors we had I am not sure we would have had sufficient to do that."

Ridwyn suddenly appeared like a wraith from the early foggy valley. "They have gone, my lord. There is no sign of any of them."

"We will have to wait until the sun rises to investigate further. Ridwyn go and wake Tuanthal and ask him to mount a patrol. We will see what they can discover."

See we could that Ridwyn was correct. I sent Tuanthal off to the east to track them while I led Angus, Miach and their men across the river. We climbed over the barricade. I did not want it dismantled only to have to rebuild it again; this could be a trick. We marched in a shield wall warily watching for ambush but, as with the other camp, it was deserted. I began to fear that Raibeart was right. They had stolen a march on us and headed north. They would be able to destroy King Morcant Bulc and his men and then defend the impregnable fortresses of Bernicia. I had been outwitted. "We can dismantle the barrier now. Miach keep the archers on the ridge to watch for the Saxons in case this is a trick to lure us away."

By noon the villagers were back in their homes, weapons had been sharpened and the army waited for an order. The prince, King Gwalliog and I had spent some time with Myrddyn debating our course of action. King Urien was coming to our aid and we could wait a day. That still left the problem of the Bernician army which could, even now, be lying slaughtered just north of us. It was with some relief that we saw a jubilant Tuanthal and his patrol return to Dunelm.

"Great news! It is the Bernicians; they are half a day away, coming along the river."

Prince Ywain asked the question which was on all of our minds. "And the Saxons are they north or south of the river?"

"King Morcant Bulc had not seen them but he had seen their ships sailing down the river. They looked to be empty and the land across from the camp was very muddy." He hesitated. "If I were to make a guess I would say they have crossed the river."

We had been outwitted again and Aella had gained at least half a day on us. "Tuanthal send another patrol on the road south and tell them to find the Saxons. They could head west and take the Roman Bridge or travel to Elmet and devastate that land. We must know where he is." I could see the fear in Gwalliog's eyes as I suggested the unthinkable. His army was here and his land was defenceless. "Do not worry King Gwalliog. His army is on foot. You can have all of our horses to pursue him if we discover that he is south of the Dunum."

The Bernicians arrived in the late afternoon. He had brought just a thousand warriors and fifty horses. Aella must have feared he was being caught in a trap but had he stayed he would still have outnumbered us. *Wyrd*! The camp cheered Morcant Bulc and his men as though they were heroes. I still did not like the man and I did not see him as a hero. Had he come quicker then Adair and many others would be alive. But he was here and he revelled in his moment of glory. He looked as happy as I had ever seen him and he embraced first his brother king, then Ywain and finally me. "I want to thank you for helping me to drive the Saxons from my land." I threw a look of disbelief at Raibeart who gave a slight shake of the head; the effrontery of the man. It was us who had fought, bled and died while he had vacillated his way south.

"And now we just wait for my father and we can finish this job once and for all."

King Morcant Bulc laughed and shook his head. "Aella and his men are a finished force. He will crawl back to the lands of the Saxons beyond the seas."

It was obvious that they had not seen the Saxons. "Does your majesty know how many men Aella has?"

Morcant Bulc pointed at the dead fires. "We passed through their camp and counted the fires. If there were two thousand I would be surprised."

I had to hold in my anger at both the arrogance and the incompetence of the man. "On the other side of the river there were more than three thousand men. He has five thousand and he has lost very few. He will not return home just yet."

I saw him start and his face drained of colour. He looked around at the camp. "But we have less than two thousand men here. We cannot defeat him."

Prince Ywain showed that he was his father's son. "We could give a good account of ourselves as we have for the last six days but it would be wiser to wait a couple more days and await the men of Rheged and Strathclyde. Lord Lann and I achieved what we were ordered to do; we denied the Saxons the crossing of this river which would have allowed them to devastate the whole of Bernicia."

He gave a weak smile, "And I am grateful. Where shall I camp my men?"

I pointed across the river. There is a huge area on the ridge over the river. As you can see we are somewhat crowded on this side."

As he led his men away Raibeart and Ywain joined me. "I see he has not changed Lann."

"No Prince Ywain and I wonder if he thought we had defeated them and that is why he joined us."

Raibeart laughed. "I like the way you let him have the shithole that is the Saxon camp."

I shrugged but I could not keep the smile from my face. The Saxons were not known for their clean camps. My men dug latrines daily but the Saxons just did it where they would. We had watched them. The Bernicians would be paddling through excrement to try to find a clean part. I suddenly saw Riderch and the remaining Bernicians. "Are you not going with your king?"

He gave me a feigned look of innocence. "I thought I was still attached to Lord Lann's vanguard; as did my men." It is truly said that you cannot buy loyalty, you earn it. The king of the Bernicians had yet to learn that lesson.

The second patrol returned just after dark. Tuanthal looked exhausted. Rather than delegate he had led the patrol himself. "They left the Roman Road about twelve miles south of here. They headed for the Dunum."

Prince Ywain asked eagerly, "Are they leaving by ship?"

Tuanthal shook his head. "We saw their fleet. It is much smaller now. I do not think he has enough ships to return home. He has occupied a hill and ridge which is surrounded on all sides by tidal marches, bogs and swamps. There is a causeway to reach it. One of the men I took with me knows the area. Sometimes the river and the tide combine to make the hill accessible from the sea."

The two kings were not battle hardened enough to understand what Aella was about but the rest of us could. Their puzzled looks were testament to their lack of experience, despite their age. "He means to do as we did here and break our armies upon his defences. We will not be able to use our horses and, by the time we reach his sanctuary, he will have made defences against out archers. He means to make us fight warrior to warrior for he will then outnumber us and defeat us and he can always escape with his fleet. It may not be large enough at the moment to take off his army but with losses he would be able to do so. Why he could even embark and return here or at Metcauld. The battle we will have to fight is bound to result in a weaker allied army. He is clever and I am just glad that soon we will have a mind which is superior to Aella, King Urien." With the exception of King Morcant Bulc everyone looked pleased about that.

King Urien and King Rhydderch Hael arrived in the middle of the next afternoon. They had with them two and a half thousand men including two hundred horses and a hundred archers. We now had a chance, however slim, to catch Aella and end this war.

The king of Rheged knew that he had a role to play and he went first to his brother kings despite the fact that I knew he would have been desperate to see his son and his injuries. He nodded to me as he greeted King Gwalliog and I could see a message in the eyes. We had assembled the last of the edible food and augmented it with some of the fresh supplies brought from Rheged. We had a feast for the kings and lords and one for the warriors. The warriors who had fought alone for so long were feted by their brothers who recognised their achievement for what it was… a miracle.

King Urien sat close by Prince Ywain and I could see the concern on his face as his son told him of our campaign. I knew whenever my name was mentioned, which was often, for the king would turn to look at me. I was seated betwixt Raibeart and Myrddyn and I enjoyed the feast for they were both the most interesting and witty men that I knew. Aelle would have made the night perfection.

When the men all relaxed with the ale brought from Strathclyde King Urien sought Myrddyn and me out. He took us to one side. "I am indebted to both of you." He looked at Myrddyn, "You for saving my son's life and you for saving the campaign. I know from speaking with my son that both of your actions were instrumental in the success we have had."

I shook my head and gave a snort of derision, "Success? I have lost most of the men. That is not a success in my world."

"Do not put yourself down. You were outnumbered but you did as I asked. I should have left sooner. Any blame is attached to me but enough of blame let us look to the future. How do we defeat this Aella?"

I looked at Myrddyn, I knew that he would have ideas but he inclined his head for me to speak. "From Tuanthal we have learned that it will be a well defended site. He will have had at least two days to improve the defences and he has seen how we do it. I expect to be facing the same defences we built."

"It will be bloody."

"At the very least."

"However your majesty, my lord, he does have one weakness; his fleet. If we can threaten his fleet he may have to withdraw and return home. He does not want, nor do his warriors, to be stuck in this land without the means to escape."

There was a pause and I asked the obvious question, "How do we threaten his fleet? We have no ships."

"I am working on that but as far as attacking a defending hill then you use Angus and his hammers."

I grinned and the king looked puzzled. When I explained he nodded. Perhaps King Rhydderch Hael has more of these weapons amongst his other warriors."

"It seems to be a specialised field but we do have the option of fire arrows which have worked before."

"And we can negate the effect of the marsh and the bogs by extending the causeway with faggots of wood. We know that they cannot dig pits such as we had and their ditches would fill with water."

"It is not all bad then?" The king gave us both a wry smile. "But tell me, Lann; are you and the vanguard ready to fight again?"

"We will be, if only to avenge the dead." I know my voice sounded cold and hard but I meant every word. It would be for the Adairs and Tadghs that I would be fighting not for King Morcant Bulc and his ambition.

We left the following morning. Tuanthal and my remaining horses and scouts formed the screen we spread out ahead. The remaining equites were detailed to guard the wagons. We did not want an ambush to rob us of our valuable supplies. The archers and slingers walked parallel to the road and guarded our flanks and the middle was the domain of the heavily armed and armoured warriors. The wounded travelled in the wagons for we would need every warrior we could lay our hands on.

Tuanthal had left a patrol to guide us from the road across country to the newly fortified ride of Aella. When we reached the ridge opposite I could see it had been chosen well. It looked like an island and the causeway was clearly visible. It was five paces wide and was a killing ground. I could also see, in the distance, the masts of his fleet. I hoped that Myrddyn had come up with a solution to our problem. King Urien halted us at the ridge. It was the driest ground around and we could camp there. We were less than a mile from the Saxon lines and we were higher which, this time, gave us the advantage of height. He sent his own equites, under Bladud's leadership to reconnoitre the fleet and the other side of the ridge. We spent the afternoon building our own defensive camp. There were almost ten thousand men within a mile of each other. The green land before us would soon turn red.

We had over two thousand warriors who could assault the stronghold but only nine hundred of them were armed and armoured as the Saxons were. The rest of our men were half trained farmers. The raiders from the sea would outnumber us, again, and we would need to find some way to equalise the numbers. This time we would be attacking uphill and they would have the advantage of just waiting for us. We issued those who had no armour and no helmet, with the ones we had captured from the Saxons. We also distributed better weapons for the men of Strathclyde who came keen and enthusiastic, but poorly armed. Garth and Riderch then drilled the men so that they could form lines when appropriate and knew when to use their weight. The men of Rheged found this easy but those from the other kingdoms found it strange. So long as the sea levels remained where they were the enemy were trapped but we had no doubts that they were well provisioned. Those who knew the area spoke of a well and streams running to the Dunum. We would not defeat them with a siege; we would need to beat them with force of arms and any deception Myrddyn could concoct.

Bladud reported back to the king although we were all present. King Urien would not divide us; we were all in the same army and we shared everything. "They have the ships moored close to the shore and they have many armed guards close to them. There is a barrier of logs between the river and the ships and it is secured on both banks." They had taken our idea of a boom and turned it against us. "The only place we can attack is here, across the causeway."

An air of depression descended over the meeting. Suddenly Myrddyn asked, "Are there guards around the whole of the stronghold?"

Bladud gave my healer a dismissive look. "They do not need to. They have warriors in their thousands near to the causeway and others near to the boats. There is nowhere else we can attack them."

"A strange and long-winded way to answer me. I assume then that the rest of the perimeter is unguarded?"

I thought that Bladud's head would explode he became so red. I intervened. "What idea is fermenting in your fertile mind?"

"I can see what Bladud means but men could cross the swamps and the waters and they could climb the small fences and walls they have built. If they did so at night then they would be unseen. If we combined that with an attack on their ships and on the front gate then a small force might break in and create so much damage that an attack might be successful."

There was a brief moment of silence and then everyone began talking at once. I could see that Bladud was not happy but King Urien had the hint of a smile on his face as though he had seen a way out of this impasse. I leaned in to Myrddyn. "How many men?"

"One hundred climbing and entering over a two hundred paces section of the wall should ensure success."

"Mailed men?"

He shook his head. "I would recommend archers or scouts. You need men who can sneak rather than battle. I, of course, will be one of them."

I shook my head. The one thing Myrddyn did not lack was confidence. The king stood and we all became silent. "I think that Myrddyn has a good plan but we first need to widen the causeway and that will mean archers protecting warriors as they build it. The equites, under my son Ywain and Bladud, will place themselves close to the ships to threaten them and prevent any warriors escaping. When the causeway is enlarged then we will consider how to gain access." He looked over at me and gave me a slight nod of the head. As he left I followed him. He gave me a shrewd look. "I saw you speaking with Myrddyn. Do you have a plan?"

"I have the beginnings of one. I will need to speak with Raibeart and Miach first. If we use archers then we can cover the walls with half of the men while the other half climb the walls and gain access. They can then demolish that section of wall and allow the archers to enter."

"You would not attack straight away?"

"We would not need to. If Bladud is right then there will be no-one guarding the wall and we will have time to make a fort within the fort. Then if we attack the main gate and the fleet at the same time the Saxons will have to decide which the most important area to defend is. The archers have already shown their skill and I have no doubt that they could keep the enemy occupied for some time."

"But how do we hurt the fleet?"

I smiled. "Angus and his men from Strathclyde. They have these hammers, huge stones and metal balls which they can hurl thirty of forty paces. If they were to hurl lighted logs then the ships would burn or have to cut their cables and flee. A few archers supporting them would create havoc. We use a three pronged attack at exactly the same moment."

I could see that he liked the idea already. "And how do we make sure they are timed correctly?"

"Garth could take one of those Roman horns we used and sound three blasts while an archer looses fire arrow into the air."

"You would be with the archers and not the warriors?"

"Riderch and Garth have shown that they are great leaders and they could force the gates. I am an archer and a swordsman as is my brother. It makes sense."

"Keep these plans to yourself. I am still aware that we did not find your spy and he may well be here with us."

"That has weighed heavily on my mind too. I will only speak of it with my brother."

The next day we began the causeway from just below our ridge. At first it was easy work. The faggots were dropped in the mud and the pools and logs dropped on top. I worked out that we would have three hundred paces before they could interfere with the work. Half way through the first morning Bladud decided that he did not want to go on patrol. He phrased it nicely and explained that his task was to guard the kings; he had suddenly become the guardian of all of them. Kling Urien acquiesced to his complaint but it suited me for it was left to Tuanthal to replace him and I wanted Miach and Tuanthal to put in place my plan to make it easier for us to sink their fleet.

I joined my two warriors as they led their fifty man patrol around the outside of the swamps. Sometimes the horses sank to their haunches but those occasions were rare and we found ourselves at a beach with the fleet less than fifty paces away. The boom was moored across the river and consisted of logs joined by ropes. Although there were a few warriors guarding it I could see that it would not take much to disrupt it and make it a menace to the fleet but the time for that was to come. More importantly they had spread their ships out so that they had sea room between them. I intended to change that. I turned to Miach. "Tomorrow, when you come with Tuanthal I want you to loose arrows at the ships furthest away. I want them closer together and nearer to the shore."

Tuanthal looked sceptical. "They will know what we are about my lord."

"True but what is the alternative? They will huddle together for self protection. When they do so then we will stop hitting them."

When we returned to our camp I confided in Raibeart and Myrddyn; they needed to know what the plans were and I wanted their ideas. Both of them made sound suggestions. I looked at the progress on the causeway. Within two days we would be in a position to attack. We had those two days to plot a way through the bogs to the walls. That night Myrddyn,

Raibeart, Pol and, I crossed over to the wall. We sank into marshes, we fell into pools but we made it to the wall. There were no guards; we went a long way in each direction, just to make sure. They were relying on the land to protect them. As we returned we marked the path with rocks which were only visible from the north. Anyone watching from within would not see them. As a test of our skill I sent two of my remaining warriors over the next night and they came back cleaner than we had; it had worked.

When I approached Angus and told him what we had planned for the Saxon fleet his face lit into an inevitable grin. Myrddyn had worked out how to make the missile burn. "We have a mixture of oil and wax with this resin from some pine trees. The problem will be the rope; you will need to be quick or it will burn through." Angus looked quite happy at that. "And the other problem we have is that we have to keep this a secret until you attack the fleet."

"That will not be a problem."

Chapter 14

The Saxons finally reacted to the causeway when it came within a hundred and thirty paces and they charged out to assault the builders; we lost our first men as we completed the last thirty paces. The eight men who died were a small price to pay and we left ten archers to discourage them from destroying our work. That night King Urien briefed the officers and kings. He made no mention of the attack on the fleet or our attack on the walls; instead he said that we would have a night attack the following night led by the warriors under the command of Riderch and Garth. King Rhydderch Hael and King Gwalliog wanted to lead their men too but King Urien persuaded them that this attack was to test for weaknesses and the real attack would come in the morning. I saw King Morcant Bulc and Bladud glance in my direction as my name had not been mentioned but they could not ask the reason without drawing attention to themselves. I had more on my mind, for we would need to dress without armour for our foray. I would be leaving my banner and Saxon Slayer at the camp; what we were about needed stealth and not brute force.

The Saxons were no fools and the building of the causeway had warned them of some impending attack. The wall facing the gateway bristled with warriors. Garth and Riderch formed the men up as though they were going to attack and to keep the Saxon's attention on our warriors. The timing would be difficult for we were not exactly certain how long it would take for us to reach the wall but, even if the attack began early, it would not matter much. I led the way hidden from prying eyes by my wolf cloak and a route which took us away from our camp and through scrubby, untidy bushes which seemed filled with thorns but gave good cover. Even though we had scouted the wall twice and seen no sentries it might just be that they chose this night to patrol. Raibeart had an arrow notched in case there was one on the wall. We were a hundred paces from the wall when the horn sounded three times, its strident notes sounding unnaturally loud in the silent night. A moment later the black night sky was lit by a flaming arrow arcing into the walls. Riderch and Garth would be leading the warriors to attack the walls at the front of the stronghold.

We hurried the last few paces to the wooden walls. They had used wooden stakes as high as a man. Two of my larger warriors held their shield and Pol jumped on to the top. They slowly raised him and he peered over. He leaned back and whispered, "Clear." Although whispering was unnecessary as the battle at the gate was raging and nothing could be heard above the clamour and clash of metal on metal. Pol lithely jumped over and all along the wall pairs of warriors hoisted over archers. Raibeart and I were the first of the warriors over with Scean a close third. We had only brought twenty warriors but they would be enough to do what we had to do; make a hole for the rest to pour through and protect the precious archers.

We attached ropes to the top of the palisade and, with the archers inside pushing and the rest of us pulling, we tore a thirty pace section of the wall out of the ground. While the archers watched for any curious Saxons, the warriors dismantled the demolished wall to build a barricade we could use as a refuge. It was infuriating for me to hear the noise of battle but neither see nor participate. We just had to do our job as best we could. We sent a scout back to tell the king that we had succeeded; we had another way into the fortress. Leaving Myrddyn in charge of four warriors and ten archers to guard our escape, should we need it Raibeart and I led the rest of our force towards the main gate.

We wandered through the untidy camp filled with dung pits and tents. We would not see the front gate for the hill ran away from us and bushes and trees hid it. The experience was nerve wracking as we watched for Saxons who could approach from any direction and for the mess we had to avoid. Suddenly we stopped as we heard a roar. For the briefest of moments I thought that we had been seen but, in the sky to the south I saw flames leaping into the air. Their fleet was afire and the roar was from the garrison. "Form a defensive line. We will soon have company."

Raibeart and I stood in the middle, Pol and Scean guarding our backs. Next to us were the forty archers and, before us the handful of warriors with locked shields. Someone had ordered a war band from the front gate to go to the river and deal with the threat there. The forty two arrows took them completely by surprise; none had their shields up and they were not looking for danger within their own camp. A second volley and a third left the handful of wounded Saxons to be despatched by my warriors. I waited for a second assault but, so devastating had been our attack that no alarm had been raised and we moved slowly forwards. The foliage ended just where the hill dropped away and we could see the bitter battle between the warriors who were armed and armoured in the same way. I had the chance to look beyond the gate and I could just make out the kings and the body of horsemen they held in reserve to assault the stronghold when we broke through.

There were more than enough targets for us but we had to choose the correct ones. Raibeart pointed. "If we concentrate our arrows on the men just behind the main gate then Garth should be able to push through."

"You heard Lord Raibeart. On my command, loose and keep loosing until we have no arrows left." We had left spare quivers at the refuge. If we failed here then we would have to make a last stand there. I hoped it would not come to that."Loose!"

The rain of arrows was devastating. The hill meant they plunged down and there were no shields to protect the backs of the warrior; it was as though they were being attacked by their own men. It had been some time since I had used my bow but I kept pulling until I thought my arm would drop off. I put my hand into my quiver and it was empty.

I saw Pol's ginning face. "That is it my lord, now it is time for the sword." He held out his hand and I gave him my bow. I drew the sword I had chosen to use. It was shorter than Saxon Slayer but it was handier in confused night fighting.

Our rain of arrows had had two effects: Garth and his men had broken through and two hundred warriors were climbing the hill towards us. If I had run out of arrows then the others would have too. If we retreated there would be two hundred less warriors to fight Garth and his men as I knew they would follow my wolf banner. "Retreat! To the refuge."

This time we took no care and ran as fast as we could oblivious to any mess and noise. I was pleased to see that the men we had left had made the barrier higher. We would have somewhere to defend. Arrows flew over our heads and I heard the screams as they struck the pursuing Saxons. We ran around the sides of the barrier and took our places behind it. The archers frantically grabbed the quivers and began killing the Saxons who had almost caught us. I punched my shield at the face which appeared before me and then sliced across his bared throat. Pol had sharpened this blade as well as Saxon Slayer but I knew that within the hour it would be dull for there were many bodies for it to kill. Raibeart had drawn his sword as had Scean and the three of us formed an island with Pol using a spear thrown at us by the Saxons to jab at any leg he saw. Ten of our warriors lay dead before us, overwhelmed by the sheer numbers but they had bought enough time for the archers to make their presence felt and the Saxons were desperate to get to me and my wolf standard.

Suddenly there were no Saxons before us. They were dead or dying. "Quickly find any arrows out there. Pol, come with me and we will see how the battle at the gate goes."

As we ran I risked a glance over my shoulder and saw that the sky was bright with the conflagration on the river. That part of our plan had succeeded. When we reached the ridge I could see that Aella had formed a huge shield wall. There had to be two thousand men in concentric circles. It seemed he had gathered all of his remaining warriors and was making his stand, much as we had attempted at Dunelm, at the top of the hill. We did not have enough archers to whittle the band down to size and it would be up to Garth, Riderch and the other warriors to resolve the conflict.

"Pol, bring Raibeart and the others here." We could, at least, keep the Saxons pinned down but I could see from my vantage point that Garth and his men had slowed up considerably.

Raibeart and the twenty archers who remained joined us. "Let us try to help Garth. Aim at the warriors before him." I knew that Garth could defeat any Saxon but, with a fresh man to deal with each time you killed one the odds soon went in favour of the enemy. When we ran out of arrows we became spectators and that was harder than anything I had borne before. The Saxon lines were shrinking but, as they did so they had more men available to face ours and when I saw Garth fall I felt sure that we had lost.

I heard the horn sound fall back. Raibeart looked at me. "We have failed."

I shook my head. "No we have not. That was not '*retreat*', that command was '*fall back*'. It is King Urien who commands and he is giving the men some rest." I pointed to the east. "Look dawn approaches and with it comes hope. They do say it is darkest before the dawn well so it is but we have not lost and," I pointed to the south, "from the fires we can see then Angus has, at least, destroyed some of their fleet." I turned to the archers. "Get yourselves swords and shields we will add our weight to the fray."

Although they did not have the mail of the heavier armed swordsmen my archers were strong and quick. They would use their speed to achieve victory. I heard the horn sound charge and looked down to see King Urien and the other kings charging the Saxons with their equites. There were three lines and I knew that would be a hundred warriors in each line. I wondered if he had taken leave of his senses for their horses would be halted by the wall of shields and they would be defeated. I held my breath as they closed to within thirty paces and then breathed again as they all hurled a javelin or a spear and retreated. The second line and the third repeated the action and then Riderch led the warriors back up the hill for a second time. They had had a brief rest but the Saxons had been decimated by the javelins and spears. I could see Aella busily reinforcing his sagging front line.

Suddenly a warrior appeared from behind me. It was one of Tuanthal's men. "My lord, we have fired the fleet and they have either fled or sunk. Lord Angus asks for instructions."

"Tell them to join me here."

My hope rose with that news but I saw the remnants of the fleet defenders join Aella. He too had been reinforced and now he knew that he was cornered. He had no escape. He either defeated us or he perished!

I had intended to join the attack but I decided to wait until I too was reinforced. Riderch and his men had closed with the Saxons and I could see that his brother was to his right. They were a formidable combination and I knew that they would hold the Saxons but I was not sure how we would break their shield wall. We were evenly matched and the Saxons had the advantage of higher ground. Tuanthal galloped up. He had thirty men with him and Angus huffed and puffed with his fifty warriors and the twenty archers under Miach. We now had enough men to cause some problems for Aella.

"Well done Tuanthal. You have done well."

He grinned. "No my lord, Angus and his men were the secret. They hurled their flaming rocks." He nodded to Myrddyn who was tending to some of the wounded. "Your concoction worked well healer. The ships were so close together that they set fire to their fellows. The ones, who could, fled and then we attacked the men on the shore. They fought well but then a messenger came to them and they withdrew."

"Have you javelins?"

"Some of us have; why?"

"I want you and your men to charge the Saxons and release your javelins at thirty paces."

Tuanthal looked at the handful of men he had left and then at the Saxon horde. "My lord it will be like spitting into the wind."

"No Tuanthal it will make Aella think we have a larger force than we do. With Miach and Raibeart's archers we can cause problems here and then Angus and I will attack their shield wall." I pointed down the hill and raised my voice so that all could hear. "We cannot win the battle; that will be King Urien's task but we can distract the enemy. We are not going to throw our lives away for when we have assaulted them we will withdraw and they will think we are retreating. When they do so then the archers will attack them and the horse can charge."

Tuanthal nodded, "I am sorry for doubting you my lord."

"Do not worry, Tuanthal, I sometimes doubt myself."

Angus thrust a huge ham like hand around my shoulder, "I like you wee man! You are a mad bugger. Life is never dull when you are around."

We formed into our lines as yet unobserved by Aella who was busily feeding more men into the front ranks as Riderch hurled his men at the Saxon lines. Tuanthal's javelins and Miach's arrows did little damage but they did alert Aella to our presence and as my standard began to move towards the Saxons he quickly moved reinforcements to that side of the perimeter. Angus was to my right and he carried a huge two handed sword. His men were to his right and to my left I had the ten warriors and archers left from our attacks. Angus swung his sword and I looked on in amazement as he sliced off three heads in one blow. I took advantage of the gap and stabbed forwards at the next man in line. The men from Strathclyde were awesome and must have terrified the Saxons.

Behind me I heard Scean. "My lord, we are about to be surrounded."

"Retreat!"

The men were ready and everyone struck out with his shield and moved swiftly back. As the Saxons tried to close with us Raibeart and Miach rained arrows at them and Tuanthal's men raced in dealing death with their long swords. Riderch and his men sensed the hesitation and pushed forwards, shrinking the perimeter even more. The Strathclyde men with their king then added their own deadly hail of rocks and hammer to pound and grind at men already reeling from continuous attacks. Whereas our men were able to gain some respite whilst another arm attacked the same Saxon warriors each faced different foes; we were on all sides now.

I heard the recall sound. "Tuanthal, when the king attacks so shall you. Raibeart and Miach support the horsemen when they charge in." I knew that our attack would be as a pinprick but if it divided the Saxon attention then so much the better. I saw Myrddyn with our wounded. His presence in this campaign had saved so many warriors that I thought about asking Brother Oswald for another three for the rest of the army.

He glanced up at me. "So far my weapon has remained sheathed."

"No Myrddyn, for you have used a more powerful weapon, the weapon of your mind."

I heard the call for the charge and the horsemen thundered in. This time they were ready with their shields but all that that did was to make the shields unwieldy as they could not free them of the javelins; when they tried the arrows ended their attempts quickly. The next attack would be the last. Riderch and Ridwyn now led a wedge towards the Saxons while Prince Pasgen and the men of Elmet led another. King Urien was making two parts of the shield wall weaker. "How many arrows brother?"

"Less than five each."

"Then loose them and arm yourselves with swords. The next time I order charge we all go in and support the king."

Their arrows fell on the unprotected backs of the men in the front ranks and I could see the shield wall was precariously thin. Then I heard the sound for the charge and the wailing of the dragon standard told me that it was King Urien and his equites who were charging. They charged in a wedge at the point between Pasgen and Riderch. It takes a brave man to stand up to charging horses and the Saxons had had enough. They broke. We too charged but it was not a wedge we all ran as individuals. My aim was not to break through but make the Saxons think we were attacking from all sides.

As the Saxons ran before the mailed horsemen Aella's bodyguards formed a defensive ring around their king; they were the elite and they were oathsworn. Other Saxons still fought but none could stand before the King, his men and his fellow kings. King Urien's blade flashed in the first light of dawn and I could see the blood running in rivers from its silvery edge. The Saxons who faced us were nervous and, glancing over your shoulder is not effective when you are fighting warriors who mean to kill you. Even Pol with his seax and small shield was able to pierce the defence of warriors who feared what was behind them as well as what was in front.

Riderch and the warriors had reformed into one wedge and were approaching the last stand of the Saxons. Tuanthal and the spare horsemen were busily pursuing the fleeing Saxons. I hacked, slashed and stabbed until there were no more enemies before me and I raced towards the Saxon elite. King Urien's horse was well trained in war and he raised his hooves to smash down on the shields of the front ranks. You could almost hear the bones breaking, along with the warrior's spirits. Mercifully the hooves then smashed their skulls and ended their lives. The king was not worrying about his horse and his sword carved a path of death towards Aella. Aella was cunning but he was also brave. The equite who preceded King Urien found that to his cost when the Saxon King's axe sliced through his horse's legs and as he was thrown to the floor, his head was neatly decapitated.

King Urien reined in and dismounted. He was taller than the Saxon king but I could see the mighty muscles on the warrior's arms. King Urien had not fought as much in the last few years and I worried that he might not last a long fight. The king's bodyguards desperately formed a ring to keep the others away as the two kings circled each other. Aella's axe flew at Urien's head but he deftly moved out of the way, hacking at the Saxon as he did so. A ribbon of blood could be seen along the Saxon king's arm but it did not seem to slow him up. Instead of going for King Urien's head he swung his axe at his shield. It gouged a lump of wood from it and I couldn't help thinking that I had asked the king to protect his shield with iron as we had. It was too late for that now. The axe had swung in full circle and King Urien saw a gap. He stabbed forwards and the point of the sword found a gap in the mail. This time blood spurted and Aella roared a shout of pain and anger. He swung his axe even harder and the shield of King Urien shattered. From the limp state of King Urien's left arm I suspected that it was broken. I stabbed at the eye of the bodyguard who faced me and he fell dead. I was desperately trying to get to my king's side but there were too many men between us. The king staggered back and I saw the look of joy on Aella's face. He might be seriously wounded but without his shield King Urien was at his mercy.

King Aella took a mighty swing with his axe and King Urien did the most unexpected thing, he stepped in to Aella's body bringing his sword up as he did so. The handle of the axe struck King Urien a blow to the head which made him stagger but by then the Sword of Rheged had penetrated the mail, the muscles and the heart of King Aella. With a shocked look on his face, he died and the slaughter of the bodyguards began.

As I joined in the killing I shouted over my shoulder, "Pol, Myrddyn, get to the king and help him." I saw a blur of movement as the two young men sprinted through warriors who were too slow to stop them. When I saw Myrddyn kneel at the king's side with Pol guarding them I turned to the bodyguards. Today was the day when the Saxons would be defeated. Even though we were all exhausted we knew that this last effort would end the problem with which we had lived for so many generations and we gritted our teeth and we killed.

Chapter 15

It was late morning when the last of the Saxons had finally been killed. The bodyguards and oathsworn fulfilled their oath and died around the body of their king. The ones who fled were chased down and slaughtered by horsemen of the allies. It was a great victory but it had come at a great cost. Many of King Urien's bodyguards had perished in the brutal battle of the hill as had Angus and Prince Rhiwallon. Of the kings only King Urien had suffered a wound, a broken arm. Garth was badly wounded in the leg but Myrddyn had gone to him as soon as he had tended to the king. I found the king still guarded by Pol.

King Urien looked up at me, "He is a brave sentinel you sent to watch over me Lord Lann. I am indebted to him and your healer." His sad eyes softened. "Your plan succeeded, you did well."

I shook my head, "No your majesty, the honour of this day belongs to you. You led the charge and it was your tactics which succeeded. For the first time since the Romans left we have finally defeated the Saxons."

"Help me up young squire." Pol helped the injured king to his feet and King Urien leaned on his shoulder. "I think this will be my last battle. I saw my death as the axe was swung and I would see my grandchildren and play with them on my knee. I will leave the defence of Rheged to young men like my sons and you." He looked around at the body and blood littered field. "It is a grim sight. How many men have we lost?"

"It is early yet and we have not accounted for all the wounded but two thousand would be a reasonable estimate."

"So many?"

"The Saxons lost far more and most of their fleet. There will be many empty hearths over the sea when the ships return unmanned."

I looked up to see Prince Ywain riding over to us. He looked sad and he must have been told of his brother's death. I did not envy him having to tell his father. There were now but two brothers left: Pasgen and Ywain. King Urien had paid a high price for his victory. I nodded to him. "I will leave you with your father. I go to collect the few men of mine who remain and work out how I can tell their families of their loss."

Raibeart, Pol, and Scean joined me as we moved around the battlefield gathering our men. When we had reached the causeway I had but thirty men left from the one hundred and ten I had brought. Raibeart had lost fewer men but the losses were still grievous. We gathered around Garth and Myrddyn. My champion tried to raise his head but Myrddyn forced it down. "Just lie there. I have not finished my work."

Garth opened his eyes and asked, "Will I fight again?"

Myrddyn grinned, "Well not tonight but some day with rest then you will fight." He nodded his head at me. "Our Wolf Warrior overcame a wound such as this and so shall you."

"Ridwyn did well my lord. He dragged me from the field. I owe my life to him."

"Aye and his brother Riderch led the last charge and did so valiantly. They are both a credit to Bernicia."

Myrddyn threw me a sharp look and then thought better of it. I wondered what he knew. When we had the time I would speak with him. I turned instead to the rest of my men. "We have done well and now we need to rest." I looked over at the small copse in the valley bottom. "Brother Raibeart, what say you and I go and try to hunt some food for our men?"

They began to protest but Raibeart laughed, "An excellent idea. The rest of you prepare our camp and we will return with food." He suddenly looked at his empty quiver. "If I can find some arrows!"

We returned at dusk with some game birds and rabbits. The marshes and swamps were not well endowed with game but it would make a hearty stew and Raibeart and I had enjoyed being brothers again. All of the allied troops were in their own camp. Each of the kingdoms had lost many men and it would be a time to sing songs and tell tales of the dead. When we returned home they would be told to the families as a reminder. We all built our own funeral pyres and said goodbye to our friends. The small and cosy camp of the warriors of the Hogan brothers gave us all a sense of belonging.

After we had eaten Myrddyn sought out Raibeart and me. "I knew that something had annoyed you. What did you see, healer?"

"When the battle was at its height Bladud and five of his men were not at the king's side. I saw them holding back. There was that warrior Garth did not like with and three others I knew not. And the Bernician king did not put himself at the fore as the other kings did. There is something afoot."

"Men may have said that we hung back on our flank. We know that we did not."

"No my lord, this was different. They were both at the rear of their warriors. I would doubt that there is mark on their armour and any nicks in their blades have come from striking at the rear of men."

Raibeart looked at me. "He may be right brother. I noticed that they were not protecting the king. Many of the bodyguard died and all have wounds except for Bladud and his cronies. We had better watch them again." He looked into the flames and sighed, sadly. "I will be glad to return to my family."

"You tire of war?"

Raibeart glanced up, "We began this war against the Saxons to avenge our parents and then to protect the king. The Saxons are no more and we can enjoy a little peace."

"I hope so brother."

Myrddyn's young face looked old and serious "I am not so sure. I know that the Saxons have gone but when I was in their camp I learned that they view this land as heaven. Their own home is being eaten by the sea and by terrible warriors from the east. We have not seen the last of the Saxon invaders."

I knew what he said was true but I still had the belief that we could not fail. "If they come again we can defeat them while they are weak. King Ida and King Aella had been here for some time and we defeated them; any newcomers would know even less. We know this land."

The healer stretched and rose, prior to retiring. "We live in the west Lord Lann. If they come again it will be in the east and do you think that King Morcant Bulc will change and suddenly become King Urien?"

As we all turned in for the night I pondered those words. He would not change and if the Saxons came again then it would be us who would be forced to fight them but King Urien would not lead us and I was not sure if Prince Ywain, after his wounds, was the warrior to lead us. Perhaps it would be Prince Pasgen who had shown, when he led the wedge into the attack, that he was unafraid and that men would follow him.

The next day we cleared the battlefield and filled carts with the armour and the weapons we had taken. King Urien insisted that it be split four ways, despite the fact that it had been Rheged who had fought the longest and lost the most. The men gathered along four sides of a square as the four kings took their leave of each other. After they had all extolled the virtues of everyone's warriors they embraced and prepared to mount. King Gwalliog held up his hand. "Before we depart I would like to thank Rheged for without King Urien and his warriors we would have lost." He knelt to the ground. "Elmet will serve you my lord as High King."

I thought it was spontaneous but King Rhydderch Hael also dropped to his knee. "And Strathclyde will serve you and your son, my lord."

The whole of the army looked at King Morcant Bulc who stood with pure hatred for his fellows etched on his face. Even though he did not swear allegiance or subservience the idea was there for all to hear. King Urien was High King. He was the first to be acknowledged as such since the time of Dux Britannica.

When he spoke it was measured and thoughtful. "I thank you. I hope that we never need the High King again and that this threat from the Saxons is over but if they return then I swear that I will lead you again for it has been my honour to serve with such brave and resourceful warriors."

He mounted and led us west to the land of Rheged. As I waited for the princes to pass I noticed that Llofan Llaf Difo was speaking with King Morcant Bulc and I wondered if he were thinking of returning to his homeland having learned his trade with the finest army in Britain. After a few moments, however, he trotted to take his place next to Bladud and the handful or bodyguards who had survived the slaughter.

We had to take our time crossing the land for we had wagons and we had wounded. Garth complained about having to travel in a wagon but Myrddyn, for all his youth could be quite strict and Garth had to lie there and suffer. Myrddyn worked miracles and he saved men and their limbs when all hope was gone. Next to King Urien he was the man held in the highest regard by all of the army of Rheged. His bravery as a scout and on the battlefield merely added to his lustre. I thanked my gods again for bringing him into our lives.

We reached Castle Perilous first and, not for the first time, I was glad that I had left so many of my warriors to guard my home. Had I taken them all then I know that they would all have died. The others did not come to my home as they were all keen to return to their own families. Aelle's survivors left too, to head south towards the Wide Water. King Urien announced that we would have celebratory games at midsummer. Until then we could all reflect on the war to end all wars which we had just fought.

I led my tiny troop through the gates. Any celebration would have to wait until we had mourned and paid our respects to the dead. Once through the gates Brother Oswald, Aideen and my children waited for me. They had seen no reports of our travails and I saw the look of relief flood over Aideen's face as she watched me dismount. I knew what she was thinking and I smiled. She was checking for fresh wounds but I had been saved this time and returned whole.

I said little, after hugging my family and greeting Brother Oswald. It had been a hard campaign and Garth's wounds were a clear reminder of the mortality of all of us, no matter how invincible we felt. Hogan appeared to have grown and my daughter, Delbchaem, now responded with giggles and smiles. Some of my hurts went away. They all left me in my silence and after we had eaten Aideen put the children to bed while I went to the solar. Myrddyn appeared quietly and sat opposite me. He said not a word, but, like me, looked to the west and the setting sun.

Eventually he spoke; not necessarily expecting a response but merely articulating his ideas. "They say, my lord, that there are lands to the west Hibernia." I said nothing but noted the thought. "Perhaps it is a place too far for the Saxons to bother us."

I looked at him sharply. This sounded like defeatist talk. "You would give up the fight against the invader? You would let all the deaths become meaningless?"

He gave me that disarming smile of his which infuriated me. "No, my lord, I was doing my job, I was healing, healing your mind. The battles and the deaths seem to have taken something from you as though you no longer wish, yourself, to finish the fight. I was merely giving you an option."

His words set me thinking. I had become morose over the deaths and there were three choices, as far as I could see: continue the, fight, join the Saxons or flee. Myrddyn had merely given me a way out. "Sometimes I think you are a wight, and far too clever for your own good. Where did you get such knowledge when you are so young?"

"I listen, my lord, and I think. It is an activity in which more men should partake." He paused and his eyes seemed to bore into my mind as though he was reading my thoughts. "You will continue to fight then?"

"Your mythical land to the west may cause more deaths than fighting and I could not, in all conscience, join with the Saxons. No I will fight and, so long as King Urien is the leader of the kings then we will prevail."

He nodded. "They will, of course return and those Saxons in the south will come north to take, first the land of Elmet and then, Bernicia. We both know that they are ripe for plucking." He of course was correct and we both knew it. "We have bought time and that is all."

Once again his astute young mind had cut through the mist to see the truth. "What would you suggest then? The old mind in such a young body?"

"There are a number of things we can do. The king could make Rheged so impregnable that the Saxons will find other land to steal."

To me, that sounded as though we had lost. "The king would not countenance that. He would defend the other kings."

"Then, my lord, become used to this feeling for it will be Rheged blood which will defend the allies and you will have to face the families of the dead." I suddenly looked at him. How did he know that was what I had been thinking? The men knew about dying on a battlefield but the families had to live with the loss. "That is the real reason you are so unhappy is it not? You do not want to see the looks on the faces of the families of the men who will not return that is what you fear, not death, not defeat and certainly not the Saxons."

I slumped in my chair. My healer was right. "I know from Aideen's face that she worries each time I leave and yet I always return. How much worse for those who do not return?"

"It is the same for every warrior but at least here in Rheged the families are not left destitute. Someone cares. It is another reason I left my home to serve Rheged. Even if I had not had the dream and the vision it seemed to me that this was a place I could live and a king and a lord I could serve."

I pondered those words. He was right and we all served King Urien because of who he was and how he acted. We were tied to him for good or all. I suddenly felt better. "Well then Myrddyn. How can we make life difficult for the Saxons?"

We talked, or rather he talked and I listened until a sulky Aideen came for me. Her ill temper was short lived as she saw the change Myrddyn had wrought upon me. After we had enjoyed each other and she slept, snuggling in my arms, my mind was filled with all that Myrddyn had said. As he had said to me, it was obvious but I had not seen it until he had pointed the way. We could not defeat them in a shield wall. They would always outnumber us. The weapons they feared were our bowmen, our horses and our castles. Now that we had the booty from the battles we could arm more horsemen and archers and improve our castles. As far as I knew the only stone buildings which stood against the Saxons were in Rheged and at Din Guardi. As the sly Morcant Bulc had shown, you could easily defend such edifices. In the time we had before the Saxons returned we would train more men to be archers and horsemen whist we toiled to improve the defences. Myrddyn was clever and had deduced that a series of ditches with offset entrances would enable our archers to slaughter an attacking army. He also recommended towers at the gates from where we could have a greater range with our bowmen. He had heard of the horse patrols the king and the prince had once undertaken and he suggested that would be a good way to watch the Saxons and slow them down. When I had finally dropped to sleep I had all of my plans made for the next year.

By the time the midsummer games arrived, Garth and the other wounded men were healed and could travel. Surprisingly many declined the invitation to visit Civitas Carvetiorum. I did not make the men go for I, above all, understood what it was to leave your families. Brother Oswald had evolved into a fine Steward who ran Castle Perilous far more effectively than I could. He had the men continue building the ditches and improving the defences. He and Myrddyn had spent long nights drawing and scribbling on pieces of parchment with the priest showing a remarkable knowledge of how the Romans used to do such things. I knew that the building would carry on well without me. In the end I took only twenty men; they were all mounted and well armed. I was not worried about the Saxons but I knew that there were still Hibernians who liked to raid the coast for easy pickings. They would find us a hard morsel to swallow.

Aideen was looking forward to the visit as she would see both my brother's wives and Prince Ywain's bride. I knew that she missed the company of other women and they did, in all fairness get on well together. It also helped having other children there for my two were lonely at my castle. The men made a great fuss of them and spoiled them but they did not have the company of children their own age; at the court of King Urien they would have.

We were all set to arrive on the same day and I met Aelle and Freja not far from my castle. He had grown in the months since I had seen him and put on more weight around the waist and the jowls. It showed me the difference between a life of peace and a life of war. Aelle was happy and comfortable. His domain was the most peaceful and prosperous in the land and he ruled it well. I knew that King Urien held him in high regard. I was always a little taken aback by how much respect he showed me. He seemed amazingly proud of his brother. It was Myrddyn who gave me the reason. "He grew up not with his own father for you told me he was a Saxon who hurt him and he had not long with your father. You are the father he has known the most, the one who protected him and the one who helped him to get to the position he is."

"He did that himself fighting for the king."

"But it was you who was responsible for that position."

Now, each time I met my brother I was acutely aware that he saw me as a father figure rather than just his big brother. It was just another responsibility I had in my already, full life. However, as we rode towards the fortress on that Midsummer's Eve, the world felt good. I could see the banners hanging from the towers as we approached from afar. Men working in the fields called out our name and applauded the wolf banner. I recognised many from our wars and noticed that some had an arm missing or limped badly but they still cheered us as we rode along the old Roman Road. They were alive and they were free.

The king and queen greeted us at the gate. I noticed that the queen was greyer; yet another son had fallen but she still gave me that welcoming smile and embrace as she always did. She leaned and whispered in my ear. "I am pleased that the Wolf Warrior still defends Rheged. It gives me hope for the future. May Jesus bless you."

I never knew what to say when the Christians asked their god to protect me. It was as though they were trying to convert me in some way. Having said that, I welcomed the protection of any man's god; the battlefield was no place to spurn their aid. "I am pleased to serve the king still. Is he mending?"

She pulled away slightly and glanced over to where her husband was embracing Aideen and Freja. "His body heals but his mind is still disturbed."

I nodded. I knew the feeling. "It is with all men who think when they return from the battlefield. Those who cannot think, like Bladud, are to be envied for they never imagine, after a battle, what might have happened had they fallen."

She laughed and suddenly looked much younger. "I share your opinion of that brute but the king still thinks highly of him." She shook her head, "I know not why. Go to him and talk for he values your opinion and it will ease his mind." She turned to our wives and children. "Come ladies let us leave the men to talk and we will see what treats the cook has for us." She was a kind and thoughtful lady and adored children. She was the grandmother my children never knew. As they wandered off Pol, my squire caught my eye. It was the first time he had been to the fortress and wonder was in his face.

"Yes Pol, you can explore but try not to get in people's way."

"Yes my lord." He raced eagerly off.

"He thinks much of you."

"He is young but he is so loyal." As the king led me by the arm I turned to him. "Well your majesty, you are looking well."

He smiled and looked older than he had ever looked. "You are kind but we both know I came within a handbreadth of death."

"But you survived your majesty and we won."

"We won that day but what of the future days?" He looked sadly to the east. "It seems Gwalliog and Bulc have just returned to their lands and not prepared to defend them against the Saxons for they will come back and they should be ready."

Myrddyn was disappearing into Brother Osric's rooms and I pointed to him. "My healer is an intelligent man and I have spoken with him. He has counselled that we make our land too difficult to take and the enemy will go elsewhere." We walked into the great hall where there were jugs of beer and platters of bread and cheese. "The hedgehog has not teeth and is easy prey for any hunters, fox, or wild pig. Yet he survives and why?"

Aelle smiled as he answered. "His back is covered in spines and he can roll into a ball. The fox soon gives up."

"And that is what we do. Make ourselves as a hedgehog and surround ourselves with spines."

"Spines?" The king gave me a curious look.

"Archers, horses and defences even better that those you have here in your fortress."

The king drank and contemplated this. "That might work but what of our allies? Do we abandon them?"

It was time for some hard talking for this kind king. "Your majesty it is the men of Rheged who died defending their lands. It is time they took responsibility for their own defence."

"And if they fail?"

"Then they fail but they know that there is a sanctuary here at Civitas Carvetiorum."

"Perhaps we could make peace with the Saxons?"

"They are like the fleas on a dog. You could make peace with one group and another would come in their place. We make Rheged a circle of stone and iron. They will go elsewhere. Look at Aelle's domain at Wide Water. No-one could capture that, no matter how many men they had and our southern borders have been safer than any; mine included."

The king looked at Aelle for confirmation. "It is true your majesty and the people prosper. Many new families have come and there are many settlements north of us for my brother's castle and mine give them the confidence that they will be protected."

King Urien smiled and the years fell away. "It is good to talk with you. When the others arrive we will continue this. I too am tired of bleeding my poor land for others."

The midsummer celebrations seemed better than the Yule ones. As Brother Osric said to me at the feast, "Perhaps our allies changed the atmosphere a little eh Wolf Warrior?" I gave him a nod of agreement but my mouth was filled with some roast fish Prince Pasgen had brought. The priest nodded towards an animated Myrddyn who was having an animated conversation with Aelle and Raibeart. "The healer worked out well I hear?"

"Do not be coy Brother Osric. I know not how but you know every single event which happens within and without Rheged. As you well know he is more than just a healer. I just thank the gods that he was sent to me."

"You mean thank God and Jesus don't you?"

I saw the twinkle in his slightly inebriated eyes and I wagged an admonishing finger. "You know perfectly well that it was the spirit of my mother who appeared to him."

"A Christian might say the Virgin Mary."

"Then they would be wrong but there is something about him which is special. It is not just his skills at healing but he has the power to hide himself as he did when he spied for us and he knows what men are thinking. Well. What I think at any rate."

"There are scientific explanations for all of that but I think I agree with you; there is something about the young man and that heartens me as I fear we have dark days coming."

"The Saxons you mean?"

He waggled his head from side to side which made me smile. "Could be the Saxons but it could be our allies too. You never did find out who your spy was did you?"

"No but many of the suspects are dead and I could not fathom out what they were doing anyway."

"I have given the matter some thought. I think he or they were watching you and what you did. Perhaps they were trying to kill you. It would have been a mortal blow to the alliance had they succeeded."

"I think you exaggerate my importance."

"And I think that you underestimate yours."

"Besides I was rarely alone. I always had my men with me."

"Is the spy still there then?"

I stared at Brother Osric; he was becoming as intuitive about me as Myrddyn. "I believe that the spy has gone. Do not ask me why; although we found no further traces once spring came."

"I know not if it is a good thing or a bad thing but you need to keep your wits about you as we all do." He downed another of the goblets of rich red wine he adored and poured himself another. "I hear Morcant Bulc is telling the tale that it was he and his men who defeated Aella."

I laughed aloud and others turned to look at me. I held up my hand in apology. "There are enough men present at the battle who know the truth and every warrior knows how careful he is on a battlefield to be as far away from danger as possible."

"I have heard that he has monks on Metcauld who are writing a history for him of his success. In fifty years time that may be the only version people know."

"In fifty years I shall be dead and I will not care."

"But your son will not and could he bear the thought of his father's name being demeaned by such as Bulc?"

His words set me thinking and I wondered again about the intentions of the King of Bernicia. Perhaps I would get Brother Oswald to write a truthful version; I was not worried for myself but I could not bear to think of my son feeling shame on my account. I wanted him as proud of me as I was of his namesake, my father.

Raibeart sought me out later in the evening. We were two of the ones who had consumed less drink than the others. I found it amusing to watch those who had consumed huge quantities as they became more and more ridiculous in their movements and their words. Prince Ywain appeared to have one foot nailed to the floor as he staggered around on his other and Pasgen affected a high pitched giggling laugh. It seemed I was the only one to notice but it taught me to control my drink when in company. I could see that Raibeart was troubled by something. "Come brother, tell me what ails you?"

"It is King Gwalliog. I fear for his kingdom."

"It is in a better position now than before we helped him."

"But he is surrounded. There are many Angles in the south east of his land and I fear he will not withstand them."

"What would you do?"

He paused and I could almost hear Maiwen begging him to help her father. "I would." He hesitated and then looked at the floor in embarrassment. "I would go and serve him."

I knew what this was costing him; he would be breaking his oath to King Urien. I looked over at the king and remembered our conversation. I knew that he would not hold my brother to his oath but I did not want Raibeart to be in Elmet. I was the one who looked after him; he was my responsibility. "You will have to ask the king."

"I know." His eyes pleaded with me. "Would you ask him for me?"

"I would rather you were closer to Aelle and myself. You are right, Elmet is in danger but I know that if the Saxons came then King Urien would give King Gwalliog sanctuary."

He had a rueful smile on his face. "And you would seek sanctuary with another king if Rheged was overrun."

"Brother, that is exactly what we did when our family was killed." I could see that he was becoming agitated. "But I will do as you ask. Promise me one thing; if things go badly you will return here with your wife and her father. You will always have a home in Rheged."

The king was up early, as I was, the next day and he stood, as was his practice on the eastern wall peering towards the Saxons, many miles hence. I had done so at my castle. It was as though you expected them to suddenly lumber towards you in a gigantic shield wall. He turned as I approached, the two sentries nodding and moving to give us some privacy.

"Ah Lord Lann. It is a fine morning is it not?"

"It is your majesty. The winters are so long that it seems a shame not to make the most of each morning filled with sun as it is this day."

He had a contemplative expression on his face. "Aye, I am aware that my days are coming to an end and I would watch every sunrise and sunset."

I was taken aback. Was the king ill and had kept it hidden from us. "No, your majesty; you have many years to rule yet."

Shaking his head he said quietly, "My injuries have made me think of my mortality and the death of my sons... a man should not bury his children." He peered into my eyes. "Promise me that, when I am gone, you will do all you can for Ywain. He has changed but, somehow, when you are in his company he is the old Ywain. He must hold the kingdom together and he cannot do that without you." He paused and led me to the small tower at the end of the ramparts. "I would ask you to be warlord of Rheged."

This was a major decision. A warlord led a kingdom's armies. In Rheged it had always been the king. "Are you sure, your majesty? Prince Ywain is a fine leader."

"True but you are a great leader and men will follow you. Will you refuse me, Lord Lann?"

"No, your majesty, I swore an oath to you and I will never break that oath but will Prince Ywain be happy with the decision?"

He smiled, "It was his idea."

"Then I accept and now, your majesty I have a boon to ask of you."

"Whatever it is I will grant it for we owe you a great debt already."

I took a deep breath. "I will ask first your majesty and then you can reconsider your generosity. My brother Raibeart would leave your service and take his family to Elmet to aid King Gwalliog."

"So Osric was right."

"Brother Osric, your majesty?"

"Yes the priest said that he thought that Lord Raibeart would make the request. I am just disappointed that he did not approach me himself."

"Raibeart is shy your majesty and he has always looked to me. He meant no disrespect by it."

He put his hand on my arm. "I know and I am not offended. Brother Osric and I think it is a good idea. It will stiffen Gwalliog at the expense of one warrior. But we will need to put a stout man at his castle. Perhaps Lord Gildas; he looked after Rheged well while we fought Aella." Although my wish had been granted I felt as though Raibeart was being sacrificed. I knew that it was his idea but it still seemed as though he was just part of a grander plan. "We will make the announcements this morning. I believe it will let the king know of our intentions."

I managed to speak with Raibeart before the announcements and he had the grateful look of a child whose wishes have come true. Everyone seemed pleased with my appointment, everyone that is, except for Aideen who looked as though she had sucked on one of Brother Osric's precious lemons. I would have bridges to build when we returned home.

Raibeart and Maiwen left that morning, both eager to travel to Elmet whilst the weather was so clement. It was a sad parting for Aelle, Raibeart and myself. We were to be separated and who knew when we would meet again.

"If you need any help in Elmet, Raibeart, then you must promise to let me know."

Raibeart looked both sad and proud at the same time. "You are now warlord, brother, and your first duty will be to Rheged but do not fear I am taking twenty men with and we will soon train Elmet archers who are as good as Rheged's."

We took our farewells and I felt tears in my eyes; I had not felt such sadness since the Saxons took my parents. It felt like the end of all things. In many ways it was for, after that glorious summer nothing else was ever the same.

Chapter 16

As we rode home two days later I had much to think on. Aideen had understood that I could not refuse the king's offer but she felt that it put me in more danger. I had argued that it did not as I would be the one making the decisions about the battles and the wars and would not actually be fighting. She seemed mollified by that but I could see that it still rankled that I would not be at peace. I had also met with Prince Ywain. It was largely to clear the air between us for, although I believed the king I had to be sure that I not only had his support but also his heart. I was confident that he would be a good king. I made sure that I spoke with Aelle. With Raibeart gone and the threat to our borders coming from the south and east we needed to establish good communications. We revived the despatch riders which had largely fallen into abeyance since the spring war. We both believed that when the riders matured they became better warriors and we decided on seven each. That meant they could ride just once a week between our forts. Out of all the decisions I made I felt that this was the one in which I had the most confidence.

Finally I met with Brother Osric and Myrddyn. I could tell that the priest had also had a hand in the decision to make me warlord; he always appeared to be looking after my interests despite our religious differences. The two thinkers agreed on most things and they came up with a plan to improve the defences of both castles as well as finding the arms and weapons that we would need. Their differences of opinion were in what Osric called supernatural nonsense and Myrddyn called magic. I cared not. So long as Myrddyn's magic worked for me I would use it. The magic of Myrddyn proved to be the saviour of me and my family; I often wondered if Brother Osric regretted his scepticism, although knowing the old man as I did I doubted it.

I knew that, with midsummer over the days would soon shorten and we could not waste the precious time we had been given. All of us, Myrddyn, Oswald and Garth, threw ourselves into recruiting and training despatch riders, archers and warriors. In those days we were still rich with the bounty of the war and we used it wisely. Aideen was with child again and that always had a soothing and calming effect on her. She seemed happiest when she had a child within her. Myrddyn said one day, after he had caught the sharp end of Aideen's tongue that perhaps I should keep her perpetually pregnant!

Miach and Tuanthal proved themselves to be invaluable as they trained the archers and the horsemen leaving Garth and me to work with the warriors. The two had seen how men could die from poor training on the battlefield and both were determined that they would not fight with half trained men. All of my captains were happy now that I was warlord as it meant others would not make the rash decisions which they thought had cost men their lives.

By the time autumn had come we had thirty horsemen, fifty warriors and twenty archers. It was too large a force to be supported by such a small burgh but Osric provided extra money, armour and weapons. Myrddyn told me that he saw me as the gate to Rheged and he would make it as strong as possible. My wounds, from the previous year, and Garth's from the recent one had healed up completely but we both had the look of battle scarred veterans. The men found it reassuring that warriors could suffer such horrendous wounds and not only survive but become better warriors.

One autumn evening, when we had lit our first fire of the year in the solar, I sat with Oswald, Garth and Myrddyn. We enjoyed this pleasure two or three times a week. Sometimes we talked of important things but at others we just told stories and remembered the dead, as warriors do. Brother Oswald had just told a ribald story about one of the village girls and an old me and we sat in companionable silence. There had been an itch I wanted to scratch but I had been unable to. "Garth, who do you think our spy was?"

He shrugged. "I have thought of that many times my lord but I cannot honestly say that I have any idea. I still cannot believe that one of the men who fought so hard beneath our banner could be an enemy and certainly not a Saxon lover."

"That is my opinion too."

Brother Oswald drank a little of the mead he had made with his precious honey. "I think, my lord, that some men are more devious than others and can hide their feelings and their intentions well."

"Myrddyn?"

"I think I know who it was, is."

We all stared at the young man who had a propensity for making statements which made your jaw drop. "Well do not keep us in suspense. Who?"

"It was quite obvious who it was when the spy stopped meeting in the woods. You remember, my lord, that we talked, last winter, each week about the spy and suddenly there were no more signs. I had worked out that the spy was not spying for the Saxons but for someone else. All of the trails which led to their meeting place came from the north or the west."

I suddenly realised he was right and I had missed that important fact. "If not the Saxons, then who?"

"It occurred to me that one of our allies or someone who fought for Rheged might have an ulterior motive. I just didn't and still don't know what. I deduced then that there were three possibilities: the spy had stopped his spying, he had died or he had left. The first I dismissed as nothing had changed here or in Rheged to make one of our allies stop requesting information. No one died during that time which left one possibility. Someone had left."

"Llofan Llaf Difo."

It was Myrddyn's turn to look at Brother Oswald in amazement. You are right but …"

He waved a dismissive hand, "I keep the records and he was the only name I had to scratch out in red." He saw my curious look and added, "Black is for those who have died and red for those who leave us. His is the only name with a red line through it. Each time I write in a new name the red line jumps out at me."

It was my turn to make the connections. "Which means it was Bladud who sent him here."

"That was my assumption too, especially as he rejoined Bladud and the king's men. Perhaps Bladud had him here to kill you or hurt your family."

The thought made me shudder. "But we have no proof."

Garth's voice was tight with anger. "No my lord but there is much evidence. Remember how the two of them and two others held back at the battle. The king nearly died."

"My lord, you should tell the king."

I shook my head. "No Oswald for he would not believe me. All of this evidence is like Myrddyn's magic; it is hard to see clearly."

Myrddyn smiled and gave a slight nod of his head. "And I believe I know their paymaster."

In my heart I knew the answer before he uttered it but I did not want to hear it for it was like the knell of doom on the last of the Britons. "Who?"

"King Morcant Bulc. Llofan came from Bernicia and we know that Bladud and their king are close. You are the danger to him; you and King Urien."

"That is what I feared. But now that we know we will watch them all much more closely. Perhaps now that I am warlord we can keep a better eye on Bladud and our spy."

In my arrogance I believed that I was the one who could control events but, as Myrddyn pointed out some time later, there were higher forces than we who were manipulating our lives. *Wyrd* was the thing which meant I could never believe in the White Christ for *wyrd* was unpredictable and even the gods could not make it bend to their will. But I was puissant and I had never been bested, I thought it would remain that way forever. What did not change was my attitude towards Bladud and Llofan; I now knew, even without hard evidence, that they were working, certainly against me and probably against Rheged.

When autumn came we received the bad news from Elmet that the Saxons were pressing their borders. Raibeart did not ask for help and I could detect, from his messages, that he had stiffened the defences and the Saxons would not find Elmet an easy nut to crack. King Gwalliog had made a series of forts and fortifications which circled his stronghold and he used his horse warriors to keep the Saxons at bay. With winter approaching then they would be safe but I hoped that they would use the cold times well for the Saxons would return in the spring.

The message spurred me to accompany Tuanthal on his patrols. We had learned our lessons and we varied our route in case any scouts were watching. I could not confide in Miach and Tuanthal that I suspected Bladud but I managed to watch the land to the north and west as well. We rode without armour but with javelins and shields. We had tried to use bows from the backs of horses but it was unsuccessful; the bow was too big. Brother Oswald's research mentioned horse warriors from the east, Parthians who destroyed thousands of Romans with their bows but they were shorter and their design unknown to us. My men could, however throw a javelin and we all carried three with the last used to strike at men who cowered on the ground. We saw no Saxons but there were bandits and brigands who preyed on the isolated farms and farmsteads. When we found them we left their heads on poles at crossroads to warn others the penalty for robbery in Rheged. Gradually they moved elsewhere, I suspect to Bernicia where King Morcant Bulc still squatted, like the over grown toad he was becoming, in Din Guardi. Already the Saxons were encroaching back towards the Dunum and much of our hard fought gains were lost. We patrolled as far as the Roman Bridge and then south towards Elmet. King Gwalliog had a fort at the old Roman town of

Cataractonium. Sometimes we met Elmet warriors close to the old hill fort where my family died. The Saxons did not come near us.

We were supposed to visit the king for Yule again but the weather intervened. After the bone fires the snows came early and the ground was frozen solid. Normally it meant that it would thaw and brighten but this was the year of the wolves and it did not. The snow grew deeper and we were almost besieged in our castle by snow. We took to patrolling closer to home, just to make sure that the villagers and farmers did not suffer. There were plenty of forests and wood aplenty but food was scarce. Brother Oswald's goat and sheep cheeses became valuable sources of food and my men hunted whenever possible.

We called it the wolf winter for the wolves returned. I had not seen them in large numbers since my parent's deaths but I still recalled the death of the young family. My men took the opportunity of wolf hunting for they all wanted a wolf cloak such as I wore and Garth. They knew that any man could wear one as long as he had killed the wolf himself. It was a week before Yule and I joined the ten warriors who had been selected to hunt the wolf. We took a variety of men each day, some archers, some warriors and some horsemen. It helped the men to feel part of my army. We also took a slinger or a despatch rider to teach them the skills of scouting which they would need.

As the men checked their equipment I turned to Brother Oswald. "Who is the young boy? Is he a despatch rider? He looks familiar."

The priest looked sad, "That is because he is Aedh, the younger brother of Adair."

Now it made sense. I could see the brave dead despatch rider in his hair and his eyes. I knew he had had a brother but thought he was too young to fight. Then I remembered Aelle and Raibeart fighting when they were even younger. No-one had a long childhood but I would watch Aedh; his family had sacrificed enough for me already.

One of the archers led us out. The wolves hunted at night normally but the snow meant that they had become bold. They still liked to have a lair in the rocks which they could use for shelter. We headed towards the east and the rocky crags above the deep forests. If we found their lair we might kill any cubs and females whilst still enabling us to track them through the snow. I walked in the middle and Aedh was in front of me; it was not an accident. A couple of miles from the castle we came upon tracks. They were not fresh but they led to the south and a tumble of rocks known locally as Fainch's Den from some ancient witch who had lived there before the Romans. I did not need to give a command for the men knew what to do and they formed a thin line. I was on the extreme left.

As we neared the rocks the musky, pungent smell of animal and death drifted towards us on the wind. We had, through good fortune, approached upwind. Most of us had bows which we now strung but two of the horsemen had their javelins with which they were more familiar. The closer we came to the den the slower we went. There were five paces between each man to enable us freedom of movement in case they attacked.

At thirty paces from the rocks we halted and two of the more experienced archers slithered forwards on their bellies. They went to the left and the right, seeking slightly higher ground where they could look down into the tumbled rocks. When they were in position they waved and we moved forwards. The two archers lay down on the rocks so as not to give themselves away. We were ten paces from the rocks and the two archers were rising when disaster struck. One of the warriors slipped on the snow and his bow fell with a crash to the rocks at his feet. In an instant there were blurs of fur as the six wolves, which had been sheltering in the rocks, leapt over the tops at us. Brave Aedh did not run but aimed his bow at the nearest wolf and released. The arrow glanced off the thick fur and the wolf turned to attack the threat. I pulled back and aimed for the head; if I struck anywhere else then the boy would be dead for even a wounded wolf can rip a throat out in a heartbeat. It had to be an instant kill. Nodens was with me for the arrow went through his head, the force taking him away from the shocked Aedh. I closed my eyes to say a silent prayer of thanks for my aim. It had been close. As I scanned the rest of my men I saw that only one wolf had escaped whilst one had sunk its teeth into the arm of one of the archers. It was a wound which would take some healing.

Aedh turned to me, his face drained of blood, "My lord, I owe you my life. I thought he had had me."

I smiled and ruffled his hair. "Next time aim for the chest. If he moves left or right you still have him. You did well Aedh, brother of Adair."

His eyes opened even wider. The warlord knew his name. "I will do better next time."

"I know you will. Remember keep practising until; you feel you cannot practise anymore and then do another hour!"

The men had put the dead animals onto their javelins and carried them between them. I looked at the dead wolf. "Come then Aedh or would you have your lord carry our kill by himself?"

He grinned and grabbed a javelin. I smiled as he struggled to push it through its mouth. I shook my head. "Up its arse. I can open its mouth and make it easier for you to get it out." Understanding flooded his face and soon we had it between us. There was a height disparity which meant that I had the heaviest load to carry but I did not mind. It had been a good day. The meat would feed many farmers and villagers and, more importantly, there were fewer wolves to prey on my people.

As we entered the gate we were cheered by the guards and I saw Aedh swell with pride. Pol was waiting anxiously. He had wanted to join us but I was strict; only one young warrior was allowed with each patrol. As Aedh had discovered, hunting the wolf was a dangerous occupation. The young rider turned to me. "Can I help you prepare your wolf skin my lord?"

I affected a serious look. "Do you think the one I wear is threadbare and needs replacing?"

He looked confused. "No my lord I …"

I relented and smiled, noting the annoyance on Pol's face. "I was just teasing you Aedh. I need not the skin and you were brave not to run. You may have the skin but you cannot wear it until you become a warrior."

The delight on his face was like a breath of sunshine on this cold day. As he ran off to get a skinning knife Pol said, somewhat peevishly, "That is not fair my lord. I should have been the one to kill the wolf."

"Fear not Pol, your day will come. Let Aedh have his day." My face became serious. "Adair was his brother and this may go some way to making up for the loss."

Understanding flooded my squire's face. "I am sorry my lord. I should have known that you would be making a wise decision. Please forgive me."

"There is nothing to forgive; now take my weapons. I shall be with Lady Aideen."

The snow lasted for many weeks and, despite all our efforts many people died. The fact that they were the old, the young and the sick made it harder for the warriors to take. Famine was an enemy it was hard to defeat. The men who survived were angry and frustrated that, in spite of their efforts against the Saxons to protect their families, they had still suffered. Brother Oswald was saddened because many of the followers of the White Christ reverted to the old pagan ways arguing that this benevolent god had done little to help them in their time of need. The messages from Aelle were also disturbing; like us he had suffered deaths but his mighty defence, the Wide Water, had frozen over. Had there been Saxons around they could easily have taken his stronghold. He would have to strengthen in the summer for who knew if we might suffer another winter as bad.

As soon as it thawed and the roads became usable I took Pol and half a dozen men and rode to Civitas Carvetiorum to consult with the king. He looked as grey as the land when I saw him. "It has been a hard winter for our people Lann. Many have died."

"And with me also."

"Ywain's son was taken. He is deeply saddened for he is now without children." I could not conceive of a pain as deep as that suffered by my friend. If I lost Hogan I would not want to live. I would have to find the time to speak with him. He was a deep thinker and I knew that he would brood on the death. He gave me a wan smile. "But I suspect that you too have had your problems eh?"

As he walked with me to his hall I told him of Aelle's problems, the reversion to paganism and the wolf hunt. "But our losses were neither as severe nor as personal as yours your majesty."

"Still it is strange that the wolf plays such a large part in your life. I can see why your warriors feel that there is something mystical and magical about you, your sword and your healer." He gave me a curious look. "They say that your Myrddyn is a wizard or a witch and can make himself disappear."

I laughed. "Men talk your majesty. He is clever and resourceful and he does use the old ways but I have yet to see him disappear." As we sat before the roaring fire I asked him of news from beyond our borders.

"You know of Elmet's woes but your brother is preventing any losses. However it is the Bernicians who perplex and confound me. Why they did not fortify the high ground south of the Dunum I have no idea. They would have been able to deny the Saxons the use of that river; as it is they now defend north of there and that puts us in danger."

"We patrol as far as the Roman Bridge but there are many miles twixt there and my castle. The Saxons could capture that land if they chose and it would not take much effort."

"I know but I feel that they will see Bulc as the weak link and will strike there first." I stopped with the beaker of warmed ale half way to my lips. The king gave me an apologetic look. "I know that does not sound like me but we have gone to the Bernicians aid on three occasions and they still do not take responsibility for their own defence. I fear that they are a lost cause. I also fear that the winter deaths have taken many who might have swelled the ranks of our warriors in future years, this may be a bigger disaster than losing a battle."

When I returned home I was even more worried than when I had left. We felt like an island surrounded by enemies from another country who did not want our way of life and wanted to replace it with their own. This would be a fight to the death and only one culture would survive. Unless we could end this strife then the land would be devoid of the people who had lived here since before the Romans.

When the weather became better I doubled our patrols. I asked Aelle to patrol to the east and I used Garth, Tuanthal and myself to send out patrols every day. It meant that we only had one day in three to rest but I wanted advance notice of the enemy. If they were to return, then now would be the time. We kept the same men with us. I was able to leave Ridwyn in charge of the castle during our absence as he had proved himself to be a valiant and reliable warrior. Besides which Miach and his archers provided a solid force of sentries to protect our families, all of whom now lived within the castle and its periphery. I took Aedh as my scout and kept Pol with me.

It was Garth who found the first signs of the Saxons. It was in the area north west of Aelfere. Now that Elmet was besieged the horsemen of Gwalliog could not control their borders and as the Bernicians had abandoned the land south of the Dunum it was a perfect place for the Saxons to infiltrate.

I told Tuanthal to head for the Roman Bridge and explore the Dunum estuary while I took my men to Aelfere. It was a long ride and the men would be tired when we returned but, if Garth had seen signs to the north then it seemed logical that they had reinvested the village we had secured. The tops of the moors were cold but the majority of my men had wolf cloaks. I felt sorry for Aedh and Pol who shivered. Aedh was obviously thinking that he had a wolf cloak of his own but he could not yet wear it. It was a clear day and when we reached the eastern side of the divide we could see tendrils of smoke which spoke of inhabited settlements. I hoped that they were our people but I feared that they were not.

My brothers and I had visited Aelfere when we had fled Stanwyck and I could remember that it was on a low ridge. We would have to be circumspect when we approached. Aedh had proved himself to be a clever scout and, when we saw the stockade which surrounded the town he slipped from his pony and scampered off through the brush and thin woods which surrounded it. I ordered the men to feed themselves and their horses whilst Pol and I kept watch. I had learned that you ate when you could. Aedh was away some time and Pol and I had managed to eat some dried meat and feed some grain to our mounts.

He was breathless and his clothes were torn. I wondered had he been seen but his enthusiastic grin told me that he had not. "Well Aedh?" I gestured at his clothes.

"It was a bramble bush my lord but it enabled me to hide close to their gate. They are Saxons." I did not need to know how he knew that for we all could recognise the guttural sounds which made up the Saxon language. "There were a few armed men but not an army."

"Well done Aedh. Get some food." They were settling. This would not worry me yet but it meant that they had returned. Tuanthal's report would tell me if we had a problem or not.

We reached Castle Perilous before Tuanthal and after dark. The men were exhausted. Garth would have to take the longer patrol the next day for my men and Tuanthal's need recovery time. When my Captain of horse returned it was with more bad news. There were Saxon ships in the Dunum. Not an army but enough to make me worry. "But my lord the worse news is that they have begun rebuilding the old fort at the mouth of the Dunum. They control the river."

The fact that we had no ships was immaterial but if they were making a stronghold then they had learned their lesson. This time they would have a refuge in case they had to retreat and I knew the site he had mentioned. It was almost as good as Din Guardi and Stanwyck. To take it would bleed an army dry. "You have done well. At least we now know the problem, even if we can do nothing about it."

That evening Myrddyn and Oswald joined me in the solar. "I could infiltrate their camp again my lord. Aella is dead."

"No Myrddyn. It is a brave offer but there may be someone left who would recognise you and we would gain nothing from it. We know where they are. This time we will not oppose them if they choose to cross the Dunum, that is up to King Morcant Bulc. We will stop them if they come west." I pointed at the defences. "Thanks to the cleverness of the priest and the magician we have a castle which will halt them."

They both nodded at my praise and then Brother Oswald coughed and said, "My lord, if I might suggest?" I waved my hand for him to continue. "If we had beacons on the high places then, when the Saxons come we could light them and the people could take refuge here."

"It would be a little cramped I feel."

"The land to the west will be safe. We could build huts there and then the ones not fighting would be safe."

I suddenly realised that what he said made perfect sense. I did not want Aideen and the other women subject to accidental death because they were close to the fighting. "Good idea. Begin building tomorrow." The huts were wattle and daub. My men could erect twenty in a week.

"We could also build a wooden wall between the huts and our eastern wall. If we fell it would give them time to escape."

Myrddyn's words brought a chill to my heart. Even the optimistic young man thought we might lose. "You think they will win Myrddyn?"

"They may but I have learned that it is as well to make plans for all eventualities."

I was intrigued. "What plan then if they do defeat us?"

Brother Oswald leaned forward, equally interested as Myrddyn took the jug of wine and the three goblets we had used. "The jug is Rheged." He placed one to the west, one to the north, quite close to the jug, and one a little further away to the south west. "If Rheged fell then we could go north to King Rhydderch Hael's kingdom." He pointed to the goblet to the north. Or we could flee to Hibernia." He held up Brother Oswald's goblet which was to the west. "Or," and here he held his own goblet which was the one furthest from the jug, "we could go to my home in the mountains of Wales."

"You may drink your wine brother Oswald I think that the Hibernians would be as the Saxons are."

"Thank you my lord and I agree."

"North is attractive but if Morcant Bulc's land also fell then it would be surrounded." I picked up my goblet and drank it off. "Which leaves your goblet. Explain how that would help us."

"Your brother holds the gateway to the south. He could join us or delay the enemy." I felt a cold sensation rundown my spine. I could not fault Myrddyn's logic but it seemed callous to allow my young brother to sacrifice himself for us. "The land between Wide Water and Wales is flat and we could make good time using horses. The land has few people and, if we avoided the coast then we would be safe from the slavers. The mountains are easily defended and we would be safe once we reached there."

I pondered his ideas and there was silence. "We would need to build wagons and make sure we had enough horses capable of pulling the wagons." I looked up as Oswald spoke. He was already making plans.

"And we would need to send a small party to scout out a site which was suitable."

Both of them seemed set on the idea. "I have not decided yet and we have not lost. Why make the plans?"

"Because, my lord, as I found when the Hibernians came and you found at Stanwyck, when disaster strikes you have no time to rescue those who are not warriors. Would you have the women and children enslaved or killed?"

He was right and that was the day we began to plan for defeat.

Chapter 17

As spring grew towards summer we increased our patrols and I urged the others to be more aggressive. We no longer hid and we rode up to their settlements martially dressed and with aggression. I wanted the Saxons to know that they would not catch us unawares. As they had few, if any horsemen, we were safe enough and my men were wary and careful enough to avoid ambushes. The ploy worked and the Saxons did not come any further west. On the other hand it allowed them to focus their attention on Elmet and Bernicia. Raibeart's new defences threw them back and his well trained archers discouraged their attentions. So it was that their king, Aethelric, launched an attack north of the Dunum and the forces sent by King Morcant Bulc were soundly beaten. We heard this second hand from some of the survivors who escaped towards and beyond Roman Bridge.

Garth brought two of the badly injured warriors to Castle Perilous where Myrddyn healed them. After they had recovered enough they told us of the battle. It seems that King Morcant Bulc had sent Riderch with a thousand men to oppose the Saxons. The numbers were insufficient as the Saxons fielded twice that number and he had sent neither archers nor horsemen to support them. Despite Riderch's leadership and the bravery of the Bernician warriors they had been routed although the wounded men assured us that my friend still led them as they left the field.

"So Myrddyn, it seems the Bernician king has not learned his lesson yet. He still tries to hide behind his walls."

"I think, my lord, that he thought that Rheged would come to his aid again and turn the tide. From what I have seen of the man he wants the glory without the risk. The Saxons do not fear him and they have his measure. Even if he did lead the men on the battlefield it would not deter the Saxons."

"And what do you know of this Aethelric?"

"He was the leader of a warband and he was close to Aella. He seemed to be very sure of himself and he did survive the slaughter on the Dunum so we can assume he has cunning."

I turned to Oswald. "I think we will be going to war sooner rather than later. Make sure we have a healthy supply of arrows and javelins and all of the men have armour."

"What of the farmers? Do you wish them called to arms?"

"No Oswald, just my oath sworn. I do not want my people to die for the Bernicians."

We were surprised a month later, a month in which little had been seen or heard of the Saxons, when King Urien, Prince Ywain and their bodyguards arrived at Castle Perilous. The king did not enter but beckoned me over. "King Morcant Bulc has asked to meet with us close to Dunelm."

"What for? Does he wish our help?"

"He did not say. He just asked that I bring my son and you."

"I like this not, your majesty. The Saxons are north of the Dunum now. If they found you without your army it could go ill for you."

He smiled, "My Wolf Warrior, you truly do have a warrior's mind. I know what you fear which is why I only bring my bodyguards and Ywain's for they are mounted. "

"Then I will join you." I turned to my captains, Brother Oswald and Myrddyn." "Tuanthal, Garth mount the horsemen we follow the king. Miach, mount twenty archers. Myrddyn you are coming. Ridwyn and Brother Oswald take charge. Pol bring my sword, bow and armour." One or two looked as though they might argue but one look at my face sent them scurrying to obey.

My wife, of course, had no such dilemma. "My husband do you go to war again?" Her voice was harsh and her eyes flickered annoyance between me and the king.

King Urien answered for me. "No, my Lady Aideen; he goes with me to meet with the King of Bernicia. There will be neither war nor deaths; we go for a meeting only."

The king's noted honesty made her sigh with relief. "I am sorry your majesty, my husband, but I do not want war again."

"And neither do I." The king's voice was filled not only with sincerity but a power which had been missing for some time. The old king was back.

As we tagged along as a rearguard I noticed that Myrddyn was also armed. It was not like him. "Do you know something I do not?"

"No my lord, but like you I am suspicious. Especially as the four men behind the king are Bladud, Llofan and their two evil faced companions. As we are meeting the man we believe is behind the deceit last year I thought it best to be prepared." I smiled. I had felt foolish voicing my fears before the king but now I felt justified.

We reach Dunelm just before dusk and we could see that the people there had already repaired the damage suffered the previous year but of Morcant Bulc there was no sign. The king did not seem to have noticed the slight. "Make camp here. Perhaps we are early."

It was after dark when we heard the sound of a horse galloping along the Roman Road. We stood to until we recognised that it was a Bernician rider. "Your majesty. King Morcant Bulc requests that you meet him, further north at the old Roman fort of Vinovia."

The rider was a young warrior I remembered from our last campaign. He was an affable young man and a brave warrior. "Now?" The king's voice displayed his disbelief and I saw the embarrassment on the warrior's face. "We would be travelling through dangerous lands after dark."

"I will tell my king that you will meet him tomorrow." The young man kicked his horse and they galloped off towards the distant fort.

"I do not like that your majesty; it was at best discourteous and at worst dangerous. We could be riding into a trap."

"I think you are right Lord Lann. We will keep our wits about us tomorrow and we will make sure we are prepared for all eventualities."

We rode north the following morning; I do not know about the others but I wondered at this strange turn of events. We were now in Bernicia; it struck me that we could have stayed at Dunelm and awaited their king there and I worried that we might be heading into an ambush of some type but, for the life of me, I could not work out the reason. "Myrddyn, do not take your eyes off Bladud and the others."

"That will be easy to do if not very pleasant." Garth and I smiled for Bladud was large and distinctive but as he rarely smiled his ugly features did not warrant close scrutiny.

We saw the old fort loom up in the distance and we could all see that the Bernicians had repaired it and re-hung the gate. King Morcant Bulc and his twenty bodyguards awaited us at a table erected beneath a canopy in front of the fort. I relaxed a little. It would not be a trap after all. We could see all around the fort and there was no sign of Saxons.

King Urien and Ywain reined in close to a wood which would afford shade for the horses and the equites. I saw the two men walk towards King Morcant Bulc followed by six of the king's bodyguards. "Tuanthal, Garth, come with me and Myrddyn. Tell the men to be alert." I looked at Pol. "You come too and bring my bow." I did not know why I wanted my bow but something smelled wrong and I needed to be prepared. "Stay close to me. Understand?"

"Yes, my lord." He looked determined and I was happy to be followed by four such loyal warriors.

King Morcant Bulc had a self satisfied and smug expression on his face as we approached. There was a chair opposite him, presumably for King Urien but the Bernician made no effort to show respect to the man who had been elected the High King and he remained seated. Ywain threw me a look which showed that he was as confused as I was. The Bernician bodyguards formed a half circle behind their king and I saw that there was no Riderch; obviously he was still out of favour.

King Urien frowned as he sat down. "I am confused, King Morcant Bulc. Why did you feel it necessary to meet with me and why here and why," he spread his arms at the empty space, "why the formality?"

Morcant Bulc gave a silky smile which I did not trust for an instant and my hand went involuntarily to Saxon Slayer. I watched the Bernician bodyguards but they made no movement and seemed amused by the events.

"As you may have heard King Urien my army suffered a defeat at the hands of the Saxons. I had thought that, as High King, you would have come to my aid."

The three of us looked at each other. I was about to speak but the king held up his hand. "Forgive me, King Morcant Bulc but may I ask why you did not defend your own land. It seems to me that you could have prevented the Saxons from establishing a base on the Dunum."

He affected a shocked look, "Oh, so it is my fault then? I should have fought the Saxons alone."

"It would have been a first at any rate."

King Urien threw me an irritated look and held up his hand to silence me but Morcant Bulc stared coldly at me. "Ah the famous Wolf Warrior; still hunting glory are you?" If he thought to annoy me he had failed. I was cold inside. But I could not work out what his intentions were. He leaned forward and glared at King Urien. "You are not fit to be High King. The High King would protect the whole of the land and not just his own." Again, there was no answer to this nonsense and I wondered how long the king would suffer the abuse he was being dealt. He leaned back and smiled. "I have decided that I will be High King now."

I could not help myself and I laughed out loud. Ywain and Urien still looked confused. King Urien shook his head. "I did not ask to be High King. That position was forced upon me by the other kings but I will serve as High King until they decide otherwise." He shook his head. "Men have told me of your weaknesses King Morcant Bulc and I did not believe them." He looked at me and gave me an apologetic nod. I was gratified by the look of hatred which erupted on the Bernician's face. "However, I have my own kingdom to rule. This journey was a waste and I am saddened by your attitude. Had you given the same attention to the defence of your own land rather than this hunt for glory then perhaps your kingdom would be more secure. I will return home."

He started to rise and I saw the look of unmitigated exultation on Morcant Bulc's face. I heard Myrddyn yell, "Treachery!" And I saw the sword in Llofan Llaf Difo's hand stab down into King Urien's back.

Suddenly the Bernician bodyguards formed a shield wall around their gleeful king. Things happened really quickly. I saw Myrddyn dive to the king's side. Bladud turned to strike his sword at a shocked Prince Ywain and the other four bodyguards rushed at me and my men.

"Pol, get the men!" My squire dropped my bow and quiver and ran shouting for aid.

I had Saxon Slayer out in an instant and the first bodyguard lost his head before he could even make a stroke. I ducked under Llofan's blade and stabbed at Bladud, more in hope than expectation. I was lucky or perhaps it was wyrd but Saxon Slayer caught him behind his knee and his blow failed to strike the prince. He turned angrily towards me and swung his sword at my head. I had no shield and I just dropped to one knee. As I did so I stabbed forwards. His sword swung harmlessly over my head and Saxon Slayer slid along the rings of his mail ripping open the rings and coming away red.

Bladud did not seem worried and he snarled at me. "There will be no one to save you this time."

"I never needed help against you. You were always overrated and now I find that you are a treacherous traitor. You will die slowly." As we turned to face each other I caught sight of Garth about to despatch Llofan. "I want the killer alive Garth!"

Bladud took advantage of my inattention and swung his sword at my side. I wore my mail gauntlets and I grabbed hold of the blade. It was not as sharp as mine but I felt the blood as it sliced into my palm. I was too close for a blow and so I head butted him. I heard his nose break as blood erupted like water from a waterfall. I stepped back. He now had three wounds and I knew that I would win for the blood loss would weaken him. As we turned around each other I saw that my men had despatched the killers and Garth held his sword at Llofan's neck. The rest of my men stood between the Bernicians and their dying king. I could now concentrate on the traitor I was about to kill.

Bladud did not look so confident and I caught him flick a glance in the direction of Morcant Bulc. It confirmed my suspicions. I met Bladud's next blow with Saxon Slayer and I saw chips of metal fly from his blade. He saw it too and knew that mine was the superior weapon. My left hand was wet with the blood from my wound and I held it behind me. As Bladud swung again I pirouetted around so that he struck fresh air and Saxon Slayer hacked through the mail protecting his back. I heard the crack as bones were broken and saw blood once again. This time he gave a scream of pain and when he faced me, for the first time he looked afraid. "It will not be swift, believe me Bladud. You are going to pay for your treachery!" He was moving slowly now and when his next clumsy attempt at a blow slid harmlessly off my sword I hacked at the leg I had not stuck. It sliced through the muscle and the bone and he collapsed in a heap, his weapon falling harmlessly from his hand.

I stood over him. "Who paid you for this?"

I heard Morcant Bulc shout, "Kill the murderer!" I did not know if he meant me or Bladud but I shouted, "Pol! My bow!"

The bow was in my hand almost instantly and I notched an arrow and aimed it at King Morcant Bulc. "If any of your men move a muscle then you will die." I grinned; it was not a happy grin but the grin of a wolf about to devour his prey. "And you know I never miss!"

"You would threaten a king?" His voice sounded shocked.

I laughed a cold heartless laugh which echoed above the stunned silence of the moment. "No, I would kill a king and a piss poor one at that." I did not look down but said, "Tell me who paid you Bladud and I will end your life swiftly otherwise you will die slowly."

He spat blood at me. "Fuck you!"

I could see that he would not speak and I went over to Llofan. "You have the same choice traitor."

His words sounded strong but there was no conviction. "Do your worst."

Still aiming my arrow at Morcant Bulc I said. "Garth, take down his breeks and castrate him. Let us see how he faces the next world without balls."

"No, please, you wouldn't!"

"Garth!"

Garth and Tuanthal pulled down his breeks and Garth grabbed his knife. "It was King Morcant Bulc. He paid us to kill the king."

I drew the arrow back further and saw the terror in the Bernician's face. I was a heartbeat from releasing when Myrddyn shouted, "The king says there must be no more blood. He commands you to let him live."

I saw that Myrddyn did not agree with the order but I was oathsworn. "Leave now Bernician but this is not over. Watch for me in the night. There will come a reckoning for this!" The cowardly king ran as fast as he could with his bodyguards retreating slowly. "Garth, find out all you can about the plot."

"And then?"

"End it!"

I dropped my bow and taking my sword I cut Bladud's hamstrings. I peered into his eyes. "You will lie here and die and I will watch you die and then we will strip your body, remove your dick and your heart and leave your body for the birds, the rats and the vermin."

I saw terror in his eyes. "Kill me now. Let me die like a warrior."

I laughed. "You were never a warrior and you can now think of what you could have done as your life seeps into the ground." I turned and dropped to King Urien's side. Myrddyn gave me a slight shake of the head, but I could see from the blood that it was a mortal wound. The king gave me a weak smile. "We must not do the Saxon's work for them. Lann, watch over my son and my kingdom and..." and then the last great king of Britain died, cradled in his weeping son's arms. It was the end of any hope we had of defeating the Saxons and all of Morcant Bulc's treachery brought him naught.

Prince Ywain looked as though it was he who had been wounded and not his father. He was covered in blood. Myrddyn took off my gauntlet and began to dress the wound which

I had forgotten. I heard the sound of Llofan's throat being cut and then Garth stood next to me. "He confirmed what we thought my lord. It was he who met with Bladud in the woods. They had planned on killing you but the opportunity never arose."

It was cold comfort to know that we had been right but at least we had Myrddyn's warning which had saved the prince. "Let us take the king home to his queen. The king is dead. Long live King Ywain."

It was a solemn and yet angry band of warriors who escorted the dead King Urien back to Civitas Carvetiorum. We all knew, at that moment that the Saxons had won. What irked and galled the most was that they had won through a king of Britain. King Morcant Bulc would pay for his treachery just as the poor land that had been Roman Britannia would pay for his perfidy as they succumbed to waves of Saxons who would claim the land for their own.

The End

Glossary

Characters in italics are fictional

Name-Explanation

Adair-Despatch rider and scout

Aedh-Despatch rider and scout, Adair's brother

Aelfere-Northallerton

Aella-King of Deira

Aelle-Monca's son and Lann's step brother

Aethelric-King of Deira (The land to the south of the Tees)

Aidan-Priest from Metcauld

Alavna-Maryport

Ambrosius-Headman at Brocavum

Artorius-King Arthur

Banna-Birdoswald

Belatu-Cadros-God of war

Bladud-Urien's standard bearer

Blatobulgium-Birrens (Scotland)

Brocavum -Brougham

Civitas Carvetiorum-Carlisle

Cynfarch Oer-Descendant of Coel Hen (King Cole)

Din Guardi-Bamburgh Castle

Dunum-River Tees

Dux Britannica-The Roman British leader after the Romans left (King Arthur)

Erecura-Goddess of the earth

Fanum Cocidii-Bewcastle

Freja-Saxon captive

Garth-Lann's lieutenant

Gildas-Urien's nephew

Glanibanta-Ambleside

Hen Ogledd-Northern England and Southern Scotland

Hogan-Father of Lann and Raibeart

Icaunus-River god

King Gwalliog-King of Elmet

Lann-A young Brythonic warrior (Lann means sword in Celtic)

Llofan Llaf Difo-Bernician warrior

Loidis-Leeds

Maiwen-The daughter of the King of Elmet

Metcauld-Lindisfarne

Miach-Leader of Lann's archers

Monca-An escaped Briton and mother of Aelle

Morcant Bulc-King of Bryneich (Northumberland)

Myrddyn-Welsh warrior fighting for Rheged
Niamh-Queen of Rheged
Nodens-God of hunting
Osric-Irish priest
Oswald-Priest at Castle Perilous
Pasgen-Youngest son of Urien
Pol-Slinger and Lann's squire
Radha-Mother of Lann and Raibeart
Raibeart-Lann's brother
Rhiwallon-Son of Urien
Rhun-Son of Urien
Rhydderch Hael-The king of Strathclyde
Ridwyn-Bernician warrior fighting for Rheged
Roman Bridge-Piercebridge (Durham)
Sucellos-God of love and time
Tuanthal-Leader of Lann's horse warriors
Urien Rheged-King of Rheged
Vindonnus-God of hunting
Wachanglen-Wakefield
wapentake-Muster of an army
Wide Water-Windermere
Wyrd-Fate
Ywain Rheged-Eldest son of Urien
-

Historical note

All the kings named and used in this book were real figures, although the actual events are less well documented. Most of the information comes from the Welsh writers who were used to create the Arthurian legends. It was of course, *The Dark Ages*, and, although historians now dispute this, the lack of hard evidence is a boon to a writer of fiction. Ida, who was either a lord or a king, was ousted from Lindisfarne by the alliance of the three kings. King Urien was deemed to be the greatest Brythionic king of this period.

While researching I discovered that 30-35 was considered old age in this period. The kings obviously lived longer but that meant that a fifteen year old would be considered a fighting man. If the brothers appear young then I suspect it is because most of the armies would have been made up of the younger men without ties.

The Angles and the Saxons did invade towards the end of the Roman occupation and afterwards. There appear to be a number of reasons for this: firstly the sea levels rose in their land inundating it and secondly there were a series of plagues in Central Europe. This caused a mass movement towards the rich and peaceful lands of Britannia. Their invasion was also prefaced by the last Roman leaders using Saxon mercenaries to fight the barbarians to the north and the west. At the same time Irish and the Scots took advantage of the departure of the Romans and engaged in slave raids and cattle raids. It was not a good time to live in the borders. Carlisle, by all accounts, was a rich fortress and had baths and fine buildings. It exceeded York at this period. Rheged stretched all the way from Strathclyde down to what is now northern Lancashire. Northumbria did not exist but it grew from two British kingdoms which became Saxon, Bernicia and Deira and eventually became the most powerful kingdom until the rise of Alfred's Wessex. Who knows what might have happened had Rheged survived?

Morcant Bulc was king of Bernicia and he was jealous of King Urien who was considered the last hope of Romano-Britain. All of the writings we have from this period come from Wales which is some way from Rheged and perhaps they were jaundiced opinions. In the years at the end of the Sixth century the kingdoms all fell one by one. Rheged was one of the last to fall.

I do not subscribe to Brian Sykes' theory that the Saxons merely assimilated into the existing people. One only has to look at the place names and listen to the language of the north and north western part of England. You can still hear anomalies. Perhaps that is because I come from the north but all of my reading leads me to believe that the Anglo-Saxons were intent upon conquest. The Norse invaders were different and they did assimilate but the Saxons were fighting for their lives and it did not pay to be kind. The people of Rheged were the last survivors if Roman Britain and I have given them all of the characteristics they would have had. This period was also the time when the old ways changed and Britain became Christina but I have not used this as a source of conflict but rather growth. I mainly used two books to research the material. The first was the excellent Michael Wood's book "In Search of the Dark Ages" and the second was "The Middle Ages" Edited by Robert Fossier. I also used Brian Sykes book, "Blood of the Isles" for reference. In addition I searched on line for more obscure information. All the place names are accurate, as far as I know and I have researched the names of the characters. My apologies if I have made a mistake.

The story will continue as the Saxons inexorably take over what was Britannia and make it, what became England.

Griff Hosker May 2013

Other books

by

Griff Hosker

If you enjoyed reading this book, then why not read another one by the author?

Ancient History

The Sword of Cartimandua Series (Germania and Britannia 50A.D. – 128 A.D.)

Ulpius Felix- Roman Warrior (prequel)

Book 1 The Sword of Cartimandua

Book 2 The Horse Warriors

Book 3 Invasion Caledonia

Book 4 Roman Retreat

Book 5 Revolt of the Red Witch

Book 6 Druid's Gold

Book 7 Trajan's Hunters

Book 8 The Last Frontier

Book 9 Hero of Rome

Book 10 Roman Hawk

Book 11 Roman Treachery

Book 12 Roman Wall

The Aelfraed Series (Britain and Byzantium 1050 A.D. - 1085 A.D.

Book 1 Housecarl

Book 2 Outlaw

Book 3 Varangian

The Wolf Warrior series (Britain in the late 6th Century)

Book 1 Saxon Dawn

Book 2 Saxon Revenge

Book 3 Saxon England

Book 4 Saxon Blood

Book 5 Saxon Slayer

Book 6 Saxon Slaughter

Book 7 Saxon Bane

Book 8 Saxon Fall: Rise of the Warlord

Book 9 Saxon Throne

The Dragon Heart Series

Book 1 Viking Slave

Book 2 Viking Warrior

Book 3 Viking Jarl

Book 4 Viking Kingdom

Book 5 Viking Wolf

Book 6 Viking War

Book 7 Viking Sword

Book 8 Viking Wrath

Book 9 Viking Raid

Book 10 Viking Legend

Book 11 Viking Vengeance

Book 12 Viking Dragon

Book 13 Viking Treasure

Book 14 Viking Enemy

Book 15 Viking Witch

Bool 16 Viking Blood

Book 17 Viking Weregeld

Book 18 Viking Storm

The Norman Genesis Series

Rolf

Horseman

The Battle for a Home

Revenge of the Franks

The Land of the Northmen

Ragnvald Hrolfsson

The Anarchy Series England 1120-1180

English Knight

Knight of the Empress

Northern Knight

Baron of the North

Earl

King Henry's Champion

The King is Dead

Warlord of the North

Enemy at the Gate

Warlord's War

Kingmaker

Henry II

Crusader

The Welsh Marches

Irish War

Border Knight 1182-1300

Sword for Hire

Modern History

The Napoleonic Horseman Series

Book 1 Chasseur a Cheval

Book 2 Napoleon's Guard

Book 3 British Light Dragoon

Book 4 Soldier Spy

Book 5 1808: The Road to Corunna

Waterloo

The Lucky Jack American Civil War series

Rebel Raiders

Confederate Rangers

The Road to Gettysburg

The British Ace Series

1914

1915 Fokker Scourge

1916 Angels over the Somme

1917 Eagles Fall

1918 We will remember them

From Arctic Snow to Desert Sand

Wings over Persia

Combined Operations series 1940-1945

Commando

Raider

Behind Enemy Lines

Dieppe

Toehold in Europe

Sword Beach

Breakout

The Battle for Antwerp

King Tiger

Beyond the Rhine

Other Books

Carnage at Cannes (a thriller)

Great Granny's Ghost (Aimed at 9-14-year-old young people)

Adventure at 63-Backpacking to Istanbul

For more information on all of the books then please visit the author's web site at http://www.griffhosker.com where there is a link to contact him.

Made in the USA
Middletown, DE
16 January 2021

31758030R00093